PENGUIN BOOKS

THE BLESSING

Nancy Mitford was born in 1904. Her childhood in a large remote country house with five sisters and one brother is described in the early chapters of *The Pursuit of Love*, which, said Miss Mitford, are largely autobiographical. She was, she said, uneducated except for being taught to ride and to speak French. She lived in Paris and she periodically contributed articles on life there to the *Sunday Times*. In 1956 she edited *Noblesse Oblige*, a collection of essays on U-usage.

Nancy Mitford wrote several novels and edited two books of Victorian letters, *The Ladies of Alderley* and *The Stanleys of Alderley*. She also translated into English Madame de La Fayette's classic novel *La Princesse de Clèves*, and wrote four biographies, *Madame de Pompadour*, *Voltaire in Love*, *The Sun King* and *Frederick the Great*. Her adaptation of a play by André Roussin ran for years in London under the title *The Little Hut*. She was awarded the C.B.E. in 1972 and died in 1973.

THE BLESSING

Nancy Mitford

PENGUIN BOOKS

in association with Hamish Hamilton

PENGUIN BOOKS

Published by the Penguin Group
Penguin Books Ltd, 27 Wrights Lane, London W8 5TZ, England
Penguin Putnam Inc., 375 Hudson Street, New York, New York 10014, USA
Penguin Books Australia Ltd, Ringwood, Victoria, Australia
Penguin Books Canada Ltd, 10 Alcorn Avenue, Toronto, Ontario, Canada M4V 3B2
Penguin Books (NZ) Ltd, Private Bag 102902, NSMC, Auckland, New Zealand

Penguin Books Ltd, Registered Offices: Harmondsworth, Middlesex, England

First published by Hamish Hamilton 1951
Published in Penguin Books 1957
19 20 18

Printed in England by Clays Ltd, St Ives plc

PART I

Chapter One

'THE foreign gentleman seems to be in a terrible hurry, dear.'

And indeed the house, though quite large, what used to be called a family house, in Queen Anne's Gate, was filled with sounds of impatience. Somebody was stamping about, moving furniture, throwing windows up and down, and clearing his throat exaggeratedly.

'Ahem! Ahem!'

'How long has he been here, Nanny?'

'Nearly an hour I should think. He played the piano, very fast and loud, for a while, which seemed to keep him quiet. He's only started this shindy since John went and told him you were in and would be down presently.'

'You go, darling, and tell him he must wait while I change out of these trousers,' said Grace, who was vigorously cleaning her neck with cotton wool. 'Oh, the dirt. What I need is a bath.'

The drawing-room door was now flung open.

'Do I see you or not?' The voice was certainly foreign.

'All right – very well. I'll come down now, this minute.'

She looked at Nanny, laughing, and said, 'He might go through the floor, like Rumpelstiltskin.'

But Nanny said, 'Put on a dress dear, you can't go down like that.'

'Shall I come upstairs?' said the voice.

'No, don't, here I am,' and Grace ran down, still in her A.R.P. trousers.

The Frenchman, tall, dark and elegant, in French Air Force uniform, was on the drawing-room landing, both hands on the banister rail. He seemed about to uproot the delicate woodwork. When he saw Grace he said 'Ah!' as though her appearance caused him gratified surprise, then, 'Is this a uniform? It's not bad. Did you receive my note?'

'Only now,' said Grace. 'I've been at the A.R.P. all day.'

They went into the drawing-room. 'Your writing is very difficult. I was still puzzling over it when I heard all that noise – it was like the French revolution. You must be a very impatient man.'

'No. But I don't like to be kept waiting, though this room has more compensations than most, I confess.'

'I wouldn't have kept you waiting if I'd known a little sooner – why didn't you . . .'

He was no longer listening, he had turned to the pictures on the walls.

'I do love this Olivier,' he said. 'You must give it to me.'

'Except that it belongs to Papa.'

'Ah yes, I suppose it does. Sir Conrad. He is very well known in the Middle East – I needn't tell you, however. The Allingham Commission, ah! cunning Sir Conrad. He owes something to my country, after that.' He turned from the picture to Grace looking at her rather as if she were a picture, and said, 'Natoire, or Rosalba. You could be by either. Well, we shall see, and time will show.'

'Papa loves France.'

'I'm sure he does. The Englishmen who love France are always the worst.'

'The worst?'

'Each man kills the thing he loves, you know. Never mind.'

'You've come from Cairo?' she said. 'I thought I read Cairo in your letter and something about Hughie? You saw him?'

'The fiancé I saw.'

'And you've come to give me news of him?'

'Good news – that is to say no news. Why is this picture labelled Drouais?'

'I suppose it is by Drouais,' said Grace with perfect indifference. Brought up among beautiful things, she took but small account of them.

'Indeed? What makes you think so?'

'Are you an art dealer?'

'An art deal-ee.'

'But you said you had news. Naturally I supposed it was the reason for your visit, to tell this news.'

'Have you any milk chocolate?'

'No, I'm sure we haven't.'

'Never mind.'

'Would you like a cocktail – or a glass of sherry?'

'Sherry, with delight.'

'Did you enjoy Cairo? Hughie says it's great fun.'

'The museum is wonderful – but of course no pictures, while the millionaires, poor dears, have wonderful pictures, for which they've paid wonderful prices (from those ateliers where Renoirs and Van Goghs are painted on purpose for millionaires), but which hardly satisfy one's cravings. Even their Corots are not always by Trouillebert. You see exactly how it is. So this afternoon I went to the National Gallery – shut. That is war. Now you will understand what an oasis I have found in Sir Conrad's drawing-room, though I must have a word with him some time about this Drouais, so called.'

'I'm afraid you won't see many pictures in London now,' said Grace. 'Papa has sent all his best ones to the country, and most people have shut up their houses, you know.'

'Never mind. I love London, even without pictures, and English women I love.'

'Do you? Don't we seem terribly dowdy?'

'Of course. That's what make you so amusing and mysterious. What can you possibly do, all day?'

'Do?'

'Yes. How do you fill those endless eons of time when French-women are having their hair washed, trying on hats, visiting the collections, discussing with the *lingère* – what is *lingère* in English?'

'Underclothes-maker.'

'Hours they spend with the underclothes-maker. What a funny word – are you sure? Anyhow, Frenchwomen always give one to understand that arranging themselves is full-time work. Now you English, like flowers in a basket, are not arranged, which is quite all right when the flowers are spring flowers.' He gave her another long, approving look. 'But how do you fill in the time? That is the great puzzle.'

'I'm afraid,' she said, laughing, 'that we fill it in (not now, of course, but before the war) buying clothes and hats and having our hair washed. Perhaps the results were not quite the same, but I assure you that great efforts were made.'

'Please don't tell me. Do leave me in the dark, it makes you so much more interesting. Do let me go on believing that the hours drift by in a dream, that those blind blue eyes which see nothing, not even your father's pictures, are turned inward upon some Anglo-Saxon fairyland of your own. Am I not right?'

He was quite right, though perhaps she hardly knew it herself. She thought it over and then said,

'Just before the war I used to have a terribly thrilling dream about escaping from the Germans.'

'One must always escape from Germans. They are so very dull.'

'But now my life is as flat as a pancake, and I can hardly bear it. I quite – almost – long for bombs.'

'I am sorry to have to say that when life is flat it is your own fault. To me it is never flat.'

'Are you never bored?'

'I am sometimes bored by people, but never by life.'

'Oh how lucky.'

'Perhaps I'll take you out dancing. But where? The night clubs here must be terrible.'

'It depends on who you go with.'

'I see. Like all night clubs everywhere. So, I pick you up at eight? I love the black-out. I am trained to be a night bomber – I have flown behind the German lines dropping delightful leaflets, so of course I can find my way by the stars. This gives me confidence, sometimes misplaced I am obliged to own. Then we'll dine at the Connaught Hotel, where I'm staying, and where they have a very good *plat sucré*. What is *plat sucré* in English? – don't tell me, I know, pudding.'

'How d'you know such wonderful English?'

'My mother was. Still it is rather wonderful, isn't it? I can recite the whole of the *Excursion,* but not now. So eight o'clock then.'

'I'll be quite ready,' said Grace.

The Frenchman ran downstairs and out of the house, and she saw him from the window running towards St James's Park. Then she went up to her room, pulled a lot of clothes from various drawers and cupboards, laid them on her bed, and hovered about wondering what on earth she should wear. Nothing seemed somehow quite suitable.

Nanny came in. 'Good gracious! The room looks like a jumble sale.'

'Run me a bath, darling. I'm going out to dinner with that Frenchman.'

'Are you, dear? And what's his name?'

'Bother. I never asked him.'

'Oh well,' said Nanny, 'one French name is very much like another, I dare say.'

Chapter Two

His name was Charles-Edouard de Valhubert. About a month later he said to Grace, 'Perhaps I will marry you.'

Grace, in love as never before, tried to keep her head and not to look as if about to faint with happiness.

'Will you?' she said. 'Why?'

'In ten days I go back to the Middle East. The war will begin soon, anything may happen, and I need a son.'

'How practical you are.'

'Yes. I am French. *Mais après le mariage – mince de – nettoyage, – La belle-mère! – on s'assied dessus!'* he sang. He was for ever singing little snatches of songs like that. 'But you won't have a *belle-mère*, unfortunately, since she died, poor dear, many years ago.'

'I must remind you,' said Grace, 'that I am engaged to somebody else.'

'I must remind you that your behaviour lately has not been the behaviour of a faithful fiancée.'

'A little flirtation means nothing at all. I am engaged, and that's that.'

'Engaged. But not married and not in love.'

'Fond.'

'Indeed?'

'You really did see Hughie in Cairo?'

'I saw him plain. He said, "Going to London are you? Do

look up Grace." Not very clever of him. So I looked up. He is
very dull.'

'Very handsome.'

'Yes. So perhaps on Wednesday?'

'Wednesday what?'

'The marriage? I will now go and call on your father – where
can I find him?'

'At this time of day he'll be at the House.'

'How little did I ever think I should end up as the son-in-law
of the Allingham Commission. How strange is one's fate. Then
I'll come back and take you out to dinner.'

The next day Sir Conrad Allingham went to see Mrs
O'Donovan, a widow with whom he had had for many years a
loving friendship. Sir Conrad preferred actually making love, a
pastime to which he devoted a good deal of energy, with those
whose profession it is, finding it embarrassing, never really able
to let himself go, with women whom he met in other circumstances. But he liked the company of woman to an extent rare
among Englishmen, and often went to chat for an hour or so
with Mrs O'Donovan in her light sunny little house which
looked over Chelsea Hospital. She was always at home, always
glad to receive a visitor, and had a large following among the
more intellectual of the right-wing politicians. Her regard for
Sir Conrad was special; she spoke of him as 'my Conrad' and
was out to other callers when he came to see her. It was said that
he never took a step without asking her advice first.

He said, without preamble, 'Have you seen Charles-Edouard
de Valhubert?'

'Priscilla's son?'

'Yes.'

'Is he in London?'

'He's been in London several weeks, courting Grace so it
seems.'

'Conrad! How extraordinary! What's he like?'

'Really, you know, irresistible. Came to see me at the House
yesterday – wants to marry her. I knew nothing – but nothing. I
thought Grace was buried in that First Aid Post, and, of course,

I've been busy myself. Rather too bad of her really – here I am presented with this *fait accompli*.'

'Well, but what about Hughie?'

'What indeed? Mind you, my sympathies with Hughie are limited – he ought to have married her before he went away.'

'Poor Hughie, he was longing to. He thought it wouldn't be fair.'

'What rubbish though. He leaves a position utterly undefended, he can't be surprised if it falls into – well, Allied hands. I never cared for him, as you know, quite half-baked and tells no jokes. However, she didn't ask my advice when she became engaged to him, nor did she ask it before breaking the engagement (if, indeed, she has remembered to do so). Clearly it doesn't matter what I think. So much for Hughie. He has made his exit all right.'

'I can see that you're pleased, really.'

'Yes and no. Valhubert is quite a chap I will say, tall, attractive (very much like his father to look at, much better dressed). He is clearly great fun. But I don't like the idea of Grace marrying a frog, to tell the truth.'

'Conrad! With your love for the French?' Mrs O'Donovan loved the French too. She had once spent several months in Paris as a child; it had touched her imagination in some way, and she had hankered to live there ever since. This love was one of the strongest links between her and Sir Conrad. They both belonged to the category of English person, not rare among the cultivated classes, and not the least respectable of their race, who can find almost literally nothing to criticize where the French are concerned.

'Only because of Grace's special character,' he said. 'Try and picture her mooning about in Paris society. She would be a lamb among wolves; it makes me shudder to think of it.'

'I'm not sure – after all she's a beauty, and that means a great deal more in France than it does here.'

'Yes, with the men. I'm thinking of the women. They'll make short work of our poor Grace, always in the clouds.'

'Perhaps her clouds will protect her.'

'In a way, but I'm afraid she's deeply romantic, and Valhubert

13

has a roving eye if ever there was one. Don't I remember that Priscilla was very unhappy? There used to be rumours —'

Mrs O'Donovan delved in her mind for everything she had known, long ago now and buried away, about Priscilla de Valhubert. Among other things she brought to the surface was the memory that when she had first heard of Priscilla's engagement she had felt exactly what she was feeling now, that it was really rather unfair. Mrs O'Donovan was as much like a Frenchwoman as it is possible for any Anglo-Saxon to be. She spoke the language faultlessly. Her clothes, her scent, the food she ate, the wine she drank, all, in fact, that makes life agreeable, came from France. There was a *bidet* in her bathroom; she had her afternoon rest on a chaise-longue; she hardly read a word of anything but French; her house was a centre for visiting Frenchmen; the cheese appeared before the pudding at her table, and her dog, a poodle, was called Blum.

In London she was considered the great authority on everything French, to all intents and purposes a Frenchwoman, and she had therefore, quite naturally, come to have a proprietary feeling with regard to France. So it had seemd unfair then that Priscilla, just as it seemed unfair now that Grace, ordinary, rather dull English girls, should marry these fascinating men and sink back with no further effort to the enjoyment of all the delights of French civilization.

Mrs O'Donovan had never wanted to marry any particular Frenchman, and had been exceedingly happy with her own husband, so that this feeling was nothing if not irrational. All the same, as jealousy does, it stung.

'Yes, very unhappy,' she said, 'partly because she never felt comfortable in Paris society (she never quite learnt French) but chiefly, as you say, owing to the terrible unfaithfulness of Charles-René, which really, I believe, killed her in the end.'

'Oh – killed her,' said Sir Conrad. 'I don't suppose she died of love all the same. French doctors, more likely. When did Charles-René die?'

'Years ago. Fifteen years I should think – very soon after Priscilla. Is old Madame de Valhubert still alive? And Madame Rocher?'

'No idea – never knew them.'

'Madame Rocher des Innouïs is, or was, Madame de Valhubert's sister. Madame de Valhubert herself was always a kind of saint, as far as I can remember, and Madame Rocher was not. I knew them when I was a child, they were friends of my mother.'

'Oh well,' said Sir Conrad testily, 'nobody tells me anything. Nothing was said about any relations. I just talked with the chap for half an hour, mostly about my Drouais, which, according to him, is by some pupil of Nattier. Terrible rot. I did ask him why he wanted to marry her. They won't have many interests in common, unless Grace makes an effort to educate herself at last.' Grace's dreamy illiteracy always exasperated her father.

'What did he say?'

'He said she is so beautiful and so good.'

'And so rich,' said Mrs O'Donovan.

'It can't be that, my dear Meg. The Valhuberts have always been immensely rich.'

'Yes, but nobody, and especially no French person, ever minds having a bit more, you know.'

'I don't somehow feel it's that. Wants a son before he gets killed, more likely. The marriage, if you please, is tomorrow.'

'Tomorrow?'

'Yes, well, what can I do? Grace is of age – 23, time she did marry, in fact – and in love, radiant with love, I must say. Valhubert is more than old enough to know his own mind, 28 it appears, and is off to the war. They have decided, without asking me, that they will marry tomorrow. It remains for me to make a settlement and look pleasant.'

In spite of all this peppery talk, Mrs O'Donovan, who knew him so well, could see that 'her' Conrad was not really displeased at the turn of events. He always rather liked the unexpected, so long as it did not interfere with his personal comfort, and was infinitely tolerant towards any manifestation of love. He had taken a fancy to Valhubert, who, since he was off to the war, would not be removing Sir Conrad's housekeeper and companion for months, possibly years to come. He who was so fond of Paris would be glad to have a solid family foothold there when the war was over, while the incompatibility of the couple, as well as Grace's broken heart, were, after all, only matters for speculation.

'Where are they to be married?' she asked. 'Shall I come?'

'I hope so indeed, and to luncheon afterwards. Twelve o'clock at the Caxton Hall.'

Mrs O'Donovan, who was, of course, a Roman Catholic, was shocked and startled. 'A civil marriage only? Conrad, is that wise? The Valhuberts are an intensely Catholic family, you know.'

'I know. I did think it rather odd. But Grace is not a Catholic yet, though I suppose in time she will become one. Anyway,' he said, getting up to go, 'that's what they've arranged. Nobody asked my advice about any of it, naturally. When I think how I used to turn to my dear old father – never moved a step without his approval —'

'Are you sure?' she said, laughing. 'I seem to remember a river party – something about the Derby – a journey to Vienna —'

'Yes, yes, I don't say I was never young. I am speaking about broad outlines of policy —'

*

Grace went out and bought a hat, and dressing for her wedding consisted in putting on this hat. As the occasion was so momentous she took a long time, trying it a little more to the right, to the left, to the back. While pretty in itself, a pretty little object, it was strangely unbecoming to her rather large, beautiful face. Nanny fussed about the room in a rustle of tissue paper.

'Like this, Nan?'

'Quite nice.'

'Darling, you're not looking. Or like this?'

'I don't see much difference.' Deep sigh.

'Darling! What a sigh!'

'Yes, well I can't say this is the sort of wedding I'd hoped for.'

'I know. It's a shame, but there you are. The war.'

'A foreigner.'

'But such a blissful one. Oh dear, oh dear, this hat. What is wrong with it d'you think?'

'Very nice indeed, I expect, but then I always liked Mr Hugh.'

'Hughie is bliss too, of course, but he went off.'

'He went to fight for King and Country, dear.'

'Well, Charles-Edouard is going to fight for President and Country. I don't see much difference except that he is marrying me first. Oh darling, this hat. It's not quite right, is it?'

'Never mind, dear, nobody's going to look at you.'

'On my wedding day?'

But when Charles-Edouard met them at the registry office he looked at her and said, 'This hat is terrible, perhaps you'd better take it off.'

Grace did so with some relief, shook out her pretty golden hair, and gave the hat to Nanny, who, since it was made of flowers, looked rather like a small, cross, elderly bridesmaid clasping a bouquet.

They went for their honeymoon to Sir Conrad's house, Bunbury Park, in Wiltshire, and were very happy. When, during the lonely years which followed, Grace tried to recall those ten short days, the picture that always came to her mind was of Charles-Edouard moving furniture. The central block of the house having been requisitioned by soldiers, he and Grace occupied three rooms in one of the wings, and Charles-Edouard now set himself the task of filling these rooms with objects of art. He seemed not to feel the piercing cold of the unheated hall, with its dome and marble floor, where most of the furniture had been put away, but bustled about in semi-darkness, lifting dust sheets, scrambling under pyramids of tables and chairs, opening cupboards and peering into packing cases, like a squirrel in search of nuts. From time to time, with a satisfied grunt, he would pounce upon some object and scurry off with it. If he could not move it alone he made the soldiers help him. It took eight of them to lug the marble bust of an Austrian archduke up the stairs into Grace's bedroom. Nanny and the housekeeper clearly thought Charles-Edouard was out of his head, and exchanged very meaning looks and sniffs while the archduke was making his painful progress. One of Marie Antoinette's brothers, bewigged and bemedalled, the Fleece upon his elaborately folded stock, he now entirely dominated the room with his calm, stupid, German face.

'He looks dull,' said Grace.

'But so beautiful. You look too much at the subject – can't you see that it's a wonderful piece of sculpture?'

'Come for a walk, Charles-Edouard, the woods are heavenly today.'

It was early spring, very fine and dry. The big beeches, not yet in leaf, stood naked on their copper carpet, while the other trees had petticoats of pale green. The birds were already tuning up an orchestra as if preparing to accompany those two stars of summer, the cuckoo and the nightingale, as soon as they should make their bow. It seemed a pity to spend such days creeping about under dust sheets.

'Nature I hate,' said Charles-Edouard, as he went on with his self-appointed task. So she walked in the sunny woods alone, until she discovered that if she could propose an 18th-century mausoleum, Siamese dairy, wishing well, hermit's grotto or cottage orné as the object for a walk, he would accompany her. He strode along at an enormous speed, often breaking into a run, seizing her hand and dragging her with him. *'Il neige des plumes de tourterelles'*, he sang.

Her father's park abounded in follies, quite enough to last out their visit. What did they talk about all day? She never could remember. Charles-Edouard sang his little songs, made his little jokes, and told her a great deal about the objects he found under the dust sheets, so that names like Carlin, Cressent, Thomire, Reisener and Gouthière always thereafter reminded her of their honeymoon. Her room became transformed from a rather dull country house bedroom into a corner of the Wallace Collection. But he hardly talked about himself at all, or his family, or life in Paris, or what they would do after the war. A fortnight from their wedding day he left England and went back to Cairo.

Grace soon realized that she was expecting a child. When the air raids began Sir Conrad sent her to live at Bunbury, and here, in a bedroom full of works of art collected by his father, Sigismond de Valhubert opened his eyes upon the calm, stupid face of an Austrian archduke.

Chapter Three

'He is a little black boy – oh, he is black. I never expected you to have a baby with such eyes, it doesn't seem natural or right.'

'I don't know,' said Grace. 'I think one gets tired of always gazing into these blue eyes. I like this better.'

'Such a funny sort of name, too,' Nanny went on, 'not like anything. If he'd had been called after his father he could have been Charlie, or Eddy, but Sigi —! Well, I don't care to say it in the street, makes people look round.'

'But you're so seldom in streets, darling.'

'Salisbury. People stop and look at him as it is.'

'That's because he's such a love. Anyway, I think he's a blessing.'

And so of course did Nanny, though she would have thought him an even more blessed blessing had he resembled his mother more and his father less.

Grace stayed on at Bunbury. She had not meant to, she had meant to go back to London and the A.R.P. as soon as Sigi was weaned, but somehow, in the end, she stayed on. She fell into various country jobs, ran a small holding, and looked after the baby as much as Nanny allowed. Sir Conrad went down to see her at week-ends, and sometimes she spent a few days with him in London. So the years of the war went by calmly and rather happily for Grace, who never much minded being alone. She had a placid, optimistic nature, and was never tortured by anxious thoughts about Charles-Edouard, or doubted that he would return safely in due course. Nor did she doubt that when, in due course, he had safely returned, their marriage would be one of Elysian happiness.

Her father and Mrs O'Donovan selected many books for her to read, in preparation for a French life. They told her she ought to be studying the religious writings of the 17th, the drama and philosophy of the 18th, the prose and politics of the 19th centuries. They sent her, as well as quantities of classics and many novels and *mémoires*, Michelet in sixteen morocco volumes and

Sainte-Beuve in sixteen paper ones; they sent her Bodley's *France* and Brogan's *Third Republic*, saying she would feel a fool if she did not understand the French electoral, judicial, and municipal systems. Grace did make spasmodic efforts to get on with all this homework, but she was too mentally lazy and untrained to do more than nibble at it. In the evenings she liked to turn on the wireless, think of Charles-Edouard, and stitch away at a carpet destined to be literally laid at his feet. It was squares of petit point, in a particularly crude Victorian design of roses and lilies of the valley and blue ribbons. Grace thought it too pretty for words.

She lived in a dream of Charles-Edouard, so that as the years went on he turned, in her mind, into somebody quite divorced from all reality and quite different from the original. And the years did go on. He came back for three hectic days in July 1940 which hardly counted, so little did Grace see of him, and after that seemed to go farther and farther away, Fort Lamy, Ceylon, and finally Indo-China. When the war ended he was not immediately demobilized, his return was announced again and again, only to be put off, so that it was more than seven years after their wedding when at last the telephone bell rang and Grace heard his voice speaking from Heath Row. This time he was unannounced; she had thought him still in the East.

'Our Ambassador was on the plane with me, and he is sending me straight down in his motor,' he said. 'It seems I'll be with you in an hour or two.'

Grace felt that, whereas the seven years had gone in a flash, this hour or two would never never end. She went up to the nursery. Sigi was having his bath before bedtime.

'Don't let him go to sleep,' she said to Nanny. 'Guess what, darling – his father will be here presently.'

Nanny received this news with the air of one resigned to the inevitable fact that all things, especially good things, have their term. She gave a particularly fearful sniff and said, 'Well, I only hope he won't over-excite the poor little fellow. You know what it's like getting him off, evenings, as well as I do.'

'Oh, Nanny, just for once, darling, it wouldn't matter if he stayed up all night.'

She left the nursery and wandered down the drive to the lodge, where she sat on one of the stone stumps that, loosely chained together, enclosed grassy mounds on either side of the gates. There was no traffic on the little road outside the park, and beyond it, bordered by clumps of wild rose bushes, the deep woods were full of song. It was high summer now, that week when cuckoo and nightingale give their best, their purest performances. The evening was warm, but she felt glad of a cardigan; she had begun to shiver like a nervous dog.

At last the motor drove up. Charles-Edouard sprang out of it and hugged her, and then she remembered exactly what he was like as a real person, and the other, dream Charles-Edouard, was chased into the back of her mind. Not quite chased away, she often thereafter remembered him with affection, but separated from reality.

They got back into the motor and drove up to the house.

'You are looking very beautiful,' he said, 'and very happy. I was afraid you might have become sad, all these years and years down here, away from me.'

'I longed terribly for you.'

'I know. You must have.'

'Don't tease, Charles-Edouard. But if we had to be separated I would rather have been here than anywhere. I love the country, you know, and besides, I had plenty to do.'

'What did you do?'

'Oh, goats and things.'

'Goats must be very dull.'

'No, really not. Then of course there was Sigi. Are you excited for him?'

'Very very much excited.'

'Come then, let's go straight up to the nursery.'

But outside Grace's bedroom Charles-Edouard caught her hand and pointed sternly to the door. 'I must see if the archduke is still there,' he said, and they went in.

Grace said presently, 'If you had been killed in the war, it would have finished me off.'

'Ah! Would you have died? That's very nice.'

'Yes, I couldn't have gone on living.'

'And would it have been a violent death by poison or a slow death by misery?'

'Which would you prefer?'

'Poison would be very flattering.'

'All right then, poison. Now come on, let's go to Sigi.'

In the day nursery Nanny's face was a picture of disapproval. 'Funny thing,' she said, 'I thought I heard a car quite half an hour ago. Time he went off to sleep, poor mite.'

They went through into the night nursery. Sigi was standing on his bed. He had black, silky curls and clever little black eyes, and he was always laughing.

'Have you ever seen me before?' he said to his father.

'Never. But I can guess who you are.'

'Sigismond de Valhubert, a great boy of nearly seven. Are you my papa?'

'Let me present myself – Charles-Edouard de Valhubert.' They shook hands.

'What are you?'

'I am a colonel in the French Air Force, retired. And what are you going to be?'

'A superman,' said the child.

Charles-Edouard was much gratified by this reply. 'Always the same old story,' he said, '*l' Empereur, la gloire, hommage à la Grande Armée*. I shall have a lot to tell you about the Marshal of France, your ancestor. Do you know that at home we have a standard from the battlefield of Friedland?'

Sigi looked intensely puzzled, and Grace said, 'I'm afraid his superman isn't Napoleon, not yet at least, but Garth.'

'Goethe?'

'Oh dear – no. Garth. It's a strip – I can't explain, I'll have to show you some time. It's rather horrible really, but we don't seem able to do without it.'

'Garth, you know, in the *Daily*,' Sigismond said. His grandfather had forbidden him to call it the *Mirror* so he compromised with the *Daily*. 'When I'm big I'm going to have a space ship like Garth and go to the —'

'But what do you know, Sigismond? Can you count? Can you read, and can you name the forty Kings of France?'

'Forty?' said Grace. 'Are there really? Poor little boy.'

'Well eighteen are Louis and ten are Charles. It's not as bad as it sounds. I always forget the others myself.'

'Isn't he a darling?' said Grace, as they went downstairs.

'A darling. Rather dull, but a darling.'

'He's not dull a bit,' she said indignantly, 'though he may be a little young for his age. It comes from living all alone with me in the country, if he is.'

'So perhaps tomorrow I take you both home to France.'

'Tomorrow? Oh no, Charles-Edouard, not —'

'We can't stay here. I've seen all the leaning towers and pavilions and rotundas and islands and rococo bridges, I've moved the furniture and rehung the pictures. There's nothing whatever to do, and we have our new life to begin. So —?'

'Oh darling, but tomorrow! What about the packing?'

'Don't bother. We're going straight to Provence, you'll only want cotton dresses, and you must have all new when we get to Paris, anyhow.'

'Yes, but Nanny. What will she say?'

'I don't know. The plane is at twelve, giving us time to catch the night train to Marseilles. We leave here at nine. I've arranged everything and ordered a motor to take us. I suppose you've got the passports as I told you to last year?'

'But Nanny —' wailed poor Grace.

Charles-Edouard began to sing a song about sardines. *'Marinées, argentées, leurs petits corps decapités ...'*

Chapter Four

CHARLES-EDOUARD, Grace, Sigismond, and Nanny arrived at Marseilles in a torrid heat wave. Grace and the child were tired after the night in the train, but Charles-Edouard and Nanny were made of sterner stuff. His songs and jokes flowed like a running river, except when he was actually asleep, and so did Nanny's complaints. These were a recitative of nursery grievance in which certain motifs constantly recurred. 'No time to write to Daniel Neal – all those nice toys left behind – the beautiful rocking-horse Mrs O'Donovan gave us – his scooter with rubber tyres and a bell – poor little mite, grown out of his winter coat, how shall we ever get another – what shall I do without my wireless? –

the Bengers never came, you know, dear, from the Army and Navy – shall we get the *Mirror* there and my *Woman and Beauty*? Oh, I say, I never took those books back to Boots, what will the girl think of me – that nice blouse I was having made in the village —' Then the chorus, much louder than the rest. 'Shame, really.'

They were met at the station by Charles-Edouard's valet, Ange-Victor, in a big, rather old-fashioned Bentley. Ange-Victor was crying with joy, and it seemed as if he and Charles-Edouard would never stop hugging each other. At last they stowed the luggage into the motor, Grace and Sigi crammed into the front seats beside Charles-Edouard, with valet and nurse behind, and he drove hell for leather up the narrow, twisting, crowded road which goes from Marseilles to Aix.

'I'm a night bomber, have no fear,' he shouted to Grace as she cringed in her corner clasping Sigi. The hot air rushed past them, early as it was, the day was already a scorcher. Charles-Edouard was singing '*Malbrouck s'en va'-t-en guerre et ne reviendra pas.*'

'But I am back,' he said triumphantly. 'Never never did I expect to come back. Five fortune-tellers said I should be killed.'

And he turned right round, in the teeth of an enormous lorry, to ask Ange-Victor if Madame André, in the village, still told the cards.

'Shall I tell your fortune now?' said Grace. 'If you don't drive much more carefully there will soon be a widow, a widower, an orphan, and two childless parents in this family.'

'Try and remember that I am a night bomber,' said Charles-Edouard. 'I have driven aeroplanes over the impenetrable jungle, how should I have an accident on my old road I've known from a baby? Here we turn,' he said, wrenching the motor, under the very bonnet of another lorry, across the road and down a lane to the left of it. 'And there,' he said a few minutes later, 'is Bellandargues.'

The Provençal landscape, like that of Tuscany which it so much resembles, is marked by many little hills humping unexpectedly in the middle of vineyards. These often have a cluster of cottages round their lower slopes, overlooked by a castle, or the ruin of a castle, on the summit. Such was Bellandargues. The village lay at the foot of a hill, and above it, up in the blue sky, hung the castle, home, for many generations, of the Valhubert family.

As they drove into the village it presented a gay and festive appearance, all flags for the return of Charles-Edouard. A great streamer, with *'Vive la Libération, Hommage à M. le Maire'*, was stretched across the street; the village band was playing, and a crowd was gathered in the market-place, waving and cheering. Charles-Edouard stopped the motor. M. Mignon, the chemist, made a long speech, recalling the sad times they had lived through since Charles Edouard was last there, and saying with what deep emotion they had all heard him when he had spoken on the London radio in July 1940.

'Hm. Hm.' Charles-Edouard had a certain face which betrayed, to those who knew him well, inward laughter tinged with a guilty feeling. His eyes laughed but his mouth turned down at the corners. He made this face now, remembering so well the speech at the B.B.C.; how he had been exchanging looks as he delivered it with the next speaker, on the other side of a glass screen. She was a pretty little Dutch girl, and he had taken her out to tea, he remembered, before going back to Grace. M. Mignon made a fine and flowery peroration, Charles-Edouard spoke in reply, the village band then struck up again while he and Grace shook hundreds of hands. Great admiration was lavished upon Sigi, pronounced to be the image of his papa; he jumped up and down on the seat, laughing and clapping, until Nanny said he was thoroughly above himself and pinned him to her lap.

'Well,' said Grace, when at last they drove on, 'if you never thought you'd be son-in-law to the Allingham Commission, it certainly never occurred to me that I should marry a mayor.' She turned round and said, 'Wasn't that delightful, Nan?'

'Funny-looking lot, aren't they? Not too fond of washing, if you ask me. Fearful smell of drains, dear.'

The road up through the village got steeper and steeper, the side alleys were all flights of steps. Charles-Edouard changed down into bottom gear. They bounced through a gateway, climbed another slope, came out on to a big, flat terrace, bordered with orange trees in tubs, and drew up at the open front door of the castle. The village was now invisible; far below them, shimmering in the heat and punctuated with umbrella pines, lay acre upon acre of vivid green landscape.

As she got out of the motor Grace thought to herself how different all this was going to look in a few weeks, when it had become familiar. Houses are entirely different when you know them well, she thought, and on first acquaintance even more different from their real selves, more deceptive about their real character than human beings. As with human beings, you can have an impression, that is all. Her impression of Bellandargues was entirely favourable, one of hot, sleepy, beautiful magnitude. She longed to be on everyday terms with it, to know the rooms that lay behind the vast windows of the first floor, to know what happened round the corner of the terrace, and where the staircase led to, just visible in the interior darkness. It is a funny feeling to visit your home for the first time and have to be taken about step by step like a blind person.

An old butler ran out of the door, saying he had not expected them for another half-hour. There was more hugging and crying, and then Charles-Edouard gave him rapid instructions about Nanny being taken straight to her rooms and a maid sent to help her unpack.

'And Madame la Marquise?' he said.

The butler replied that Madame la Marquise must be in the drawing-room. He said again that they had arrived before they were expected.

'Come, then,' Charles-Edouard said, taking Sigi by the hand. 'Come, Grace.'

'Go with the butler, Nan,' said Grace. 'I'll be up as soon as I can.'

'Yes, well, don't keep Sigi too long, dear. He's filthy after that train.'

Her words fell on air, Grace was pursuing husband and son into the shadows of the house and up the stairs. Somewhere a Chopin waltz was being played, but Grace did not consciously hear it, though she remembered it afterwards.

'Wait, wait, Charles-Edouard,' she cried. 'Who is this Marquise?'

'My grandmother.'

'Charles-Edouard, dearest, stop one minute, I didn't know you had a grandmother – oh, do stop and explain —'

'There's nothing to explain. In here.' He held open a door for her. Grace walked into a huge room, dark and panelled, with a painted ceiling. Furniture was dotted about in it; like shrubs in a desert the pieces seemed to grow where they stood, following no plan of arrangement, and dotted about among them were human figures. There was an old man painting at an easel, an old lady at a piano playing the Chopin waltz, while another old lady, in the embrasure of a window, was deep in conversation with an ancient priest. She looked quickly round as the door opened, and then ran towards Grace.

'So soon?' she cried, 'and nobody downstairs to meet you? It's that wretched stable clock, always slow.' She kissed Grace on both cheeks, and then again, saying, 'A beauty! What a beauty! Well done, Charles-Edouard,' she said, hugging him. 'This is wonderful happiness, my child.'

Now there was a perfect hubbub of greetings and introductions. 'Tante Régine – M. le Curé, how are you? Yes, yes, I quite realized that,' said Charles-Edouard when M. le Curé began to explain that he had not been down in the village because M. Mignon was in charge of the welcome there. 'Grace, this is M. de la Bourlie, and this is M. le Curé, Grace, who has been M. le Curé here – for how long?'

Madame de Valhubert said, 'M. le Curé arrived here, a young priest, the same summer that I arrived, a young bride. We shall have seen sixty grape harvests together this year.'

Tante Régine became rather fidgety while her sister was speaking, and said to Grace in an aside, 'But I am much younger, I was always the baby – fifteen – twenty years younger than Françoise.'

Their faces were the same, soft, white faces with black eyes, but while Madame de Valhubert's was framed in soft white hair and her clothes were very much like those of a nun, Madame Rocher, painted and powdered, had her red hair cut in the latest way and wore such a beautiful, simple, desirable cotton dress that Grace could look at nothing else in the room.

'Dear Tante Régine, I'm very much pleased to see you,' said Charles-Edouard. 'And Octave?'

Octave was her late husband's nephew, the present holder of his title, whom Madame Rocher had brought up and then, because he bored her, had pushed into the army. The old Marquis had left her every penny of the enormous fortune which came to him through his mother, so she was able to behave in a very high-handed manner with his relations.

'Oh poor Octave, no luck at all, as usual,' said Madame Rocher. 'He is still with his regiment, still only a captain. Of course, if it hadn't been for this wretched war he would be at least a colonel by now.'

'Hm. Hm,' said Charles-Edouard, bursting with inward laughter. 'And I, in spite of this wretched war, am a colonel, do you know that? Grandmother, did you know that I am a colonel?'

'Yes, yes, we know a great deal about you here. Little Béguin, who was invalided home after the Libération, was full of your exploits.'

'Indeed I did splendidly,' said Charles-Edouard, laughing. 'I am a colonel and I have a son – where is this son, by the way?'

He dragged Sigi out from behind a curtain, where he was hiding in a most unusual state of shyness.

'Sigismond, come and kiss the hand of your ancestress. Now that you are a French boy we should like to see some manners, please.'

Sigi became quite scarlet with embarrassment, but the old lady, taking two boxes of sweets from a table, held them out to him and said, 'You can kiss my hand another time, darling, but now choose which you'll have, a chocolate or a marron glacé. A little bribery never spoils anything,' she said to Charles-Edouard as Sigi carefully made his choice. 'Well?'

'Well, I do love chocolate, certainly I do, but I suppose I ought to choose the one with the silver paper on account of the poor lepers.'

'What, my child?'

'You see Nanny – well you haven't met her yet – she keeps a silver-paper ball, and when it weighs a pound she sends it up and one poor leper can live on that – oh for years, probably. They hardly need anything at all Nanny says, quite contented with a handful of rice from time to time, but it's ages now since Nanny sent up, silver paper is so terribly rare in these days. She will be pleased.'

'But this child has saintly thoughts!' cried Madame de Valhubert. 'M. le Curé, did you understand? The little one is already planning for the lepers. It is wonderful, so young. How he does look like you, Charles-Edouard, the image of what you were at that age, though I don't remember that you had such gratifying preoccupations.'

'Yes, isn't he the very picture,' said Charles-Edouard, 'but I'm afraid he's not as brilliant as I was. Now if you will excuse us perhaps I'll show Grace the rest of the house before luncheon, and take St François Xavier up to his nursery.'

Outside on the staircase, Nanny was hovering with a face of leaden reproach. She pounced upon Sigi and hurried him off, muttering her recitative under her breath. She was very slightly in awe of Charles-Edouard, and would only let herself go, Grace knew, when alone with her. The words 'unbearably close, here' were just distinguishable, a look of terrifying malice flashed in the direction of Charles-Edouard, and she was gone. Grace absolutely dreaded the day when she would be obliged to have it out with him about Nanny. She had known, as a child, that her father and mother used to have it out at intervals, until her mother, by dying, had saddled Sir Conrad with Nanny for ever. She gave Charles-Edouard a nervous, laughing look, but he did not notice it; he put his arm round her waist, and they went slowly up the stairs.

Then she went back to what she had been wondering as they came out of the drawing-room. 'But why didn't you tell me about your grandmother – well, really, all these people?'

'I have one very firm rule in life,' he said, 'which is never to talk to people about other people they have never seen. It is very dull, since people are only interesting when you know them, and furthermore it can lead to misunderstandings. You and my grandmother, having no preconceived ideas about each other —'

'You haven't got a wife hidden away in some other room, I hope?'

'No wife.'

'Oh good. But of course it's just like in *Rebecca*. By degrees I shall find out all about your past.'

'Oh my past! It's such a long time ago now.'

'So tell me more, now I've seen them. Who is the old man?'

'M. de la Bourlie? He is my grandmother's lover.'

'Her lover?' Grace was very much startled. 'Isn't she rather old to have a lover?'

'Has age to do with love?' Charles-Edouard looked so much surprised that Grace said,

'Oh well – I only thought. Anyway, perhaps there's nothing in it.'

He roared with laughter, saying, 'How English you are. But M. de la Bourlie has visited my grandmother every single day for forty-six years, and in such a case you may be sure that there is always love.'

'He doesn't live here, too?'

'No. He has a beautiful house in Aix. He generally comes over in the afternoon, but today, of course, he has come early, dying of curiosity to see l'Anglaise. They all must be, we shall have the whole neighbourhood over. It will be very dull. Never mind.'

'Why don't they marry?' said Grace.

'Who? Oh my grandmother. Well, but poor Madame de la Bourlie.'

'Poor her anyway. In England, when there is a long love affair like that people always end by marrying.'

'And in America if you hold a woman's hand you are expected to go round next day with the divorce papers. The Anglo-Saxons are very fond of marriage, it is very strange.'

'I've never seen a pale green wig before.'

'He's worn that wig ever since I was a little boy. He has been a tremendous lady-killer in his time, wig and all.'

'And when I am old like your grandmother, will you love me still?'

'It depends.'

'How horrid. Depends on what?'

'It all depends, entirely, on you.'

'Charles-Edouard, was the reason you didn't tell me about your grandmother because you thought I wouldn't like the idea of sharing my house with another woman?'

Charles-Edouard looked immensely surprised. 'It never

occurred to me for a single minute,' he said. 'It's not your house, exactly, but a family house, you know. But we shall hardly ever be here.'

'Oh! I thought it was my new home?'

'One of them. Our real home is in Paris, and there my grandmother, though she lives in the house, has a separate establishment. You will love her, you know. For one thing, French people (and you are French now) always love their relations, and then my grandmother is a saint.'

'Yes,' said Grace, 'I see that. I know I shall. It was so charming the way she gave those chocolates to Sigi when she saw he didn't want to kiss her hand. But how sad, Charles-Edouard, to have this lovely house and not to live in it?'

'Oh dearest Grace, for living the country is really impossible. It is too dull. I am obliged to come down here on business, but I could never never live here.'

'What business?'

'I must explain that, whereas in England the country is for pleasure and the town for business, here it is the exact opposite. We French have all our pleasure in Paris, where we have nothing to do except amuse ourselves, but we work really hard in the country. I have a lot of work when I am here, local business, since I am the mayor, and much family business, looking after my property.'

They had reached a wide landing, arranged like a room, with old-fashioned, chintz furniture. Two great windows from floor to ceiling were open upon an expanse of pale blue sky. Charles-Edouard led her through one of them on to a balcony, and, waving at the green acres far below, he said,

'There grows the wealth of the Valhubert family.'

'D'you mean that vegetable? But what is it? I was wondering.'

'Vegetable indeed! Have you never been in the country in France before! How strange. These are vineyards.'

'No!' said Grace. She had supposed all her life that vineyards were covered with pergolas, such as, in Surrey gardens, support Miss Dorothy Perkins, heavy with bunches of hot-house grapes, black for red wine, white for champagne. Naboth's vineyard, in the imagination of Grace, was Naboth's pergola, complete with crazy paving underfoot.

However she did not explain all this to Charles-Edouard, but merely said, 'I've never seen one before. I thought they would be different, somehow.'

Grace's bedroom was at the top of the house. It was a large, white-panelled room with many windows, from most of which, so high up was it, so hanging in the firmament, nothing was visible but sky. But on one side two French windows opened on to a tiny garden of box hedges and standard roses, which looked like a stage set forming part of the room itself.

'Very English,' said Charles-Edouard, 'you will feel at home here.'

It had been arranged by his mother with old-fashioned chintz and embroidered white muslin.

'The garden!' said Grace. 'I never saw anything so lovely.'

'Every floor of this house has a terrace. It is built on the side of a hill, you see. Here are your bathroom and dressing-room, and here are my rooms. So we are all alone together.'

'Literally in heaven,' said Grace, with a happy sigh.

'Now perhaps I'll take you to the nursery; we go down again and up this little staircase. Here we are.'

'Oh, what a lovely nursery – isn't it lovely, Nan, much the biggest we've ever had, and so light – and what a view!'

This was Grace's technique with Nanny. She would open an offensive of enthusiasm, hoping to overcome and silence the battery of complaints before Nanny could begin firing them off. It almost never worked, she could see it not working now, though for the moment she was shielded by the presence of Charles-Edouard. Nanny remained silent and went on with what she was at, grimly unpacking toys from a hamper.

'I'll come back,' said Charles-Edouard. 'I want a word with Ange-Victor.'

Grace's heart sank, but she rattled bravely on. 'You've got a garden, too, isn't it delightful? I love it being surrounded by those pretty red roofs against the sky, like Kate Greenaway. Look at the plants growing out of them, what are they, I wonder? Doesn't it all smell delicious? I long for you to see my bedroom; it is so pretty. Tell you what, darling, I'll get you a garden chair, then you'll be able to sit out here of an evening.'

Nanny looked over her shoulder to make sure that Charles-

Edouard had gone, and then spoke. 'Horribly draughty I should think, with all those roofs. Smutty, too, I daresay. Aren't the stairs awful? I shan't be able to manage them many times a day, in this heat. Well, I've been trying to unpack, but there's nowhere to put anything, you know – shame, really – no nice shelves for our toys. No mantelpieces, either, for my photographs and the ornaments. Funny sort of rooms, aren't they? Not very homy. I'd like to show you the bathroom and lavatory, dear – nothing but a cupboard – no window at all, really most insanitary – it would never be allowed at home.'

'How fascinating,' said Grace, 'look, it's built in the thickness of the wall, this big bathroom.'

'Perhaps it may be. Then what is that guitar-shaped vase for, I wonder? Oh, well, it'll do to put the things to soak. Not very nice, is it? Leading out of our bedroom like that?'

'Never mind, in this lovely weather you can leave everything wide open – it's quite different from England.'

'Different!' a deep sniff, 'I should say it is.'

'Look at the swing! How amusing! That will quite make up to Sigi for leaving his rocking-horse behind.'

'Yes, well it's a funny place for a swing, in our bedroom.'

'It's all so huge, isn't it? And like being out of doors, with these great windows everywhere. Heavenly, really. Look, here's a cupboard, darling – the size of a room, too. Hadn't you noticed it? You can put everything here – and see, there's a light for it. That is nice.'

'Just smell inside, dear – horribly musty, I'm afraid. Then I was wanting to speak to you about these roofs – the little monkey will be up on them in no time. My goodness! I knew it! Come down this instant, Sigi, what did I tell you? You are not to climb on those roofs – what d'you think you're doing? It's most dangerous.'

'I'm Garth on the mountains of the moon.'

Charles-Edouard reappeared, saying, 'Oh, do be Napoleon crossing the Alps. This Garth is really too dull. The roofs are quite safe, Nanny, I lived on them when I was his age, mountaineering and exploring. I must get out my old *Journal des Voyages* for him, since I suppose he is rather young for Jules Verne?'

33

Nanny having retreated into the nursery, 'don't know how you can stand the glare,' Charles-Edouard pulled at the neck of Grace's cotton dress and implanted a kiss on her shoulder.

'Ugh! You soppy things,' said Sigismond, 'I don't like all this daft kissing stuff.'

'You'll like it all right one day,' said Charles-Edouard. 'That big bell means luncheon time. Good appetite, Sigi.'

As they went back through the nursery a man-servant was laying the table on a thick, white linen tablecloth. 'Good appetite, Nanny,' said Charles-Edouard. Nanny did not reply. She was looking with stupefied disapproval at a bottle of wine which had just been put down in front of her.

Chapter Five

VERY hungry, accustomed to English post-war food, Grace thought the meal which followed the most delicious she had ever eaten. The food, the wine, the heat, and the babel of French talk, most of which was quite incomprehensible to her untuned ear, induced a half-drunk, entirely happy state of haziness. When, after nearly two hours, the party rose from the table, she was floating on air. Everybody wandered off in different directions, and Charles-Edouard announced that he was going to be shut up in the library for the afternoon with his tenants and the agent.

'Will you be happy?' he said, stroking Grace's hair and laughing at her for being, as he could see, so tipsy.

'Oh I'm sleepy and happy and hot and sleepy and drunk and happy and sleepy. It's too too blissful being so drunk and happy.'

'Then go to sleep, and when I've finished we'll do whatever you like. Motor down to the sea if you like, and bathe. I'm sleepy myself, but the *régisseur* has convened all these people to see me – they've been waiting too long already – I must go to them, so there it is. See you presently.'

'All right. I'll go and have a little word with Nanny and then a lovely hot sleep. Oh the weather! Oh the bliss of everything! Oh how happy I am!'

Charles-Edouard gave her a very loving look as he went off.

He thought he was going to like her even more in France than in England, and was well satisfied to have come back accompanied by this happy beauty.

Alas for the hot, tipsy sleep! Nanny sobered and woke her up all right, her expression alone was a wave of icy water. Grace did not even bother to say 'Wasn't the luncheon delicious? Did you enjoy it?' She just stood and meekly waited for the wave to break over her head.

'Well, dear, we've had nothing to eat since you saw us, nothing whatever. Course upon course of nasty greasy stuff smelling of garlic – a month's ration of meat, yes, but quite raw you know – shame, really – I wasn't going to touch it, let alone give it to Sigi, poor little mite.'

'Nanny says the cheese was matured in manure,' Sigi chipped in, eyes like saucers.

'I wish you could have smelt it, dear, awful it was, and still covered with bits of straw. Makes you wonder, doesn't it? Well, we just had a bite of bread and butter and a few of Mrs Crispin's nice rock cakes I happened to have with me. Not much of a dinner, was it? Funny-looking bread here, too, all crust and holes, I don't know how you'd make a nice bit of damp toast with that. Poor little hungry boy – never mind, it's all right now, darling, your mummy will go to the kitchen for us and ask for some cold ham or chicken – a bit of something plain – some tomatoes, without that nasty, oily, oniony dressing, and a nice floury potato, won't you, dear?'

These words were uttered in tones of command. An order had been issued, there was nothing of the request about them.

'Goodness, I've no idea what floury potato is in French,' said Grace, playing for time. 'Didn't you like the food, Sigi?'

'It's not a question of like it or not like it. The child will eat anything, as you know, but I'm not going to risk having him laid up with a liver attack. This heat wave is quite trying enough without that, thank you very much, not to mention typhoid fever, or worse. I only wish you could have smelt the cheese, that's all I say.'

'I did smell it, we had it downstairs – delicious.'

'Well it may be all right for grown-up people, if that's the sort of thing they go in for,' said Nanny, with a tremendous sniff,

35

'but give it to the child I will not, and personally I'd rather go hungry.' This, however, she had no intention of doing. 'Now, dear,' she said briskly, 'just go and get us a bite of something plain, that's a good girl.'

'I'm so dreadfully starving, Mummy, I've got pains in my tummy. Listen, it rumbles, just like Garth when he'd been floating for weeks on that iceberg.'

Sigi looked so pathetic that Grace said, 'Oh all right then. I don't know where the kitchen is, but I'll see what I can do. I think it's all great rubbish,' she added in a loud aside as she slammed the nursery door behind her.

She wandered off uncertainly, hardly able, in that big, complicated house built at so many different dates, on so many different levels, to find her way to the first-floor rooms. At last she did so, looked into the drawing-room, and was almost relieved that there was nobody there. Her mission seemed to her absurd, and really so ill-mannered, that she quite longed for it to fail. She assumed that everybody except Charles-Edouard would be happily asleep by now, and only wished that she were too. Loud French voices came from the library, apart from them the house was plunged in silence. She stood for a moment by the library door but did not dare to open it, thinking how furious Sir Conrad would be at such an interruption. The dining-room was empty; no sign of any servant. She went through it, and found a stone-flagged passage, which she followed, on and on, up and down steps, until she came to a heavy oak door. Perhaps this led to the kitchen; she opened it timidly. A strangely dark and silent kitchen, if so, with cool but not fresh air smelling of incense. She stood peering into the gloom; it was quite some moments before she realized that this must be a chapel. Then, not two yards from her, she saw Madame de Valhubert, a lace shawl over her head, praying deeply. Grace shut the door and fled, in British embarrassment, back to the nursery.

'I can't find the kitchen, or one single person to ask,' she said, in a hopeless voice. Nanny gave Grace a look. 'Where's Papa then?'

'At a meeting. Well Nan you do know, we should never have dared disturb my papa at a meeting, should we? I don't see how

I can. Are you sure you haven't any food with you, to make do just for now?'

'Nothing whatever.'

'No groats?'

'Groats isn't much of a dinner. The poor little chap's hungry after all that travelling. We didn't get much of a dinner yesterday if you remember, in that aeroplane, expecting every moment to be our last.'

Sigismond now began to grizzle. 'Mummy I do want my dinner, please, please Mummy.'

'Oh all right then,' said Grace, furiously. There was clearly nothing for it but to set forth again, to summon up all her courage and put her head round the library door. Abashed by the sudden silence that fell and the looks of surprise and interest on eight or ten strange masculine faces, she said to Charles-Edouard, who was the furthest from her so that she had to say it across the whole room, 'I'm so sorry to interrupt, but could I possibly have a word with you?'

He came out at once, shut the door, put his-arms round her, and said, 'You were quite right to come. It was very dull in there, and now we'll go to your room.'

'Oh no,' said Grace. 'It wasn't for that.'

'How d'you mean? it wasn't for that. What is "that", anyway?' he said, laughing.

'Oh don't laugh at me, it was terrible going in there. I was so terribly frightened, but I had to. It's about Nanny.'

'Yes, yes, I know. We must have a long talk about Nanny, but not now. First we go upstairs – what must be must be, and quickly too.'

'No, first we go to the kitchen and ask for a floury potato for Nanny, who is waxy, in a bait, I mean, because they've had no luncheon.'

Grace, by now, was really rather hysterical.

'Had no luncheon!' cried Charles-Edouard, 'this is too much. I must find my Grandmother.'

'Oh they had it all right, they just couldn't eat it.'

'What d'you mean, Grace? I'm sure they had the same as we did. You said yourself it was delicious.'

'Yes, of course it was, and I'm furious with Nanny for complaining, but the fact is Nannies never can bear new food you know, it's my own fault, I ought to have remembered that. Now dear, dearest Charles-Edouard, do come to the kitchen and help me to find something she can eat.'

'Very well. And tomorrow we send her back to England.'

There. Grace's heart sank.

'But who would look after poor little Sigi?'

'M. le Curé must find him a tutor. This child is quite un-lettered, I had a long talk with him in the train. He knows nothing, and can't even read.'

'But of course not, poor little boy. He isn't seven yet!'

'When I was five,' said Charles-Edouard, 'I had to read all Dumas, *père.*'

'I've noticed everybody thinks they themselves could read when they were five.'

'Ask M. le Curé.'

'Anyway you must have been too sweet for words,' said Grace. 'I only wish I'd known you then.'

'I was exceedingly brilliant. Now here is the kitchen, and here, by great good luck, is M. André, the head chef. Will you please explain exactly what it is that you do want?'

While some of the household slept (though sharp attacks of insomnia characterized that afternoon) and Madame de Val-hubert prayed, Madame Rocher des Innouïs and M. de la Bourlie took themselves off to a little garden, deeply shaded by an ilex tree, to have a nice chat about Grace. One summer long ago they had conducted a violent love affair under the very noses of Madame de Valhubert, Madame de la Bourlie, M. Rocher, and Prince Zjebrowski, the lover of Madame Rocher. It had really been a *tour de force* of its kind; they had succeeded in hood-winking all the others, none of whom had ever had the slightest suspicion of it. After that they had remained on cosy, rather conspiratorial terms.

'We must begin by saying that she is beautiful – more beauti-ful, perhaps, than Priscilla.' Madame Rocher spread out the ten yards of her Dior skirt and settled herself comfortably with cushions. 'But not, as anyone can see, a society woman. Of good family, yes perhaps, but perfectly green in worldly matters. She told me, at luncheon, that she has hardly been out in society since the war, but spent all those years looking after goats. Of course the English are very eccentric, you don't know that, Sosthène, you have never crossed the Channel, but you can take it from me that they are all half mad, a country of enormous, fair, mad atheists. Why did she look after goats? We shall never know. But looking after goats can hardly be considered as a good preparation for life with Charles-Edouard, and I am bound to say I feel uneasy for her. They are not married religiously, by the way.'

'Oh! How do you know?'

'I asked her.'

'What an extraordinary question to ask.'

'After all, I am Charles-Edouard's aunt.'

'I meant what an extraordinary idea. It would never have occurred to me that they might not be.'

'It occurred to me. I know England, Sosthène. We went every year for the Horse Show, don't forget.'

'Shall you tell Françoise?'

'Of course not, on no account, and nor must you. It would upset her dreadfully.'

'Speaking frankly then, nothing matters very much?'

'I don't agree at all. It's true that they can easily be divorced, and that Charles-Edouard will be able to marry again without waiting for an annulment, but before that happens he will have made her totally miserable. Charles-Edouard is a good, warm-hearted boy, he won't be able to help making her miserable, but he will suffer too. Oh dear, what could have induced him to marry an Englishwoman – these English with their terrible jealousy – it will be the story of Priscilla all over again, you'll see.'

'But the English husbands then, how do they manage?'

'English husbands? They go to their clubs, their boat race, their Royal Academy – they don't care for making love a bit. So they are always perfectly faithful to their wives.'

'What about the Gaiety Girls?'

'I don't think they exist any more. You are behind the times, my poor Sosthène, it is the gaiety boys now, if anything. But they have no temperament. Now Charles-Edouard cannot – he really cannot – see a pretty woman without immediately wanting to sleep with her. What foolishness, then, to go and marry an Anglo-Saxon.'

'You talk as if Latins are never jealous.'

'It is quite different for a Frenchwoman, she has ways and means of defending herself. First of all she is on her own ground, and then she has all the interest, the satisfaction, of making life impossible for her rival. Instead of sad repining her thoughts are concentrated on plot and counterplot, the laying of traps and the springing of mines. Paris divides into two camps, she has to consider most carefully what forces she can put in the field, she must sum up the enemy strength, and prepare her stratagem. Whom can she enlist on her side? There is all society to be won over, the hostesses, the old men who go to tea parties, and the families of those concerned. Then there is the elegance, the manicurists, the *masseuses,* the *vendeuses,* the *modistes,* the *bottiers,* and the *lingères.* A foothold among the tradesmen who serve her rival's kitchen may prove very useful; we must not, of course, forget the fortune-tellers, while a concierge can play a cardinal role. The day is not long enough for all the contrivances to be put on foot, for the consultations with her women friends, the telephoning, the messages, the sifting and deep consideration of all news and all fresh evidence. Finally, and not the least important, she has her own lover to comfort and advise her. Ah! Things are very different for a Frenchwoman. But these poor English roses just hang their lovely heads and droop and die. Did Priscilla ever defend herself for a single moment? Don't you remember how painful it was to us, for years, to see how terribly she suffered? And now I suppose we are condemned to live through it all over again with this Grace.'

M. de la Bourlie thought how much he would have liked to appropriate to himself one of these loving, faithful and defenceless goddesses. When Madame de la Bourlie finally succumbed to a liver attack, he thought, why should he not take a little trip to London? But then he remembered his age.

'So hard to believe that we are all over eighty now,' he said, peevishly.

'Yes, it must be, but what has that to do with Charles-Edouard? Poor boy, he has certainly made an unwise marriage.

All the same I rather like this Grace, I can't help it, she is so lovely, and there is something direct about her which I find charming. I also think her tougher, a tougher proposition than poor Priscilla was, more of a personality. There was never any hope for Priscilla, and I'm not quite so sure about Grace. If I can help her I will. Should I try to prepare her a little while she is here? Warn her about Albertine, for instance? What do you advise?'

'I don't think it ever does much good, to warn,' said M. de la Bourlie, thinking how furious he would be, in Charles-Edouard's place, if somebody were to warn his exquisite new wife about his intoxicating old mistress.

'No good at all,' agreed Madame Rocher, 'you are quite right. And then it's not as if it were only Albertine. I'd have to warn against every pretty woman and every *jolie-laide* at every dinner and every luncheon that they go to. I'd have to warn against Rastaquouères and Ranees, Israelites and Infantas, Danes and Duchesses, Greeks and Cherokee Indians. I'd have to give her a white list and a black list, and now, I suppose, since he has just come back from Indo-China, a yellow list as well. No, it would really be too exhausting, the young people must work it out for themselves – everybody has storms and troubles at their age no doubt, and there is no point in getting mixed up in them. All the same, I do wish so very much that Charles-Edouard could have married a good, solid, level-headed little French woman of the world instead of this beautiful goat-herd.'

The long summer days went by, slowly at first and then gathering speed, as days do which are filled from dawn to dusk with idleness. Grace spent most of the morning on the terrace outside her bedroom sewing away at her carpet. Charles-Edouard liked to see her doing it; her fair, bent head and flashing, white hands made such a pretty picture, but he decided that the day the carpet was finished it would have to be overtaken by some rather fearful accident, a pot of spilt indelible ink, or a spreading burn. Charles-Edouard was not one to cherish an object, especially so large and ugly an object as this was going to be, for reasons of sentiment.

After luncheon there was the siesta, and then Charles-Edouard and she would often drive down to the sea for a bathe. He had countless friends and acquaintances on the coast to whose villas they could go and from whose rocks they could swim, but Grace's complete lack of suitable clothes protected her from a really social life, from dinner parties, and visits to the Riviera. For this she was thankful. She liked the sleepy existence at Bellandargues, though Charles-Edouard complained of its dullness. His crony there was Madame Rocher, who poured into his ears an endless saga, her own version of all that had happened to all his friends since he had last seen them in 1939. It sounded simply terrific to Grace, whenever she overheard any of it. Madame Rocher was bored herself, longing to be off to yachts and palazzos and villas at which various impatient hosts and hostesses were said to be awaiting her. But this year she had decided to obey her doctor, and to stay quietly at Bellandargues for at least a month. She kept herself amused by the overwhelming interest she took in all that happened in house, village, and neighbourhood. When Grace and Charles-Edouard went off on their bathing expeditions she was able to tell them a great deal about their hosts, and what they were likely to find in the way of a household.

'Is it today you go to the English Lesbians? The nephew of the old one is there, I believe – if he is her nephew. They've just bought a refrigerator, what extravagance!'

'The Italian *ménage à trois*? Have you explained to Grace that *she* only like boys of sixteen and *they* get them for her? An excellent cook, I hear, this year.'

'Those two pederasts? Poor people, they are being horribly blackmailed by an ex-convict who lives in the village. But their rocks have never been nicer.'

And so on.

'Your aunt sees life through a veil of sex,' Grace said to Charles-Edouard when, for the third or fourth time, the company, represented to her by Madame Rocher as steeped in lurid vice, had turned out to be an ordinary, jolly house party.

'And who's to say she's wrong?'

'Well, I do think to call Mrs Browne and Lady Adela the English Lesbians is going rather too far. Anybody can see they've never heard of such a thing, poor darlings.'

'Then it's time somebody told them. More fun for them, if they know.'

'Charles-Edouard! And that dear old Italian lady with her two nice friends and all their grandchildren. I can't believe it!'

'One must never entirely discount Tante Régine's information on these subjects.'

One day when they were going to see an intensely pompous French duke and his wife, Madame Rocher hissed through the window of the motor at Grace, 'Reds.'

'Dear Tante Régine, come now!' Even Charles-Edouard was laughing.

'That family have always been Orleanists, my dear boy, and you very well know it. Impossible to be more to the Left.'

As they drove back in the beautiful evening light Charles-Edouard said, 'Shall we go to Venice? You could buy some clothes in Cannes on our way.'

Grace's heart sank. 'I'm happy here – aren't you, Charles-Edouard?'

'The evenings here are so terrible,' he said. 'I can get through the day, but the evenings — !'

'I love them,' she said, 'they must have been exactly the same for hundreds of years.'

She dreaded leaving Bellandargues, she felt she could cope with life there. The world that awaited them outside its walls was so infinitely complicated, according to Madame Rocher.

'Very well,' said Charles-Edouard, 'if you like it so much we'll stay until we go to Paris. I like it all right except for after dinner.'

Certainly the evenings were not very gay. The party repaired for coffee and *tisane* to a small salon where they chatted or played bridge until bed-time. Hot night noises floated in through the open windows. 'Why do French ducks quack all night?' Grace had asked. 'Those are frogs, my dearest, our staple diet you know.' Sometimes Madame Rocher played Chopin. It really was rather dull. Then Charles-Edouard discovered that she knew how to tell fortunes by cards, after which there was no more Chopin and no more gossiping. Grace was left at the bridge table while Charles-Edouard bullied Madame Rocher in a corner.

'Come on, Tante Régine, to work, to work!'

'But I've told you all I can.'

'That was yesterday. Today some new and hitherto unknown factor may have changed the whole course of my existence. Come, come!'

Madame Rocher, completely good-natured, would take up the cards and go on to the end of her invention. 'No wonder those five fortune-tellers said you would be killed in the war – they simply had to, to get rid of you.'

'Once more, Tante Régine – do I cut in three this time?'

'That's it, flog the poor old horse till it drops.'

'I passed by Madame André's cottage this afternoon, and made her tell the cards. She is much more dramatic than you, Tante Régine – dark ladies and fair ladies – wicked ladies of all sorts about *chez* Madame André.'

'Yes, but I am handicapped by the presence of your wife,' said Madame Rocher, laughing.

'Oh!' said Grace, from the bridge table, 'you mustn't be. I'm not a bit a jealous person. I don't know what it is to be jealous.'

Madame Rocher raised her eyebrows, Madame de Valhubert and M. de la Bourlie looked sadly at each other across the table, and M. le Curé said, 'I declare a little slam.'

'That's very naughty, M. le Curé,' said Grace, 'now we shall be two down.'

Chapter Six

'It's about this Mr Labby, dear.'

Charles-Edouard, who always got things done at once when he had decided upon them, had produced a young abbé to give Sigismond his lessons, and of course M. l'Abbé and Nanny were, from the very first, at daggers drawn. That is to say, Nanny's dagger was drawn, but it hardly penetrated the thick, black, clerical robes of the priest, who seemed quite unaware of her existence. That was his weapon.

'Oh Nan! But he seems nice, don't you think? So gentle. And Sigi loves him.'

Indeed that was partly the trouble. Sigi was always running

off to be with M. l'Abbé, adored his lessons, had asked for longer hours, and Nanny was jealous.

'That's as may be,' she said darkly, 'you never can tell with these foreign clergymen, but it's his little brain I'm thinking of. Their little brains are so easily taxed. I wish you could hear him scream of a night. He's nothing but a bundle of nerves, all on edge – awful dreams he has, poor little fellow. I was wondering if these lessons aren't too much for him.'

'No, darling, of course not. We all learnt to read, you know. I was reading *The Making of a Marchioness* when Mummy died, I remember it so well.'

It was a memory that she always found rather disturbing. The little girl, with her nose in the book, had felt that she ought to feel sad, and yet all she wanted was to get on with the story. Sir Conrad had come into the nursery, tears pouring down his cheeks, at the very moment when Emily Fox-Seaton was setting out for the fish, and Grace had been distinctly annoyed by the interruption. Later on in life she had pondered over this apparent heartlessness with some astonishment. Did little children, then, not feel sorrow, or was it that the book had provided her with a refuge from the tragic, and perhaps embarrassing, reality?

She did not remember feeling sorrow at the loss of her mother, though she had often been seized with a physical longing for the soft lap and scented bosom of that intensely luxurious woman.

'I was only six – do you admit, Nanny?'

'Practically seven, and girls are always more forward.'

'Besides, you know, he simply must learn French.'

Nanny sniffed. 'He's learning French quick enough from that Canary. Another thing I wanted to talk to you about, when he's with Canary and all those other little devils they go off together goodness knows where, and I wouldn't be surprised if they bathe in the pond.'

'I expect they do.' Grace had, indeed, often seen them at it, and very pretty they looked popping naked in and out of the green water of a Renaissance fountain on the edge of the village. 'But it doesn't matter. Sigi's papa says he always bathed there when he was a child. It's perfectly safe.'

'Oh, perfectly safe until the poor little chap gets poliomyelitis and spends the rest of his life in a wheel chair. I wish to goodness he'd never taken up with that Canary, he's a perfect menace.'

Canari, the little yellow-headed son of Mignon the chemist, was Sigi's friend. 'M. l.Abbé is teaching me to pray. I prayed for a friend and I got Canari.'

Every afternoon, at the hottest time of the day, Sigi would race down to the vineyard to meet Canari and his band of *maquisards*. He was seen no more until Nanny rang the bell for Dick Barton, when he would race back up the hill. Nanny now had a powerful wireless installed, which turned the nursery into for ever England with 6 o'clock news, 9 o'clock news, Music While you Work, and Twenty Questions. The *Daily Mirror,* too, had begun to arrive, bringing Garth in person, and so had *Woman and Beauty,* since when the nursery front had been distinctly calmer.

'But we mustn't worry too much, Nanny darling. Sigi is a little boy, growing up fast now, he's bound to dash off, you know, that's what little boys are like. I think it's a lovely life for him here, I only wish we could stay for ever.'

'You love M. l'Abbé, don't you, Sigismond?' said Grace, next morning. He always sat on her bed while she had her breakfast, a great bowl of coffee with fresh white bread, served on old Marseilles china. It was in many ways her favourite moment of the day; she drank her coffee looking at the hot early morning sky through muslin curtains; everything in the room was pretty, and the little boy on the end of her bed, in a white cotton jersey and red linen trousers, the prettiest object of all.

'I love M. l'Abbé and I revere him, and I've got a new ambition now. I wish to be able to converse with him in Latin.'

'French first, darling.'

'No, Mummy, the Romans were civilized before the Gauls, M. l'Abbé says. He tells some smashing stories about these Romans, and I've a new idea for Nanny. Supposing we got her into an arena with a particularly fierce bear?'

'Oh, poor Nanny. Where will you find the bear?'

'One of our *maquisards* comes from the Pyrenees, and they've got three bears there, wild, to this day. I showed him a picture of Garth digging a cunning pit, covered with leaves and branches—'

'Not Garth still?' said Charles-Edouard, coming in with the morning's letters. 'Run along, Sigi,' he said, holding the door and shooing him with a newspaper.

'Why do you always say run along, Papa?' He dragged through the door, looking crestfallen.

'It's what my mother used to say to me. "Run along, Charles-Edouard." The whole of my childhood was spent running along. I did hate it, too. Off with you! That was another.' He shut the door and gave Grace her letters.

'If you didn't like it,' she said, 'I can't think why you inflict it on the poor little boy. I don't think he sees enough of us, and he never sees us together.'

'That's not the point. The point is that we see quite enough of him,' said Charles-Edouard. 'There is nothing so dull as the conversation of small children.'

'It amuses me.'

'It does sometimes amuse women. They've got a childish side themselves, nature's way of enabling them to bear the prattle. And while we are on the subject, M. l'Abbé tells me that Nanny won't leave them alone at lesson time, she's always fussing in with some excuse or other. It's very annoying. Perhaps you'd speak to her about it?'

'I do know. I was afraid you'd be cross.'

'Well, speak.'

'Yes, I'll try. But you know what it is with Nanny, I'm dreadfully under her thumb. She thinks M. l'Abbé is taxing his little brain.'

'But his little brain has got to be taxed, it's there for that. Let Nanny wait till he's reading for his *bachot* if she wants to see him taxed – going on to twelve and one at night – poor little green face – rings under his eyes – attempted suicide – breakdowns—'

'Oh, Charles-Edouard, you are a brute,' said Grace, quite horrified.

He laughed, and began kissing her arm and shoulder.

'All this loony kissing again,' Sigi appeared in the window, 'over the pathless Himalayas, that's where I've come.'

47

'Yes, I wondered how long it would be before you found the way,' said Charles-Edouard.

'Shall I tell you something? I've just seen the *Daily*, and Garth has renounced the love of women.'

'Oh, he's like that, is he?'

'He's an Effendi now. What's an Effendi, Papa?'

'Talk about taxing his brain,' said Charles-Edouard.

'Well I know, but if it wasn't for Garth and Dick Barton he'd never go near the nursery, and poor Nanny would have a stroke looking for him on the roof and in the vineyards all day.'

'Now, Sigismond, just go back over those trackless paths, will you?'

'In other words, run along and off with you. All right, if I must.'

'M. l'Abbé talks about teaching him Latin.'

'Yes?' Charles-Edouard was opening his letters.

'Seems rather a waste of time?'

'Latin is a waste of time?' he said, putting a letter in his pocket and looking at Grace with surprise. 'Surely he must learn it before he goes to Eton?'

'Well it won't be the right pronunciation. Do we want Sigi to go to Eton?'

'Why not, for a bit? Then he can be top in English when he goes to St Cyr.'

'But I don't think they can go to Eton for a bit. Oh dear, I thought the thing about being French was you had your blessing always at home.'

'Do we always want him at home?'

'I do. Anyway, you have to be put down for Eton before your parents are married now – long before you are conceived, so I think this dream will come to nothing.'

Charles-Edouard, who was still reading his letters, said, 'Brighton College then, it's all the same.'

'Please can I come to the sea with you?'

'Not today, darling. We're lunching with some grown-up people.'

'It is unfair. I want to take a photograph of a huge, frightened wave.'

'But today it will be flat calm. Next time there's a mistral we'll take you.'

'I'm so hot. I do so want to bathe.'

'Don't you bathe in the fountain, with Canari?'

'I'm *brouillé* with *le chef*.'

'Not *brouillé* with Canari?'

'Yes I am. It was *convenu* that the *maquisards* should come here and be *chasseurs alpins* on the roof one day and the next I should spend with them doing sabotage in the village. Well, they came here, and yesterday I went down to the village and he was under the lime trees with *les braves*, and he said, "*va-t-en. On ne veut pas de toi.*"'

'But why, Sigi?'

'I don't know. But I don't care, not a bit. I want to go to the sea and swim under water and spear an octopus.'

'When you are older.'

'When shall I be older?'

'All in due course. Run along now and find M. l'Abbé.'

'He is reading his *bréviaire*.'

'Well, Nanny then. Anyway, run along, darling.'

That night, at dinner, Madame de Valhubert said, 'Do you know our poor little *maquisard* spent the whole afternoon by himself in the salon? He looked the picture of woe. In the end Régine and I had to play cards with him for very pity.'

'It's that wretched Canari,' said Grace, 'he has sent him packing, and nobody knows why. Oh, I do hope they'll make it up soon, or the poor duck will have no more fun at all. I feel quite worried. Couldn't you go down and speak to M. Mignon, Charles-Edouard, and find out what it is?'

Charles-Edouard laughed, looked round the table at the others, who were all smiling, and said, 'Alas, my influence with Mignon is but limited, I fear.'

'But why? He made that nice speech.'

'That was the *solidarité de la libération*. It just held long enough for him to make the speech. Now we are back among all the old feuds again. A very good sign that peace is really here.'

'M. le Curé, couldn't you do something?' said Grace.

At this there was a general laugh. M. le Curé lifted his hands, saying that Grace did not quite grasp the situation. M. Mignon, he said, was a Radical Socialist. If Grace had not spent the years of the war so idly, stitching dreams into an ugly carpet or leading goats to browse on blackberries, if she had taken the advice of her father and concentrated instead upon Messrs Bodley and Brogan, whose works lay among a huge heap of unopened books behind the back stairs, these words would have meant something to her, and what was to follow would have been avoided. But as she looked completely blank Charles-Edouard began to explain.

'Not only is M. Mignon, *père*, a Radical Socialist of the deepest dye – Canari doesn't go to our school, I would have you observe, but to the *Instituteur* – but he is actually a Freemason.'

'Well, in that case, it's a pity my father's not here to have a word with him. They could wear their aprons, and do whatever it is together.'

Charles-Edouard tried to kick Grace under the table, but she was too far for him to reach her. She went blandly on.

'Papa is one of the top Freemasons, at home, you know. Couldn't we tell M. Mignon that? It might help.'

Silence fell, so petrifyingly cold that she realized something was very wrong, but couldn't imagine what.

Madame de Valhubert's black eyes went with a question mark to Charles-Edouard. Madame Rocher and M. de la Bourlie exchanged glances of mournful significance; M. le Curé and M. l'Abbé gazed at their plates and Charles-Edouard looked extremely put out, as Grace had never seen him look before. At last he said to his grandmother, 'Freemasons are quite different in England, you know.'

'Oh! Indeed?'

'The Grand Master, there, is a member of the Royal Family – is that not so, Grace?'

'I don't know,' said Grace. 'I don't really know much about them.'

'With the English anything is possible,' said Madame Rocher. 'What did I tell you, Sosthène?'

'Oh no, but all the same,' muttered the old man, 'this is too much.'

There was another long silence, at the end of which Madame de Valhubert rose from the table, and they all went into the little salon. The evening dragged much worse than usual, and the party dispersed for the night very early indeed.

'What have I done?' said Grace in her bedroom.

'It's not your fault,' said Charles-Edouard, crossly, for him, not knowing that it was entirely her fault for neglecting the information Sir Conrad had put at her disposal, 'but I must beg you never again to speak of Freemasons before French people. Take a lover – take two – turn Lesbian – steal valuable boxes off your friends' tables – anything, anything, but don't say that your father is a Freemason. It will need ten years of virtuous life before this is forgiven, and it will never be forgotten. *La fille du francmaçon!* Well, I'll see my grandmother in the morning and try to explain —' He was laughing again now, but Grace saw that he was really very much embarrassed by what she had done.

Madame de Valhubert having rushed to the chapel, Madame Rocher went down with M. de la Bourlie to his motor, and they stood for a moment on the terrace together.

'You see!' she said, 'daughter of Freemasons! What did I tell you? No wonder she was married by a mayor, all is now plain as daylight. Can they, I wonder, really be considered decent people in England? I must find out. Poor Charles-Edouard, I see his path beset by thorns. Terrible for the Valhuberts, especially as they have had this sort of trouble in the family once – well not freemasonry, of course, but that dreadful Marshal. All so carefully lived down ever since. No wonder Françoise is upset – she will be on her knees all night, I feel sure.'

M. de la Bourlie was greatly shocked at the whole affair. Even were he not over eighty, even were Madame de la Bourlie not still alive, a beautiful English wife now ceased to be any temptation to him. He had learnt his lesson.

Grace's blunder had one good result however. Sigi got back into the Canari set, from which he had been expelled, had he but known it, on grounds of clericalism. His adherence to M. l'Abbé had been doing him no good among the *maquisards*.

M. le Curé was unable to keep the extraordinary pronouncement of young Madame de Valhubert to himself; he told one or two gossips, and the news spread like wild-fire, causing the greatest possible sensation in the village. The Catholics, adherents of the M.R.P. and so on, were very much shocked, but the rest of the population was jubilant. The daughter of a Freemason was an unhoped-for addition to the Valhubert family. Nanny, whose resistance to M. l'Abbé stiffened every day, came to be regarded as the very champion of anti-clericalism. The position of Charles-Edouard remained anomalous, a certain mystery seemed to surround his opinions, and nobody knew exactly where he stood. On one hand there was the Freemason wife, on the other it was he and nobody else who had summoned M. l'Abbé to teach his child. Since he was popular, jolly, and a good landlord, since his war record was above reproach, and they knew, from his own voice on the radio, that he had been one of the very first to join General de Gaulle, he tended to be claimed as one of themselves by all sections of the community while they awaited further evidence from which to draw further conclusions.

Charles-Edouard did manage to convince his grandmother that freemasonry in England was regarded by decent, and even royal, families as perfectly correct. It took some doing, but finally he succeeded.

'Very well then,' she said. 'I believe you, my child. But as we are on disagreeable topics, why this marriage by a mayor? Why not a priest?'

'Ah!' he said. 'You know?'

'Yes, I know.'

'The fact is I was not quite sure. I married this foreign woman after a very short courtship, I was off to the war, perhaps for years, she was engaged to somebody else when I first met her, and might have – I didn't think so, but there was no proof – an unstable character. And she was a heathen. The English, you know, are nearly all heathens, like freemasonry, it is a perfectly respectable thing to be, over there. Should she have got tired of waiting and gone off with somebody else, I didn't want to be debarred for ever, or at any rate for years, from a proper marriage. If she, or her father, had made the least objection to the civil marriage, if they had even mentioned it, I would have got a priest, but the subject was never raised. It was very odd. They regarded the whole thing as perfectly normal and natural. Sigismond has been baptized, by the way. I wrote and asked for

52

that, and it was immediately done, just as if I had asked for him to be vaccinated.'

'And now?' said Madame de Valhubert.

'Grace is still a heathen, but you can see for yourself that she is a soul worth saving. In due course we shall convert her; it will be time enough then to be married in church.'

'Charles-Edouard, you have brought home a heathen concubine instead of a wife! You are living in mortal sin, my child.'

'Dearest grandmother, you know me well enough to know that I am generally living in mortal sin. We must trust, for my soul, to the mercy of God. As regards Grace, all will turn out for the best, you will see.'

Grace would have been intensely surprised if she could have overheard this conversation. They both spoke as if he had picked up the daughter of a cannibal king in darkest Africa, whereas she thought of herself as a perfectly ordinary Christian. Something of this occurred to Charles-Edouard.

'Please, grandmother, if you speak with Grace about this, don't say that she is only a concubine. She wouldn't like it. Trust me – I'm sure everything will be all right, meanwhile you can look upon us as fiancés.'

'Very well,' said the old lady. 'I won't say a word on any religious subject. It is your responsibility, Charles-Edouard, and you know as well as I do where your duty lies in this matter.'

'But,' she thought to herself, 'there are other things I must have out with her before they go back to Paris.'

'I suppose Charles-Edouard must seem very English to you, dear child,' she began, next time she found herself alone with Grace.

'English?' Grace was amused and surprised. For her Charles-Edouard was the forty kings of France rolled into one, the French race in person walking and breathing.

'Indeed at first sight he is very English. His clothes, his figure, that enormous breakfast of ham and eggs, his aptitude for business. But you know him very little, dearest, as yet. You have been married (if one can call it a marriage) for seven years and yet here you are, strangers, on a honeymoon, with a big child. It's a very odd situation, and not the least curious and wonderful part is that you are both so happy. But I repeat that so far you have only seen the English side of your husband. He is getting restless here (I know him so well) and very soon, probably at a day's notice, he will take you off to Paris. When you are there you will begin to see how truly French he is.'

'But he seems so French to me already. How can he seem even more so in Paris? In what way?'

'I am giving you a word of warning, just one. In Paris you and he will be back in his own world of little friends all brought up together. I advise you to be very, very sensible. Behave as if you were a thousand years old, like me.'

'You think I shall be jealous. Tante Régine thinks so too, I can see. But I never am. It's not part of my nature. I'm not insensitive, it isn't that, I can mind things quite terribly, but jealous I am not.'

'Alas, my dear child, you are in love, and there is no love in this world without jealousy.'

'And I may not have known Charles-Edouard for long, but I do know him very well. He loves me.'

'Yes, yes, indeed he does. That is quite plain. And so do we all, dear child, and that is why I am talking to you like this, in spite of everything. I tell you too that if you are very sensible he will love you for ever, and in time everything will be regulated in your lives and you will be a truly happy couple, for ever.'

'That's what Charles-Edouard tells me. All right, I am very sensible, so he will love me for ever. Don't I look sensible?'

'Alas, I know these practical, English looks and how they are deceptive. So reassuringly calm on the surface, and underneath what a turmoil. And then the world reflected in distorting glasses. Latin women see things so clearly as they are; above all they understand men.'

'I never know quite what it means, to understand men.'

'Don't you, dear? It's very simple, it can be said in a few words. Put them first. A woman who puts her husband first seldom loses him.'

'Well I daresay,' said Grace with some indignation, 'that a woman who lets her husband do exactly as he likes, who shuts her eyes to every infidelity, and lets him walk over her, in fact, would never lose him.'

'Just so,' said Madame de Valhubert, placidly.

'And do you really advise that?'

'Oh I don't advise, the old must never advise. All I do say is remember that Charles-Edouard is a Frenchman – not an Englishman with a French veneer, but a deeply French Frenchman. If you want this to become a real marriage, a lifelong union (I don't speak of a sacrament), you must follow the rules of our civilization. A little life of your own, if you wish it, will never be held against you, so long as you always put your husband first.'

Grace was thoroughly shocked. 'I could have understood it if Tante Régine had spoken like that – would have expected it in fact, but your grandmother!' she said to Charles-Edouard.

'My grandmother is an extremely practical person,' he said, 'you can see it by the way she runs this house. You can always tell by that, with women.'

The next day Charles-Edouard made one of his sudden moves and whirled Grace off to Paris. Nanny and the little boy were left behind to follow in a week or two, escorted by the faithful Ange-Victor.

Chapter Seven

THE Valhuberts' Paris house was of a later date than any part of Bellandargues, and had only been finished a month or two before the Revolution. It stood on the site of a Louis XIII house whose owner, planning to receive Marie Antoinette there, had pulled it down and built something more fashionable, to be worthy of her. The intended fête for the Queen never took place, and in the end it was Josephine, not Marie Antoinette, who was received as guest of honour in the round, white and gold music room. This was an episode in their family history very much glossed over by future Valhuberts, and most of all by Charles-Edouard's grandmother. The truth was that the eldest son of Marie Antoinette's admirer, a soldier born and bred, had not been able to resist the opportunity of serving under the most brilliant of all commanders. He had joined the revolutionary army, had risen to the rank of General before he was thirty, and was killed at the battle of Friedland shortly after receiving his Marshal's bâton.

'Most fortunately,' Charles-Edouard said when recounting all this to Grace, 'or he would certainly have ended up as a Duke with some outlandish title. I prefer to be what I am.'

'Perhaps he would have refused.'

'Perhaps. But I've yet to hear of anybody refusing a dukedom.'

The family, after his death, had once more embraced a cautious Royalism, and a veil was drawn over this unfashionably patriotic outburst. Old Madame de Valhubert always pretended that she knew nothing of it, and, if anybody mentioned the Marshal, would say that he must have been some very distant relation of her husband's. All his relics, his portrait in uniform by Gros, the eagle which it had cost him his life to recapture, his medals, his sword, and his bâton were hidden away at Bellandargues in a little outhouse, locally known as *le pavillon de la gloire,* and even Charles-Edouard would not have dared bring them back into the salon during the lifetime of his grandmother.

'It will be the same with me,' he said. 'Sigi's great-granddaughter-in-law will hide away my Croix de Lorraine, my *médaille de la résistance,* and the badge of my squadron, and say that I was some distant relation of her husband's. They are terrible, French families.'

The house, long, three-storied, lay between courtyard and garden. Old Madame de Valhubert, when in Paris, occupied one of the lodges in the courtyard. 'She moved in there during the war, after the Germans had looted the main block, and now she likes it so much that she has stayed on.' The other lodge housed the servants. The ground floor of the house itself consisted of five enormous drawing-rooms leading out of each other, the middle one being the famous round music room, masterpiece of the brothers Rousseau. Over this, the same shape and almost as elaborately decorated, was Grace's bedroom. These rooms were on the garden side, facing due south and with a wide view of trees.

'What an enormous garden, for a town,' said Grace.

'It used to be three times as long, but some of it was taken,

56

alas, in the time of Haussman to make the horrible rue de Babel, well named. However we can't complain, many houses in this neighbourhood suffered more – many wonderful houses either lost their gardens altogether, or were even pulled down. Paris was only saved from complete ruination by the fall of Napoleon III. Bismarck really saved us, funnily enough!'

As Charles-Edouard had quite openly joined the Free French under his own name, everything he possessed was confiscated during the war and would have been taken off to Germany had it not been for the initiative of Louis, his old butler, who had piled pictures and furniture in the cellar, built a wall to hide them, and, to make this wall convincing, put a wash basin with brass taps against it.

'We had so little time,' he said, when explaining all this to Grace and Charles-Edouard, 'that we had to connect the taps with an ordinary bucket of water hung up on the other side of the wall. Oh how we prayed the Germans wouldn't run them very long. All was well, however. They came, they tested the taps for a minute, just as we hoped they would, and went away again. Oh what a relief!'

'And they never requisitioned the house?'

'They didn't like this side of the river – too many dark, old, twisting streets; they felt more comfortable up by the Étoile in big, modern buildings. They just carted off everything they could see, and never came back again. Fortunately, as I've been here so long I knew which were the best pieces (we didn't dare hide everything). Later on we installed ventilation in the cellar, and the things were miraculously well preserved through those long, terrible winters. In all this we were helped by M. Saqué the builder – M. le Marquis will perhaps go and thank him.'

'Very probably I will,' said Charles-Edouard, more touched than he cared to admit by this recital. He loved his furniture and objects, and specially loved his pictures. He showed them to Grace before he even allowed her to go upstairs. It was a charming collection of minor masters with one or two high spots, an important Fragonard, a pair of Hubert Roberts, and so on. He was always adding to it, and had bought more than half the pictures himself.

The weeks which followed, spent by Grace alone with her

husband in the empty town during unfashionable September, were the happiest she had ever known. Charles-Edouard, rediscovering, after seven long years, the stones of Paris, for which he had an almost unhealthy love, walked with her all day in the streets, and sometimes, when there was a moon, after dinner as well. Grace was a good walker, even for an Englishwoman, but he was indefatigable, and sometimes, as when they went to Versailles for the day, she had to cry for mercy. He was wonderful company. He knew the long, intricate histories of all the palaces of the Faubourg St Germain and exactly where to find each one, hidden behind huge walls and carriage doorways.

'You could ring the bell there and have a peep,' he would say, 'nobody knows you as yet – but I shall remain here, out of sight.'

So Grace would ring, put her head round the wicket, apologize to the concierge, and be rewarded by a transparency of stone and glass and ironwork, placed, like her own house, between courtyard and trees. When the ground floor was the width of one room these trees would be visible through the two sets of windows.

'Well, did you like it?'

'Oh wonderful – I can't get over it, Charles-Edouard !'

'Please do not demonstrate in front of these policemen. Please remember that I am a well-known figure in this neighbourhood. Did you notice the sphinxes in the courtyard?'

Grace never noticed any details of that sort; her eye was quite untrained, and she was content to take in a general impression of beauty, to which she was very receptive. Unlike her husband, however, she really preferred natural beauty to things made by man.

'I am loving it, oh I am loving it. I didn't know Paris was like this. When I was at school here it was different – rue de la Pompe and Avenue Victor Hugo (the hours we spent in the Grand Magazin Jones !) in those days. And even so I was always happy here, but now —! I suppose it's got something to do with you as well, my happiness.'

'Something !' said Charles-Edouard. 'Everything.'

'How lucky I am ! I could never have loved anybody else half as much.'

'I know.'

'Still, I wish you wouldn't say "I know" like that. You might say that you're lucky too.'

'I'm awfully nice,' he answered, 'never could you have found anybody as nice as I am. Admit that you amuse yourself when you are with me. Now look – the Fountain of Bouchardon, so beautiful. But how foolish to put those horrible modern flats just there.'

'You ought to have a Georgian Society,' said Grace. 'Do you think you're really the whole reason for my happiness?'

'Almost certainly.'

'Oh dear, I hope not, so dangerous when it all depends on one person. Perhaps the Blessing has a bit to do with it too.' But she knew that if so it was a very minor bit, much as she loved the pretty little boy.

'Look, the gateway of the Hôtel de Bérulle, is it not a masterpiece of restraint and clever contrivance? See how a coach would be able to turn out of this narrow street, and drive in.'

'Oh yes, how fascinating!'

'Please do not demonstrate —'

But he was really delighted at the way she was taking to everything French. He saw that, in spite of her bad education, she showed signs of a natural taste which could easily be developed. As for Charles-Edouard, art was a religion to him. If he had a few moments to spare he would run into the Louvre as his grandmother would run into church for a short prayer. The museums were awakening one after another from their war-time trance, and Charles-Edouard, intimate with all the curators, spent hours with them discussing and praising the many improvements.

Grace said, 'How strange it is that you, who really take in everything through the eyes, should hate the country so much.'

'Nature I hate. It is so dull in the country, that must be why. But Art I love.'

'And pretty ladies you love?' she said, as he turned to peer at a vision in black and white flashing by in a little Rolls Royce. September was nearing its close and the pretty ladies had begun to trickle back into town, filling Grace with apprehension.

'Women I love,' he said with his guilty, interior laugh. 'But

59

also I am a great family man, and that will be your hold over me.'

But how to have a hold, she thought, unless one's own feet are firmly planted on the ground? And how can they be so planted in a strange country, surrounded by strangers at the very beginning of a strange new life?

In due course Nanny and Sigi arrived on the night train from Marseilles, and that afternoon Grace took them across the river to the Tuileries gardens. Nanny was in a wonderfully mellow mood, delighted to have got away from the heat of Provence, from Canari, and, temporarily, at any rate, from M. l'Abbé. (He was coming to Paris after Christmas, when the lessons would be resumed.) Delighted, too, to be in a town again, where a child is so much easier to control than in the country. She entirely approved of the fact that the door to the street could only be opened by the concierge, and that the garden was surrounded by walls high as the ramparts of a city. No means of escape here for little boys. She was not even entirely displeased with the nursery accommodation; arranged for Charles-Edouard by his English mother it was like an old-fashioned nursery in some big London house, and had none of the strange bleakness of the rooms at Bellandargues.

Her smiles, however, always on the wintry side, soon vanished when she was confronted with the goat carts, the donkeys, the Guignol, and the happy crowd of scooting, skating children in the Tuileries gardens. Sigi had, of course, no sooner seen the goat carts than he was in one.

'We shall never get the little monkey away from these animals – is there nowhere else for us to go, dear, more like Hyde Park? I'm not going to stand the whole winter in this draughty-looking square waiting for him to ride round hour after hour.'

'Oh no, darling, you mustn't. We must ration him. But don't you think this is a charming place for children, more fun really than Hyde Park?'

Grace had been so much looking forward to bringing Sigi here and watching him enjoy all the treats that she had overlooked the certain disapproval of Nanny.

'Grace! I'm surprised to hear you say such a thing! Think of the Peter Pan monument, and the Dell! Goodness knows what he'll pick up from all these children. Anyway there's to be no question of him going inside that filthy-looking theatre, or whatever it is. I hope that's quite understood, dear.'

'Of course, Nan, just as you say.'

Nanny took Grace's arm and said in a low voice, 'Isn't that Mrs Dexter over there?'

'Grace!'

'Carolyn!'

'I was just going to ring up your house and see if you were back. We've come to live here, isn't it lovely! I spoke to your papa on the telephone on our way through London and he gave me your number, but we've been so busy flat-hunting. Yes, now we've found a lovely one – only miles from you I'm afraid – up by the Parc Monceau. Is this Sigi? Seven, I suppose – he looks more. Poor little Foss will be rather young for him, but Nanny will be pleased to see you, Nanny, it will make all the difference. Which day can you come to tea? Then we must get together, Grace, and meet each other's husbands! Isn't it exciting?'

Carolyn Broadman was a lifelong friend of Grace. Their fathers had been friends and they had been at the same school. Carolyn was a little older and much cleverer, she was the head girl at school, revered by the others, many of whom had been passionately in love with her. She was tall, with curly, auburn hair and particularly piercing bright blue eyes. This colouring constituted her claim to beauty; her features were not very good, though her figure was excellent. She moved with more than the hint of a swagger, and Sir Conrad always called her Don Juan. She had certainly been one at school, coldly gathering up the poor little hearts laid at her feet and throwing them over her shoulder. Grace had not seen her since the war, but knew that she had married an enormously rich, important American whom she had met in Italy. As was to be expected she had become a female General in the war – were there such things as female Marshals she would, no doubt, have been one.

'Come back to tea now,' said Grace, 'and meet Charles-Edouard.'

'Darling I can't. I'm just off to our Embassy where they've got a cocktail party for some Senators – I must pick up Hector at his office and then go home and change for it. I promised I'd go early and help.'

So they chatted for a few minutes more and then parted with many plans for meeting again soon.

'Nice to see a clean English skin,' said Nanny, as they wandered back across the Pont de Solferino.

Charles-Edouard was in the hall, evidently on his way out.

'Well,' he said, 'what are the news?'

'I took Sigi and Nan – run along up darling, it's tea-time – to the Tuileries Gardens and who d'you think we met? An old friend of mine called Carolyn Dexter. Wasn't it funny?'

'Beautiful?'

'I don't know if you'd think so. Beautiful colouring.'

'That means red hair I suppose. Not my type.'

'And a wonderful figure, and she's terribly clever. She's married to a very important American called Hector Dexter.'

'So, go on. What did she tell you?'

'Well, they live up by the Parc Monceau. We must all meet some day soon.'

'Go on. What else?'

'Nothing else.'

'Ha! So you stood together in the Tuileries gazing into each other's eyes without a word?'

'You do tease me. We chattered like magpies.'

'But what about?'

'She was just off to a cocktail party at the American Embassy.'

'This is all very dull.'

'Don't be such a bully, Charles-Edouard.'

'You must tell me stories about what happens during your day, to amuse me. Do go on.'

'They have a little boy, but younger than Sigi, and Nanny is longing to go and meet their English nanny —'

Charles-Edouard's attention was wandering. *'Quand un Vicomte rencontre un autre Vicomte,'* he sang, *'Qu'est-ce qu'ils se racontent? Des histoires de Vicomtes.'* He picked up his hat.

'Are you going out?'

'Yes.'

'Back to tea?'

'No.'

Grace had her tea in the nursery, that day and subsequently. Charles-Edouard was never in at tea-time because he now resumed an afternoon habit of many years' standing, he visited Albertine Marel-Desboulles. She was one of the little friends, all brought up together, about whom Madame de Valhubert had wanted to warn Grace, and quite the most dangerous of them. She and Charles-Edouard had had the same nurse as children (passed on to Charles-Edouard's mother by Albertine's, since Albertine was older). When he was eighteen and she a young married woman they had had a short but enthusiastic love affair; this had simmered down to a sentimental friendship in which love, physical love at any rate, still played a part. Charles-Edouard found her more entertaining than anybody; she was certainly quite the reverse of dull, always having something to recount. Not plain slices of life served up on a thick white plate, but wonderful confections embellished with the aromatic and exotic fruits of her own sugary imagination, presented in just such a way as to tempt the appetite of such sophisticated admirers as he. She had endless tales to spin around their mutual friends, could discuss art and objects of art with his own collector's enthusiasm as well as with imaginative knowledge, and, what specially appealed to Charles-Edouard, would talk by the hour, also with imaginative knowledge and with collector's enthusiasm, about himself. She was an accomplished fortune-teller. Like a child who knows where the sweets are kept, Charles-Edouard always went straight to the japanese lacquer commode, in the right-hand corner of whose top drawer lay packs of cards.

'How many years since I have done this?' she said, shuffling and dealing, her long, spidery fingers bright with diamonds.

'You said I would be killed in the war, I remember,' said Charles-Edouard.

'I said I couldn't quite see in what circumstances you would be coming back. Suppose I had told you it would be complete with an English wife and a son, that would indeed have been a *coup* for me. Unfortunately I didn't foresee anything so improbable. Please cut the cards. However, I see her now, clear as daylight, surrounded by old maids, not another man in her orbit. She must be very faithful. Nice for you to have this faithful wife.

Good. Cut the cards. Yes. Now here we have a surprise, not that it surprises me very much. Not English, and not your wife, but a sparkling beauty, a brilliant. There is an enormous amount of interesting incident round you and your relationship with this brilliant. Cut the cards. This is for you. Yes, here you are and with all your talents, your charm, your wit, your good nature, watching yourself as you live your life, and fascinated by the spectacle.'

'Ah!' said Charles-Edouard, 'this is very nice. How I love being rubbed the right way.'

'Cut three times. I am bound to tell you that there will be a few little tiresomenesses, to do with the brilliant. You won't be careful enough, or you'll be unlucky – there'll be a torrent of tears, but they won't be your tears, so never mind. Cut the cards. Nothing different – you again, between the brilliant and the wife. I can't tell any more today.'

She leaned her head on her hand and looked at him with blue, lollipop eyes, which seemed out of place among her pointed Gothic features. Everything about her was long and thin, except for these round, blue eyes; she was an exceedingly odd-looking woman.

'So! How do you find marriage?'

'Rather dull,' said Charles-Edouard, 'but I rather like it, and I love my wife. She is original, she amuses me.'

'And lovely?' said Madame Marel.

'She will be, when she is arranged. No doubt you will see her at the Fertés on the 10th.'

'Yes indeed. We shall all be there, all agog. You haven't changed much, Charles-Edouard, except that you are better looking than ever.'

'Ah!' said Charles-Edouard. He got up and locked the door.

'No need to do that,' she said, smiling. 'Pierre would never let anybody else in when he knows you are here.'

Presently Charles-Edouard, lying relaxed among the cushions of an enormous sofa, said, 'So tell me, since all these years what have you become?'

'Oh it's a long story – or rather a long book of short stories.'

'Yes, I expect it is. And now —?'

'Nothing very much. I have an Englishman who is madly in

love with me – I don't believe I've ever been loved so violently with such really suicidal mania, as by this Englishman.'

'Ah, these English, they are terrible.'

'You may laugh, but it is no joke at all. The evidences of his love simply pour into the house – I don't know what the concierge can think, it is full-time work carrying them across the courtyard. Flowers, telegrams, letters, parcels, all the day.'

'Does he live here?'

'Better than that, in London. But he flies over to see me at least once a week, and then the tears, the scenes, the jealousy, the temperament. It is wearing me out, and I ought really to get rid of him.'

'Why don't you?'

'Because of the bourgeois thrift I learnt from my dear husband. Never throw anything away, it might come in useful. Besides, I do love to be loved.'

'And what is his name?'

'It's not an interesting name – Palgrave, Hughie Palgrave.'

'It is interesting to me, however,' said Charles-Edouard, 'since Hughie Palgrave was once engaged to my wife.'

Chapter Eight

As soon as she had some presentable clothes Charles-Edouard began taking Grace to see his relations. 'Very dull,' he said, 'but what must be, must be.' So at 6.30 every day they would put themselves into a little lift which shook and wavered up to the drawing-room of some old aunt or cousin of the family. These lifts, these drawing-rooms and these old ladies differed very little from each other. The rooms were huge, cold and magnificent, with splendid pieces of furniture arranged to their worst advantage and mixed up with a curious assortment of objects which had been collected during the course of long married lives. The old ladies were also arranged to their worst advantage, and covered with a curious assortment of jewellery. Prominent upon a black cardigan they generally wore the rosette of the Legion of Honour.

'We might be going in for a literary prize,' said Charles-Edouard, as for the fifth time they tottered up in the fifth little lift.

'Why might we?'

'This is how you win a literary prize in France. First you write a book – that is of no importance, however. Then you go and see my aunts, treat them with enormous deference, and laugh loudly at the jokes my uncles make over the *porto*.'

'I don't understand.'

'No wonder. All the literary prizes here are given by my aunts.'

'And won by other aunts?'

'Not usually. Their works, of an unreadable erudition, are crowned by the Academy. That is different, though my aunts have great power there also, and have managed to insert my uncles under the cupola all right.'

'Does Tante Régine give prizes?'

'Heavens no! She is in quite a different world. You will find her (she's coming back next week, by the way) at all the parties, the dress collections, the private views, the first nights. It's another product altogether. The Novembre de la Fertés, my grandmother's and Tante Régine's family, have never gone in for intellect – nor have the Rocher des Innouïs. All these clever old girls are Valhubert relations – their cradles were rocked by Alphonse Daudet and the Abbé Liszt. Ah! *Ma tante! Bonjour mon oncle*. So, this is Grace.'

'Grace! Sit here where we can see you, dear child, and tell us – so cut off from England for so long – all about Mr Charles Morgan.'

The rest of the company consisted, as usual, of earnest, dowdy young women, following in the footsteps of their elders, of old men so courtly in manner that they seemed dedicated to eternal courtship, and one or two bright, overgrown boys. They put Grace on a high-backed needlework chair facing the window, sat round her in a semi-circle, and plied her with weak port wine, biscuits, and questions. They passed from Mr Charles Morgan, about whom she knew lamentably little, to Miss Mazo de la Roche, about whom she knew less. They gave her to understand that one of the most serious deprivations caused by the war had been that of Les Whiteoaks, Les Jalna. Then they fired questions at her from all sides, wanting to know about English novelists, dramatists, lesser country houses, boy scouts, gardens, music, essayists, and the government of Britain, until she felt like an ambulating Britain in Pictures. Their knowledge of England was quite astonishing, very much like the knowledge some astronomer might have of the moon after regarding it for many a long night through a telescope.

Grace felt that they were trying to place her. Not, as Tante Régine was always trying, to place her in English society, to find out whom she knew and if her family was really, in spite of the freemason father, quite respectable, but in another way. Some of them had read Sir Conrad's *Life of Fouquet.* They pronounced it honourable, and assumed, from the fact of its existence, that Grace must have been brought up in intellectual circles. They wanted to place her views and inclinations, her turn of mind. They wanted to know if she was Oxford or Cambridge, whether she preferred *The Times* or the *Daily Telegraph,* what she felt about Shakespeare and Bacon. Their questions were not at all hard to answer, but she felt that by her answers to these, possibly deceptively, simple questions, she was being for ever judged.

She found it a great strain, and had said so to Charles-Edouard after the last tea-party.

'But that is what French people are like,' he had replied, shrugging his shoulders. 'In France you are always in a witness box. You'll get used to it. But you must sharpen your wits a little, my dearest, if you want a favourable verdict.'

The old uncles did not play much part in all this. They were still, after a lifetime of marriage, lost in admiration at the brilliance of their wives, quite wrapped up in whatever these wonderful women were doing. So when they met each other out of doors, which happened continually, as they all lived in the same neighbourhood and all had Scotties to exercise, they would shout across the street, 'Good morning, and how is Benjamin Constant going on' (or whoever it was that the other's wife was known to be studying just then). 'Splendidly, splendidly. And the old stones of Provins?'

With Grace they were charming, making her feel that she was a pretty woman and that therefore nothing she said would ever be held against her. However, she was shrewd enough to see that it was the aunts who counted. These aunts were a great surprise to Grace. She had hitherto supposed that, with the exception of a few very religious people like Madame de Valhubert, all Frenchwomen, of all ages, were entirely frivolous and given over to the art of pleasing. From which it will be deduced that the works of Mauriac and Balzac, like those of Brogan and Bodley, lay mouldering, their pages uncut, in the great heap behind the kitchen stairs at Bunbury.

'Are you happy?' Charles-Edouard said, as they walked home. It was some days, he had noticed, since Grace had said how happy she was, of her own accord.

'I am perfectly happy,' she said, 'but I can't feel at home yet.'

'You felt at home at Bellandargues, why not here?'

'Bellandargues was the country.' She found it hard to explain to Charles-Edouard how different was life in Paris from anything she had ever known, so complicated and artificial that her only refuge of reality was the nursery. The other rooms in her house, with their admirable decoration and gold-encrusted furniture, so rich that to enter one of them was like opening a jewellery box, belonged to the Valhuberts past, present, and future, but she could not feel as yet that they belonged to her. The smiling servants maintained the life of the house undirected by her; the comings and goings in the courtyard, the cheerful bustle of a large establishment, would all go on exactly the same if she were not there. In short she played not the smallest part in this place, which was, nevertheless, her home.

Charles-Edouard had quite fallen back into his pre-war existence. He spent the morning telephoning to friends whose very names she did not know; in the afternoon he ran from one antiquary to another; he was out a great deal, and always out at tea-time.

Every fortnight or so he went for the inside of a day to Bellandargues to perform his mayoral duties, and very occasionally he stayed there the night. 'I do hate to sleep out of Paris,' he used to say, and did so as seldom as he possibly could.

Grace herself was quite busy, an unaccustomed busyness, since it was all concerned with clothes. Madame Rocher's *vendeuse* had taken charge of her, and kept her nose to the grindstone, making her get more and more dresses for more and more occasions; big occasions, a ball, Friday night at Maxims, the opera, the important dinner party; little occasions, the theatre, dinner at home alone, or with one or two friends, luncheon at home, luncheon in a restaurant; and odd occasions, luncheon or dinner in the country (nothing so lugubrious as a week-end party was envisaged), and the voyage.

'Could I not travel in my morning suit?'

'It is always better to travel with brown accessories.'

'I am perfectly happy,' she repeated, 'only not quite at my ease yet. Perhaps a little homesick.'

But more than ever passionately in love with Charles-Edouard.

The first big occasion to which Grace went in Paris was a dinner given for her by the Duchesse de la Ferté. At this dinner Grace's preconceived ideas about the French, already shaken by the *porto* parties, were blown sky high. She knew, or thought she knew, that Frenchwomen were hideously ugly, but with an ugliness redeemed by great vivacity and perfect taste in dress. Perfect taste she took to mean quiet, unassuming taste – 'better be under- than over-dressed' her English mentors such as Carolyn's mother used to say. Then she imagined that all Frenchmen were small and black, at best resembling Charles Boyer, her own husband's graceful elegance being easily accounted for, in her view, by his English blood.

So all in all she was unprepared for the scene that met her eyes on entering the Fertés' big salon. The door opened upon a kaleidoscope of glitter. The women, nearly all beauties, were in huge crinolines, from which rose naked shoulders and almost naked bosoms, sparkling with jewels. They moved on warm waves of scent, their faces were gaily painted with no attempt at simulating nature, their hair looked cleaner and glossier than any hair she had ever seen. Almost more of a surprise to Grace were the men, tall, handsome, and beautifully dressed. The majority of both men and women were fair with blue eyes, in fact they had the kind of looks which are considered in England to be English looks at their best. Grace saw that these looks in the women were greatly enhanced by over-dressing, always so much more becoming, whatever Carolyn's mother might say, than the reverse. That the atmosphere was of untrammelled sex did not surprise her, except in so far as that sex, outside a bedroom, could be so untrammelled.

Madame de la Ferté took Grace by the arm and led her round, introducing her to everybody. She was so much fascinated by what she saw that the terrible up and down examination accorded to a newcomer to the herd went on without her even being aware of it, and it was a long time before she realized how under-dressed, under-painted, and under-scented she must seem. The jewels, however, which Charles-Edouard had forced her to put on against her own inclination, were second to nobody's. Her face, too, though lacking the sparkle of the French faces, had no rival in that room for beauty of line and structure.

The party waited some time for the arrival of a young Bourbon and of a certain not so young woman who, to underline the fact that she was now his mistress, liked to arrive late in queenly fashion. The affair was being discussed by the group round Grace, the rapid quality of whose talk, so precise, so funny, so accomplished, so frighteningly well-informed, positively paralysed her. Her own brain seemed to struggle along in the rear. Charles-Edouard, swimming in his native waters, was happy and animated as she had never seen him.

A moment before the arrival of the Prince, his mistress came in on her husband's arm. She curtsied lower than anybody, murmuring, 'Monseigneur!'

'They left the luncheon together, they must have been in bed the whole afternoon.'

'I don't think so. She had a fitting at Dior.'

When the late arrivals had shaken hands with the company they all went in to dinner. Grace sat beside her host, the brother of Madame de Valhubert and Madame Rocher. He seemed a thousand years old, very frail, and wore a shawl over his shoulders. Opposite her was Charles-Edouard, between his hostess and a majestic old woman who had swept in to dinner holding in one hand the train of her dress and in the other a large ebony ear-trumpet. During the hush which fell while people were finding their places and settling down she said to Charles-Edouard, in the penetrating voice of a deaf person, but with a very confidential look as if she thought she was whispering:

70

'Are you still in love with Albertine?'

Charles-Edouard, not at all put out, took the trumpet and shouted into it, 'No. I'm married now and I have a son of seven.'

'So I heard. But what has that to do with it?'

Grace tried to look as if she had heard nothing. She was wondering desperately what she could talk about to M. de la Ferté when, greatly to her relief, he turned to her and said that he had just read *Les Hauts de Hurlevent* by a talented young English writer.

'I wondered if you knew her,' he said. 'Mademoiselle Émilie Brontë.'

This was indeed a lifeline. 'I really know her sister Charlotte better.'

'Ah! She has a sister?'

'Several. They all write books.'

'But no brothers?'

'One brother, but he's a bad lot. Nobody ever mentions him.'

'This Mademoiselle Brontë tells of country-house life in England. It must be very strange – well of course one knows it is. They do such curious things, I find. I should like to read other books by her talented family.'

'I wonder whether they've been translated.'

'No matter. My concierge's son knows English, he can translate them for me.'

M. de Tournon, on Grace's other side, was handsome, blond, and young, and when the time came for them to talk he opened the conversation in English, saying, 'You are new to Paris life, so I am going to explain some very important things to you, which you may not have understood, about society here.'

'I wish you would,' she said gratefully.

'Footnotes, as it were, to the book you are reading.'

'Just what I require.'

'We will begin, I think, with precedence, since precedence precedes everything else. Now in England (and here I break off to explain that I know England extremely well; let me give you my credentials, Mary Marylebone and Molly Waterloo are two of my most intimate friends). Now what I am going to explain first is this. Please do not imagine that social life is easy here, as it is in England. It is a very very different matter. I will explain why. In England, as we know, everybody has a number, so when you give a dinner it is perfectly easy to place your guests – you look up the numbers, seat them accordingly, and they just dump down without any argument, *Placement*, such a terrible worry to us in France, never bothers you at all.'

'Are you sure,' said Grace, 'about these numbers? I've never heard of them. *Placement* doesn't bother us because nobody minds where they sit, at home.'

'People always mind. I mean the numbers in the beginning of the peerage. I subscribe to your peerage, such a beautiful book, and then I know where I am with English visitors. I only wish we had such a thing here, but we have not, and as a result the complications of precedence are terrible. There is the old French nobility and that of the Holy Roman Empire (Lorraine, Savoy, and so on). These are complicated enough in themselves, but then we have the titles created by Napoleon, at the Restoration, by the July monarchy and Napoleon III. There are the Bourbon bastards and the Bonaparte bastards. I think you have no special place for your big bastards in England?'

'I don't think there are any.'

He looked at her with pity and reeled off some well-known English family names. Grace saw that she was doing badly in this witness box.

'Mrs Jordan alone had about eighteen children,' he said. 'After all, royal blood is not nothing. But to come back to France. Suppose you have asked three dukes to dinner, which do you put first? You ring up the protocol – good, but the dukes meanwhile ring you up, each putting forward his claim. Then, my dear, you will positively long to be back in England, where you can have any number of dukes and members of the Academy at the same time. Where do you place Academicians, in England?'

'R. A.s?' said Grace. 'I don't know any.'

'Indeed! Now here, when you get to the dining-room, those of your guests who think themselves badly placed, if they don't leave at once, will turn their plates in protest and refuse the first course (though if it looks very delicious they may take it when it is handed round again).'

'Goodness!' said Grace, 'so what is the solution?'

'Do not ask more than one duke at a time.'

'But supposing they are friends?'

'Never will they be friends to that extent. But it shows how you are fortunate over there, you could ask all twenty-six – am I not right in saying there are twenty-six?'

'I haven't the faintest idea,' said Grace.

'I think so. You could ask all twenty-six to the same dinner without making a single enemy. Unimaginable. To go on with our lesson. Whereas in England the host and hostess sit at the ends of the table, here they face each other across the middle, the ends being reserved for low people, those who have married for love and so on. Two years of love, we say here, are no compensation for a lifetime at the end of the table.'

'Might not the end be more amusing?'

'No. It is not amusing to be with one's near relations and the people other people have married for love. Because near relations of the house go to the end, you and Charles-Edouard would be there tonight, except that this dinner is being given in your honour. Juliette, as you see, is there; as you also see, she is far from liking it.'

The young woman he indicated was the prettiest of them all, and the most dressed-up. She wore white tulle with swags of blue taffeta which matched her eyes, her skin looked as if a light were shining through it, and her hair fell on her shoulders in fat, chestnut curls. She was very lively and very young, hardly more than a child.

'Who is she?'

'Juliette Novembre de la Ferté, daughter-in-law of the house. The other end is her husband, watching with his jealous eye, poor Jean, and much good will it do him. She is the great success of the year.'

'How old is she?'

'Eighteen? – nineteen? Very soon she will have to begin her family, poor dear. Jean will have to take her to the country if he wants the necessary number, and wants them to be his.'

'Necessary number?'

'Yes, hasn't Charles-Edouard explained? We all have to have six nowadays if we are to prevent everything – but everything – being taken away in taxation. So most of us took advantage of the war years and just devoted ourselves to procreation. My wife

73

and I have four (we prayed for twins – in vain, alas). Very soon we shall have to make up our minds again. Oh, how we were bored, I never shall forget it. We had our house full of Germans, how they were middle-class and dreary.'

Grace, who regarded Germans as frightening rather than dreary, was very much surprised, and more so when he went on:

'There was one not so bad, a Graf, who sang little lieder after dinner, a charming baritone. But we had moments of grave disquietude, you know, caused by the *maquisards*. They were well-intentioned, but so tactless – at one moment we thought they would kill our baritone, and then, only think, there might have been a battle!'

'In wars,' said Grace, 'you rather expect battles.'

'Not in one's own château, my dear! How we were relieved when the Germans went away – just packed up one day and went – and we saw two nice young Guards officers of good family, Etonians, coming up the drive. Because please don't think I was on the side of the Germans. Why, when I saw them swarming over the hill (we lived in the unoccupied zone), I put out my hand and took down my gun. There and then I made a vow never to shoot again until they were out of France.'

'You mean, never to shoot birds again?'

'And rabbits and pigs, yes. You may not think much of this vow, but I live for shooting, it is my greatest joy.'

'Then why didn't you join the maquis and shoot the Germans?'

'Oh no, my dear, one couldn't do that.'

'Why not?'

'For many reasons. My brother-in-law joined a maquis, dreadful people, he soon had to give that up. They weren't possible, I assure you.'

'Well they may not have been possible, but they were on our side, and I love them for it.'

'Oh! my dear, we were all on your side, so you must love us all in that case.'

After dinner Charles-Edouard made a bee-line for Juliette Novembre. Grace heard him say, 'If you were Juliette de Champeaubert how is it I don't remember you? Jeanne Marie is one of my very greatest friends.'

'Oh, I've only just been invented,' she said gaily, 'but before I was invented I used to hang out of the window, waiting to see you get into that pretty black motor you had in those days. My governess used to pull me back by my hair.'

'No! But that's awfully nice,' said Charles-Edouard. 'Come – I want to see my uncle's Subleyras again.'

They went off together into another room. Somebody said, 'It was quite indicated that those two would take to each other – she might be made for Charles-Edouard.'

M. de Tournon brought his wife over to Grace. He wanted her to see for herself this uncouth girl Charles-Edouard had so oddly married, in order to be able to talk about her when they got home. Madame de Tournon was Italian, more really beautiful and more elegant than Juliette Novembre but with much less sparkle.

'I am a cousin of yours now,' she said. 'Let's all sit here. So tell me what you have been doing in Paris since you arrived – there haven't been any dinners so far, have there? We only got back ourselves last night – we came back for this.'

'Really I've done very little. I've bought some clothes.'

'Is that Dior? Yes, I could see. But are they making these high necks now?'

'I had it altered – it seemed too naked.'

'Oh no, my dear,' said Madame de Tournon, 'you've got beautiful breasts, so why hide them up like that? It spoils the line. What else?'

'I've met Charles-Edouard's aunts.'

Madame de Tournon made a little face of sympathy. 'Any cocktail parties?'

'There have been one or two, but I never go to them, I hate them. Charles-Edouard goes. I don't terribly like lunching out either,' she went on. 'If I had my way I'd never go out before dinner-time.'

The Tournons looked at each other in growing amazement as she spoke.

'But listen,' cried Madame de Tournon, 'nobody can dine out more than eight times in a week. But if one lunches every day and goes to, say, three cocktails, as well as dining out, one can go to forty houses in a week. We often have, haven't we, Eugène?'

'Sometimes more, in the summer. I wish you could see us in July, fit for a nursing home by the time we get to the seaside.'

'Where do you go to the seaside as a rule?' asked Grace, thinking of them on the sands of some French Eastbourne with their four tots.

'Always Venice. Say what you like, it's the only place in August.'

'But is it fun for the children?'

They stared at her. 'We don't take the children to Venice – poor little things, what on earth would they do there? Besides, the children don't need a change, they don't have an exhausting season in Paris, they lead a perfectly healthy outdoor life in the Seine et Marne.'

Charles-Edouard and Juliette only reappeared when a general move was being made to go home. In the hall, as they were putting on their coats, Juliette flourished a hand for Charles-Edouard to kiss, saying, 'Good-bye for the present then, wickedness, I will consider your proposition.' She and her husband then got into the lift which took them to their own apartments.

'What proposition?' said Grace, in the motor.

'No proposition.'

'Oh dear! Need we dine out very often?'

'What d'you mean?'

'Let's dine together, alone, in future.'

'It would be very dull,' said Charles-Edouard.

'Such a terrible man I sat next to.'

'Eugène? He's a friendly old thing.'

'You can't think what he's like when he talks about the war.'

'I know. I saw him at a picture dealer's the other day and we had it all. But you mustn't be too hard on old Eugène – he joined up quite correctly in '39 and fought quite bravely in '40. His father was killed quite correctly in 1917. These Eugènes are not so rotten, it is the State of Denmark.'

The Tournons, meanwhile, were discussing Grace.

'My dear, the lowest peasant of the Danube knows more than she – just fancy, she had never heard of the English order of precedence, didn't know how many dukes there are in England, and didn't seem to think any of it mattered.'

'And did you hear what she said about taking the children to Venice? She must be backward, I'm afraid.'

'Allingham. What is this name? I must write at once to Molly Waterloo and ask her if they are people one can know. Poor Charles-Edouard – I pity him really.'

'Everything will be all right. Madame Rocher told my mother they are not married religiously.'

Madame Rocher had gone to Venice the week after Grace and Charles-Edouard left Bellandargues, and there she had managed to do quite a lot of harm to Grace, not wilfully at all, not intending mischief, but because she was utterly incapable of holding her tongue on any subject of general interest. Interest was very much centred, at the moment, on Charles-Edouard and his marriage.

Everybody thought it a pity that he, with his name and his fortune, should have married an English Protestant. When it transpired that she was the daughter of a Freemason, the general disapproval knew no bounds, a Bolshevist would have been as gladly received. Those who were informed on political subjects pointed to the dire results, for France, of the Allingham Commission, and it was freely hinted that Grace was very likely in the pay of the Intelligence Service. Rather soon, however, the pendulum swung back in her favour. Older, cosmopolitan Frenchmen, writers, diplomats, and the like, who did not only live for society and yet had great influence with the Tournons of the world, had known the charming, cultivated, francophile Sir Conrad, and had read his books. They said he was by no means to the Left in politics, a rigid Conservative, in fact. Silly old Régine must have got the Freemason story all wrong, so like her, for it could not possibly be true. As to the Allingham Commission, the prime mover in that was a terrible villain called Sparks, paid by Arabs, in whose hands poor Sir Conrad had been as putty, and furthermore the results of the Commission, while annoying to the French government of the day, had not in the long run done any harm to France. It was absurd to say that the Allinghams were not the sort of people you could know; even

Eugène de Tournon was quite impressed when he saw in his peerage who Grace's mother had been.

The highbrow aunts, who, dowdy as they seemed, counted for a good deal in society, weighed in on her side, saying that, though not an intellectual, she was very nice and well brought up. Her beauty, too, was in her favour. At last the nine days' wonder came to an end, and Grace was accepted. She was a new girl, she must watch her step, but the general feeling was that she would do.

She and Charles-Edouard now dined out nearly every day, and after all these dinners Charles-Edouard would sit with Juliette Novembre, as far removed from the rest of the company as possible, until it was time to go home.

Chapter Nine

CAROLYN DEXTER and Grace saw a good deal of each other, sitting on nursery fenders, and at first this was a comfort to Grace because of her need to feel at home somewhere. She felt at home with Carolyn. But as time went on Carolyn often irritated her dreadfully. Since marriage with the important Mr Dexter the swagger and self-assurance which had made her so fascinating to the other girls at her school had deteriorated into bossiness. She was for ever telling Grace what she ought to do and whom she and Charles-Edouard ought to see, and was also for ever enlarging upon the faults of the French. She had a particular grievance against the world of Parisians which was led by such young couples as the Tournons and the Novembre de la Fertés, not, oddly enough, on the grounds of their really frightening frivolity, but because they so seldom invited herself and her husband to their houses. In view of the importance of Mr Dexter and the fact that she was the niece of a former British Ambassador to Paris, she had expected immediately to be asked everywhere, but, except for big, official parties, the Dexters moved almost entirely in an Anglo-American world. Mr Dexter did not mind this at all. When he said, as he continually did, that he despised the French, he meant it. He had no wish to meet any, except those he was obliged to work with. But Carolyn was not quite so honest. If the French annoyed her it was very largely by ignoring her presence in their town.

Carolyn thought that Grace ought to give a dinner party for her, and said so in her extremely outspoken way. Grace replied, with perfect truth, that, for the moment, she and Charles-Edouard were taken up with his many relations. Carolyn did not accept this as easily as some people would have, and often returned to the charge.

'I hear you dined last night with the Polastrons. Are they relations of your husband?' she said, before even saying hullo to Grace, who had come to tea.

'Yes, I think so.'

'How are they related?'

'Perhaps they're not. But anyway, great old friends.'

'Great old friends, but not related. I thought you were only seeing relations at present?'

'Well, but Carolyn – I leave it all to Charles-Edouard, you know.'

She felt instinctively that Charles-Edouard would find the Dexters very dull.

'Let's have a cocktail,' said Carolyn. 'I'm exhausted. I've had an awful afternoon struggling with the garage people to do something about my car. Promised for yesterday – you know the sort of thing. Really I'm fed up with these wretched French.'

'I thought you loved France. You always used to.'

'I love France, but I can't say I love the French, nowadays. They are quite different, you know, since the war. Everybody says the same.'

Grace somehow felt sure that they were not quite different at all. She really did love them. She loved the servants in her house for their friendly efficiency, their faithfulness to Charles-Edouard; she loved the highbrow aunts, now that she was getting to know them, for being so clever and so serious, and she loved the gay young diners for being so pretty and so light-hearted. She even loved their snobbishness, it seemed to her such a tremendous joke, so particularly funny, somehow, nowadays. She was beginning to love the critical spirit of all and sundry. It kept people up to the mark, no doubt, and had filled her with the desire to improve her mind and sharpen her wits. She longed to make a better appearance in the box, and be a credit to Charles-Edouard. And she loved the people in the streets for smiling at her and noticing her new clothes.

'I don't say I hate them,' said Carolyn, 'but they irritate me, and I see their faults.'

'What faults?'

'Oh, you're sold to the French, Grace, it's hardly worth talking to you about them. Faults! They hit you in the eye if you're not blind. Never punctual – don't get things done – not reliable (you should hear Hector) – dirty — The dirt! Look at the central heating here – just gusts of hot dust, impossible to keep anything clean. Then the butchers' shops – after living in America you feel ill to see them – flies all over the meat —'

'I like that,' said Grace. 'Meat can't be too meaty, for my taste.'

'Ugh! Anyhow, you can't like the rudeness —'

'Nobody's ever rude to me. They smile when they see me, even strangers in the street.'

'Trying to pick you up. And what about those dreadful policemen!'

'I always think they look like young saints, in their capes.'

'Saints! I must tell that to Hector, he'll roar.'

'I've never had anything but niceness from them – over Nanny's identity card and so on.'

'I expect your husband gives them enormous bribes.'

'Of course he doesn't.'

'I suppose even you will admit the French would do anything for money.'

'Perhaps they may – it's never crossed my path, but you may be right. Perhaps they are more frank and open about it than other people.'

'Frank and open is the word. They always frankly and openly marry for money, to begin with.'

'Charles-Edouard didn't.'

'Are you — Oh well there may be exceptions, and I suppose he wouldn't need to. But at the time when our grandfathers were marrying actresses for love their contemporaries here were all marrying Jewesses for money. I was thinking of dozens of examples last night in bed.'

'I think they were quite right. Just look at it from the point of view of their grandchildren. Honestly now, which would you prefer as a grandmother – a clever old Jewess, who has brought brains and money and Caffieri commodes into the family, or some ass of an actress?'

'I can't understand you, Grace, you used to seem so very English at home.'

'Yes, well now,' said Grace rather sadly, 'I'm nothing at all. But I would love to have been born a Frenchwoman, and I can't say more, can I?'

'Oh, you'll change your tune, I bet. By the way, I've been meaning to tell you – we quite often see Hughie.'

'Hughie! Does he live here too?'

'He was here with a military mission, now he's back in England, but he keeps coming over. Hector sees him at the Travellers and brings him in for a drink, most weeks. He's terribly in love with a Frenchwoman here, a Madame Marel-Desboulles. Hector thinks it's a disaster for him, he has heard all about this Madame Marel and says she's no good.'

'Marel – Marel-Desboulles. Don't I know her?' Grace said vaguely.

The names and faces of the French people she met had not yet clicked into place, they floated round her mind separately, many names and many faces, all wonderfully romantic and new but not adding up into real people. So the name Marel-Desboulles had a familiar ring but no face, while the brilliant woman who played conversational ping-pong with Charles-Edouard, across a dinner-table, sometimes across a whole roomful of people all delighted by the speed and accuracy of the game, volley, volley, high lob with a spin, volley, cut, smash, had not yet acquired a surname. Grace only knew her as Albertine.

'He wants to marry her.'

Carolyn looked at Grace to see if she minded, but she hardly even seemed interested.

'And will he?'

'I don't think so. He says she is very Catholic, and talks all the time of going into a convent – poor Hughie says he'll kill himself if she does. But Hector says nobody at the Travellers thinks there's much danger of that. What happened about your engagement to Hughie, Grace? I never really knew.'

'Oh, just that we were engaged, and he went to the war and I married Charles-Edouard instead. I'm afraid I didn't behave very well.'

'Pity, in a way.'

'I can't agree.'

'I meant nothing against your husband. I hear he is charming. I only meant pity to marry a Frenchman.'

Grace longed to retaliate with 'well then, what about marrying an American' but she knew that, while it is considered nowadays perfectly all right to throw any amount of aspersions on poor old France and England, one tiny word reflecting anything but exaggerated love for rich new America is thought to be in the worst of taste. She was also, by nature, more careful of people's feelings than Carolyn. So she said, mildly, that she could not imagine any other sort of husband.

The two nannies clung to each other like drowning men, and Sigi was now taken every day for air and exercise to the Parc Monceau instead of the Tuileries Gardens. He was very cross about this, and complained bitterly to his mother.

'Pascal and I are so fond of each other. I never knew such an obliging goat, and now I never see him. It's a shame, Mummy.'

'Why don't you meet Nanny Dexter in the Tuileries sometimes for a change?' Grace said to her Nan.

'Oh no thank you, dear. We don't like those Tuileries. It's the draughtiest place in Paris. I only wish you could feel the stiff neck I caught there the other day, waiting for the little monkey to finish his ride. I don't think all those smelly animals are very nice, if you ask me, and the children there are a funny lot too. Some of them are black, dear, and one was distinctly Chinese. The Parc Monceau is a much better place for little boys.'

'Oh well, Nan, it's just as you like, of course, but when I went there I thought it fearfully depressing, such thousands of children, like a children's market or something, and all those castor-oil plants. Hideous.'

'Still you do see a little grass there,' said Nanny, 'and decent railings.'

'I hate the silly little baby Parc Monceau,' piped up Sigi, 'and I loathe dear little Foster Dexter aged four. Under the spreading chestnut tree, I loathe Foss and Foss loathes me.'

'Very stupid and naughty, Sigismond. Foster's a dear little chap – so easy too. Nanny Dexter has never had one minute's trouble with him since he was born, and they've been all over the place – oh, they have travelled! I must say Mrs Dexter's a marvellous mummy.'

'In what way?' Grace asked, with interest. She tried her best to be a marvellous mummy too, but her efforts never received much acknowledgement.

'Well, she has tea in the nursery every day.'

'But, Nanny, so do I – nearly every day.'

'And gives little Foss his bath often as not, and, what's more, every Saturday and Sunday Mr Dexter gives him his bath. He is a nice daddy, Mr Dexter.'

Unfortunately Grace was stumped by this. Nobody could say that Charles-Edouard was that sort of nice daddy; he never went near the nursery. He liked the idea of Sigi, and was delighted when people said the child was his living image, but a few minutes of his company at a time were more than sufficient. He was such a restless man that a few minutes of almost anybody's company at a time were more than sufficient.

Grace said to Charles-Edouard,

'You know my friend Carolyn?'

'The beautiful Lesbian?'

'No, no, Carolyn Dexter.'

'You said she was a Lesbian at school.'

'I said we were all in love with her, that's quite different. Besides, people are all sorts of things at school – Carolyn used to be a Communist then – we used to point her out to visitors as the school Communist – and look at her now! Marshall Plan up to the eyes. Anyway, can we dine there on Thursday? – I'm to let her know.'

'You keep our engagements, it's for you to say.'

'We are quite free, but I wanted to know if you'd like it.'

'Who will be there?'

'Well, it sounded like this, but I may have got it wrong. The

Jorgmanns of *Life*, the Schmutzes of *Time*, the Jungfleisches, who are liaison between *Life* and *Time*, the Oberammergaus who have replaced the Pottses on the Un-American Activities Committee, European branch, the Rutters, who are liaison between the French Chamber of Commerce, the Radio-Diffusion Française and the *Chicago Herald Tribune*, and an important French couple, the Tournons. Are the Tournons important really?'

'Of course they are, in their way, but it won't be those Tournons. It will be what we call *les faux Tournons* – he is *chef de cabinet* to Salleté, very dull, but she is rather nice.'

'Carolyn says these are all people you ought to meet.'

'Why ought I to meet them?'

'Now darling, do be serious for once. It's all that Aid and so on. They might like you, and it's so terribly important for them to like French people because of the Aid. Carolyn's always saying so, and she's very clever, as I've told you. She says what happens is that the important Americans who come here meet all the wrong sort of French. Then they go back to the middle of America and tell the people there, who hate foreigners anyway, that the French are undependable, and so nasty it would be better to cut the Aid and concentrate on Italy, where they are undependable too but so nice, and specially on Germany, where they are dependable and so wonderful, and leave the nasty French to rot. All because they meet the wrong sort. And all this is very discouraging to Hector Dexter, who is dying to help and aid the French more and more.'

'Well of course Hector Dexter would lose his job if they cut the Aid, that's very plain.'

'There you are, being French and cynical, just like Carolyn always says. And as if it would matter to Mr Dexter whether he lost his job or not. He's far too important.'

Indeed the word important seemed, at that time, to have been coined only for Mr Dexter, and his name never occurred either in print or in conversation without it. It seemed that he was one of the most, if not the most, important of living men.

'My dear child, do you really think, when a great country like America has settled on a certain policy with regard to another great country like France, it can be deflected from it by the Jung-fleisches, meeting the wrong sort of French person?'

'Carolyn says it can.'

'And what makes you think I'm the right sort of French person for them to meet?'

'Well look at what you did in the war.'

'But the Americans hate the people who were on their side in the war. It's one thing they can never forgive. I'm surprised you haven't noticed that. Never mind,' he said, seeing her face fall. 'We'll go, and I'll do my best to be nice, I promise you.'

Chapter Ten

THE Dexters invited their guests at eight, but only sat down to dinner at nine. The intervening hour was spent drinking cocktails while Hector Dexter talked about the present state of France.

'I have known France all my life. I came here as a kid; I came during my vacations from college; I came on my honeymoon with my first wife, the first Mrs Dexter, and I was here during World War II. So I am in some sort qualified to make my diagnosis, and I have made my diagnosis, and my diagnosis is as follows, but first I would like to tell you all a little story which I think will help me to illustrate the point I am going to try if I can to make.

'Well, it was just before the Ardennes counter-offensive; we were up in this little village near the frontier of Belgium, or no, maybe it was near the frontier of Luxembourg – it makes no odds really and doesn't affect my story. Now there was this *boulanger* in the village, and I think now I will if I may describe the state of the village. Well it had been bombed by the U.S. air force, precision bombed, if you see what I mean; it had then been bombed by the Luftwaffe quite regardless I am sorry to say (sorry because I am one who hopes very soon to see the Germans playing a very very important part in the family of nations), bombed, then, quite regardless of civilian property and military objectives. It had then been shelled by U.S. infantry and taken and occupied; it had then been shelled and retaken and re-occupied by the Reichswehr, and I am sorry to say that when it was reoccupied by the Reichswehr certain atrocities took place which I for one would rather forget. It had then been shelled and retaken and occupied by the U.S. infantry. And the rain was falling down day and night. I dare say you can picture the state of this village at the time of which I am telling you. But it so happened that the habitation of this *boulanger* was still intact. It had been damaged, of course, the windows were blown in and so on, but the walls were standing, a bit of roof was left and the big oven had suffered no impairment. So I went and asked him if he would care to have some U.S. army flour so that he could bake bread for those civilians who were left in the village. But this little old *boulanger* simply said what the hell, though he said it in French of course, what the hell, the Boches will be back again this evening and I don't see much point baking bread for the Boches to eat tonight.

'Now this little story is symbolical of what I see around me and of what we Americans in France are trying to fight against. There is a malaise in this country, a spirit of discontent, of nausea, of defatigation, of successlessness around us, here in this very city of Paris, which I for one find profoundly discouraging.

'Now my son Heck junior is here temporarily with us, my son by the first Mrs Dexter, an independent, earning, American male of some twenty-two summers. He trained to be a psychiatrist. In my view, everybody nowadays, whatever profession they intend eventually to embrace, ought to have this training. Now he has a column.'

Charles-Edouard, gazing all this time at Mrs Jungfleisch, who happened to be very pretty, and wondering if there were another room he could sit in after dinner with her (but he knew really that the flat was not likely to have a suite of drawing-rooms), was startled out of his reverie by the word column.

'Doric?' he asked with interest, 'or Corinthian?'

But Mr Dexter, in the full flood of locution, took no notice.

'And my son walks in the streets of this town – he is not here with us tonight because he prefers to eat alone using his eyes and his ears in some small, but representative bistro – and he claims that he can sense, by observing the faces of the ordinary citizens, and by various small actions they perform in the course of their daily round, he claims to observe this malaise in every observable walk of life, and I am sorry to say, sorry because I am very deeply sincere in my wish and desire to help the French people, that what my son senses as he goes about this city is entirely reflected in this column.'

And so on. Grace thought it exceedingly clever of Mr Dexter to keep up such a flow, but she could see it was not quite doing for Charles-Edouard. If only he were more serious, she thought sadly, he could be just as wonderful, or more so, but he never seemed to care a bit about the things that really matter in the world. Even during the war he had done nothing, when she was with him, anyhow, but make love, sing little snatches of songs, roar with laughter, and search for objects of art on which to feast his eyes. And yet he must have a serious side to his nature since he had been impelled to leave all these things he cared for and to fight long years in the East. She knew that he could have been demobilized much sooner if he had wished, but that he had refused to leave his squadron until they all came home. She longed for him to get up and make a speech even cleverer than Mr Dexter's, in defence of his country, but he only sat laughing inside himself and looking at pretty Mrs Jungfleisch.

At last they went in to dinner. Grace, who was by now accustomed to an easy flow of French chat from her dinner partners, was completely paralysed when Mr Rutter opened the conversation by turning to her and saying, 'Tell me about yourself.' She was looking, as she always did, to see if Charles-Edouard was happy; it distressed her that he had been put as far as possible from pretty Mrs Jungfleisch. He too clearly did not admire Carolyn, who was talking to him about Nanny, a subject that did not bring out the best in him.

'Myself?' she said, and fell dumb.

However, Hector Dexter now tapped his plate for silence.

'I'm going to call on each person here,' he said, 'to say a few words on a subject with which we are all deeply preoccupied. I mean, of course, the A-bomb. I think Charlie Jungfleisch can speak for the ordinary citizen of our great United States of America, as he is just back from there. Aspinall Jorgmann will tell us what they are saying behind the Iron Curtain (Asp has just done this comprehensive six-day tour and we all want to know his impressions), Wilbur Rutter can speak of it as it will, or may, affect world prosperity, M. Tournon represents the French government at this little gathering, and M. de Valhubert —'

'Perhaps I will listen without joining in,' said Charles-Edouard, much to Grace's disappointment, 'as an amateur of *pâte tendre*, you will understand, I find the whole subject really too painful. My policy with regard to atom bombs is that of the ostrich.'

'Just as you like,' said Mr Dexter. 'Then I call on Charlie. There is one thing we here in Europe are very anxious to know, Charlie, and that is what, if any, air-raid precautions are being taken in New York?'

'Well, Heck, quite some precautions are being taken. In the first place the authorities have issued a very comprehensive little pamphlet entitled "The Bomb and You" designed to bring the bomb into every home and invest it with a certain degree of cosiness. This should calm and reassure the population in case of attack. There are plenty of guidance reunions, fork lunches, and so on where the subject is treated frankly, to familiarize it, as it were, and rob it of all unpleasantness. At these gatherings the speakers stress that the observation of certain rules of atomic hygiene ought to be a matter of everyday routine. Keep a white sheet handy, for example, since white offers the best protection against gamma rays. Then the folks are told what to do after the explosion. The importance of rest can hardly be over-estimated; the protein contents of the diet should be increased – no harm in a glass of milk as soon as the bomb has gone off. If you feel a little queer, dissatisfied with your symptoms, send at once for the doctor. You follow me, it is elementary, of course, but these things cannot be too much emphasized. If the folks know just what they ought to do in the case of atomic explosion, such explosion is robbed of half, or one-third, its terrors.'

'Thank you, Charlie,' said Mr Dexter. 'I for one feel a lot easier in my mind. There is nothing so dangerous as a policy of *laisser-aller*, and I am very glad that the great American public, if I may say so, M. de Valhubert, without offending your feelings, is not hiding its head in the sand, but is looking the Bomb squarely in the eye. Very glad indeed. And now I shall call on

Asp for a few words. Tell us what they are thinking in the Russian-occupied countries, Asp.'

'Well, I have just had six very very interesting days in Poland, Czechoslovakia, Roumania, Bulgaria, the East or Russian-occupied part of Germany, and the East or Russian-occupied part of Austria, and I'm here to tell you that these countries, if not actually preparing for war, which I think they are, are undeniably being run on a war-time basis.'

'And did you talk with the ordinary citizens of these countries, Asp?'

'Why, no, Heck. For reasons of which I suppose you are all cognizant I did not, but I saw the key men and key women of our embassies and missions in these countries, and I gleaned enough material for three, or two, very very long and interesting articles which I hope you will all be reading for yourselves —'

And so it went on. Fortunately some more very important people came in after dinner, so Grace and Charles-Edouard were able to slip away without looking too rude. Charles-Edouard never managed to have a word with Mrs Jungfleisch, who had settled down to a cosy chat with Mr Jorgmann about conferences, vetos, and what Joe Alsop had told her when she saw him in Washington. Pretty Mrs Jungfleisch, like Mr Dexter, was deeply concerned about the present state of the world, and had no time for frivolous Frenchmen who preferred *pâte tendre* to atom bombs.

Charles-Edouard was particularly nice to Grace about this dinner, and insisted on asking the Dexters back the following week. The two couples dined alone together, rather quickly, and went to *Lorenzaccio*. If Charles-Edouard had suffered from boredom at the Dexter dinner, he had more than his revenge on Hector, who really could hardly sit still at *Lorenzaccio,* and said, quite rudely, in the entr'acte, that whoever would take this play to Broadway was heading for a very very serious financial loss indeed.

'But my dearest,' said Albertine, 'dinner with the wife's best friend and the best friend's husband is a classic. I could have warned you about that, as much a part of married life as babies,

89

nannies, and in-laws. Of course a jolly bachelor like yourself had never envisaged such developments.'

'I wish I understood Americans,' said Charles-Edouard. 'They are very strange. So good, and yet so dull.'

'What makes you think they are so good?'

'You can see it, shining in their eyes.'

'That's not goodness, that's contact lenses – a kind of spectacle they wear next the eyeball. I had an American lover after the liberation and I used to tap his eye with my nail file. He was a very curious man. Imagine, his huge, healthy-looking body hardly functioned at all by itself. He couldn't walk a yard; I took him to Versailles, and half-way across the Galerie des Glaces he lay on the floor and cried for his mother. He couldn't do you know what without *lavages*, he could only digest yoghourt and raw carrots, he couldn't sleep without a sleeping draught or wake up without benzedrine, and he had to have a good strong blood transfusion every morning before he could face the day. It was like having another automaton in the house.'

'You had him in the house?'

Albertine, who hated too much intimacy, had never done this with any of her lovers.

'For the central heating, dearest,' she said apologetically. 'It was that very cold winter. Americans have no circulation of their own – even their motors are artificially heated in winter and cooled in summer. I never shall forget how hot he kept this room – my little thermometer sprang in one day from *"rivières glacées"* to *"vers à soie"*, and even then he complained. Finally it reached Sénégale, all the marquetry on my Oeben began to spring, and I was obliged to divorce him. We were married, by the way.'

'Married?' Charles-Edouard was quite astounded.

'Yes, he could do nothing in bed without marriage lines. I tried everything, I even got an excellent aphrodisiac from the doctor. Useless. We had to go to the Consulate together, and after that he was splendid. The result is I've got an American passport, which never does any harm.'

'And what has become of him now?'

'Oh he's got the cutest little wife and the two loveliest kids, and he sends me boxes of cleansing tissues every Christmas.'

Chapter Eleven

MADAME DE VALHUBERT died suddenly the very day she was to have left Bellandargues for Paris. She made the journey all the same, and was buried in the family grave at the Père La Chaise. Charles-Edouard was very sad, cast down as Grace had never seen him. He said they must go into mourning in the old-fashioned, strict way which has been greatly relaxed in France since the war; it was a tribute, he said, that he owed to his grandmother. So Grace was no longer subjected to an enormous dinner party, reception or ball nearly every day, and this was a great comfort to her. Not a truly social person, these parties, as soon as they had ceased to frighten, had begun to bore her, and she envisaged almost with horror the endless succession there would be of them to the end of her life. She was very much happier now that, for the moment, they were ruled out. She did not have much more of her husband's company than usual; he continued to spend whole days at the sale-rooms in the Hôtel Drouot and with the antique dealers, and was still always out at tea-time. They never spent an evening at home together quietly; the moment he had swallowed his dinner he would drag Grace to a film, a play, or a concert.

Charles-Edouard's long absences from his house had never surprised her or struck her as needing an explanation. She had been brought up in the shadow of Parliament, Brooks's, White's, and Pratt's; her own father was practically never at home, and she supposed that all men were engaged, for hours every day, on some masculine business, inexplicable, at any rate never explained, but quite innocent and normal.

But although she saw rather little of him it seemed to her that Charles-Edouard was cosier, more at home with her now, than when they had first arrived in France. It had never even occurred to her that she was, perhaps, more in love than he was. In her eyes, all the evidence pointed to a great deal of love on his side. He was very nice to her, he made love continually, and she had not enough experience to look for any of the other signs that indicate the condition of a man's heart. Now that they were no longer going out she never saw Juliette, and assumed that Charles-Edouard never did either. This was certainly a relief, though the affair had annoyed rather than worried her. It seemed to her that it was too open to matter, she had taken it half as a joke, and teased him about it.

So Grace regarded herself as a perfectly happy woman whose marriage was entirely satisfactory, with one very small reservation.

'You know, Charles-Edouard,' she said to him, 'I can't help thinking it's a pity you never set eyes on our Blessing. I often wonder whether I see enough of him, but you are an absolute stranger to the poor little boy. Sigi,' she called, hearing him outside on the stairs, 'come in here. Who is this gentleman?'

'Papa!'

'Yes, quite right, but how did you guess?'

He looked his mother up and down. 'I say, Mummy, you are getting Frenchified.'

'Don't you think we all are, now we live in France?'

'Nanny isn't, and Nanny Dexter isn't, and Mrs Dexter isn't.'

'Well, perhaps not. Are you just going out?'

'Oh yes, boring old Parc Monceau as usual.'

'Does he go to the Parc Monceau?' said Charles-Edouard. 'This is very foolish. Why not the Tuileries, or the Luxembourg, or the beautiful garden of the Musée Rodin? I should hate it if my childhood memories were of the Parc Monceau.'

'His little friend goes there.'

'My little friend indeed! Nanny's little friend. I loathe him. Anyway, I like grown-up people.'

'Ha!' said Charles-Edouard. 'How I agree with you, so do I. Will you chuck the Parc Monceau today and come for a walk with me instead?'

'With delight. And Mummy too?'

Grace thought it would be much better if they went off alone, without her, and said, 'I can't, darling. I've got to try on a hat. Go with Papa and I'll be here for tea when you get back.'

'Always hats! Wouldn't be much good in a tight fix with interior tribes, you and your old hats.' He was not displeased, however. His experience of walking with two grown-up people was that they chatted away together up there in the air while you were left to look for francs in the gutter.

'I think you underestimate the value of hats,' said Charles-Edouard. 'They can have a very civilizing influence on interior tribes. Look at Mummy —'

'Oh shut up, Charles-Edouard.'

'Cut the necking,' said Sigi.

'Where does the child learn this sort of language?'

'It's what I tell you. If he was more with us —'

'Where shall we go, Papa?'

> *'Promenons-nous dans le bois*
> *Pendant que le loup n'y est pas.'*

'No, not *dans les bois*. A street walk.'

'The most beautiful walk in the world then. Across the Beaux Arts bridge, through the Cour Carrée, under the Arc du Carousel (averting the eye from Gambetta) and across the Place de la Concorde. How would that be?'

'Then we could have a word with Pascal on the way?'

'Who is Pascal?'

'My goat.'

'Ah no. No words with goats.'

They set off hand in hand, Charles-Edouard dragging the child along at a furious speed. At the Arc du Carousel Charles-Edouard began reciting *'A la voix du vainqueur d'Austerlitz* – when you know that by heart,' he said, 'I'll give you a prize.'

'What sort of prize?'

'I don't know. A good sort.'

'How can I learn it?'

'It's written up there on the arch. At your age I used to read it every day. Oh how I loved the Emperor, at your age.'

'How can I read it when we never come here?'

'You must come. You must refuse the Parc Monceau and come.'

'But Papa —'

'No excuses. Nothing so dull.'

Sigi waved at Pascal with his free hand, but was dragged on.

'You are too old for goats. I'll show you some horses. There, the flying horses of Coysevox, are they not wonderful?'

'Look, look, Papa! Mrs Dexter in her lovely new Buick.'

'Come on, she's not my type. What is a Buick?'

'Papa! It's a motor, of course.'

'Ha! You know Buick and you've never heard of Coysevox. What a world to be young in. Now here are the *chevaux de Marly* – are they not beautiful?'

'Can I get up there and ride on one of them?'

'Ride on the *chevaux de Marly*? Certainly not, what an idea.'

They hurried on to Charles-Edouard's destination, the shop of an art dealer who had written to him about a pair of vases. Here Sigi was put to sit, kicking his heels, on one of those stools which, at Versailles, were kept exclusively for dukes. 'So now,' said the dealer, 'you are *duc et pair de France.*'

Charles-Edouard began an exhaustive examination of everything in the shop: the vases, a tray of jewelled boxes, an inkstand which had belonged to Catherine the Great, a pair of cherubs said to be by Pigalle, and so on. He always asked the price of everything, like a child in a toy shop, and roared with derisive laughter when he was told. He was the flail of the dealers, his technique being to arrive with the words, loudly enunciated before the other customers, 'Why don't you burn all this rubbish and get some decent stock?' But they respected his knowledge and his love of beautiful things.

Sigi gazed out of the plate-glass window. It was very dull being *duc et pair de France* for so long. In a window across the road there was a great heap of mattresses, as in the story of the Princess and the pea. The sight of these mattresses, combined with the endless aeons of inactivity so terrible to a child, filled him with a great longing to jump up and down on them.

Presently Madame Marel came into the shop. Charles-Edouard, who had forgotten that he had half arranged to meet her there, was a little bit put out at being found with Sigi. He knew that all would be reported to Grace.

'How are you, my dear Albertine? Here are the vases – not bad, what do you say? But the price is the funniest thing I ever heard. M. Dupont does love to make me laugh. Now what of this bronze? I am thinking of it most seriously. I do love Louis XIV bronze, so delightfully solid, so proof against housemaids. Once you fall into Louis XV you are immediately in the domain of restored *terre cuite* and broken china, of things which must

94

go behind glass in any case. I love them too, far too much, but there is something comfortable about this old satyr. As soon as M. Dupont has mentioned its real price I shall buy it – at present he is in the realms of romance. Such an imaginative man, such an artist in figures, M. Dupont. So – this is Sigismond.'

Sigi, rather unwillingly, but forced to it by a severe look from his father, kissed her hand.

'This is Sigi? Now all is explained – he is well worth it. Have you been here long? Very long? Poor little boy, not very amusing for you, sitting on that *tabouret* and thinking of what, I wonder? What were you thinking of, Sigismond?'

'The mattresses over there. I would like to jump and jump and jump and roll and roll and roll on them.'

'Already?' she said. 'How like your father. I'll tell you what, darling, shall we go over there and jump while he goes on breaking poor M. Dupont's heart? Shall we? Come on.'

'No, Albertine, certainly not. I am a well-known figure in Paris, please try and remember. It is quite out of the question.'

'He wants to so badly.'

'But this child has the most peculiar ambitions. On the way here he wanted to chat to a goat and to ride on the *chevaux de Marly*.'

'What a lovely idea, and how well I can understand it. Why don't we arrange it for him?'

'Try not to be foolish, Albertine. Flirt with the child if you can't help it, but keep within reason.'

'Your father has this pompous side to his nature, you know. When one comes up against that there's nothing to be done. Will you come to tea with me one day, if I collect some little friends?'

'He loathes little friends.'

'So much the better, he can come alone. There are lots of things in my house to amuse you – things that you wind up which do tricks. A dancing bear, a drinking monkey, a singing dog. Will you come?'

'Oh yes please,' said Sigi. He took greatly to this lady who was so nice to him and who smelt so delicious.

'Today?'

'Not today,' said Charles-Edouard rather hastily. 'I'm taking him home now, he has been out long enough. Say good-bye, Sigismond.'

Madame Marel said, in French, which she presumed the child would not understand, 'Then come straight on to me – tea will be ready and I've got many things to tell you.'

'Did you enjoy your walk with Daddy?' Grace asked as they sat down to tea. The two nannies had at last found an English grocer, so their tables were laden now with (for export only) such delicacies as Huntley and Palmer's biscuits, good black Indian tea, Tiptree's strawberry jam, Gentleman's Relish, and rich fruit cake.

At luncheon, chutney, Colman's mustard, and horseradish sauce made it possible to swallow the nasty foreign-looking meat swimming in fat, and hardly a day went by without a sago pudding or castle cakes with Bird's custard.

Grace never went to the nursery without feeling rather like the maiden in the fairy story whose husband allowed her to have one room in the castle lined with nettles to make her feel at home again.

'I enjoyed it very much indeed. We saw Pascal in the distance, but he didn't see me.'

'You didn't have a drive?'

'Papa was in such a hurry. Then we saw Mrs Dexter in her Buick but she's not his type, then we saw the *chevaux de Marly* but he was in too much of a hurry to let me ride on them, then we saw a huge heap of mattresses and I wanted to jump and jump up and down on them, but Papa wouldn't let me even though the lady we met said he ought to because it would be very amusing, and she said it was just like Papa, wanting to jump and roll on the mattresses.'

'You met a lady?'

'Yes, she smelt heavenly and Papa has gone to tea with her. I think she is his type.'

'A pretty lady?'

'Very Frenchified.'

'So on the whole you had a good time?'

'Smashing,' said Sigi with conviction, his hour of restless boredom on the *tabouret* quite forgotten.

When Charles-Edouard got back he found Grace in the little library next door to her bedroom where she generally sat when she was alone. She was tucked up on a chaise-longue looking pretty and comfortable and a little fragile, since she was expecting a child.

'Who was it you met on your walk? She's made a great hit with Sigi, he said she smelt too delicious.'

'Yes. I wish I knew what scent she uses, but it has always been a state secret. Albertine Marel-Desboulles.'

'Marel. Oh! Isn't that the woman Hughie's in love with?'

'Exactly. She tells me she has fourteen English suitors, it's very amusing.'

'Not very amusing for poor Hughie. He's terrified that she'll go into a convent, according to Carolyn. Do you think it's likely?'

Charles-Edouard roared with laughter. 'Convent indeed! Never, in a long life, have I heard anything so funny.'

'Where does she live?'

'Just round the corner in the rue de l'Université, in that house you always look at with the two balconies.'

'Oh, the lovely house. Does she live there?'

'As you would know if you ever listened to what I say. She has extraordinary furniture, and the most famous collection of old toys in the world. Her husband's family made all the toys for the French court from the time of Henri II to the Revolution.'

'Does she live with her husband?'

'He is dead. He was vastly rich and he died.'

'And she's an old friend of yours?'

'Since always. We had the same nurse.'

'Take me to see her one day?'

'Perhaps – I'm not sure. Albertine is not very fond of women.'

Three or four days later Grace was driving home at tea-time when she saw Charles-Edouard leaning against the great double doors of Madame Marel's house. He had evidently just rung the bell. A small side door flew open and he disappeared through it. For the first time since her marriage Grace felt a jealous, heart-sinking pang. By the time he came in, some two hours later, she was so nervous that she thought it better to speak.

'But Charles-Edouard,' she said, 'you went to tea with Madame Marel again today?'

Charles-Edouard always acted on the principle with women, of telling the truth and then explaining it away so that it sounded highly innocent.

'Yes,' he said carelessly. 'It's an old habit of all my life. I go there every day, at tea-time.'

'Then you are in love with her?'

'Because I go to tea?' He raised his hand and shook his head reassuringly, but with his inward, guilty laugh.

Grace was not reassured. 'Because you go there every day. That's why you never come and have tea with us, in the nursery.'

'Only partly why.'

'When you told me about M. de la Bourlie visiting your grand-mother every day you said in such a case there is always love. I remember so well, they were your very words, Charles-Edouard.'

'Now listen, my dearest Grace. As life goes on each person develops many different relationships with many different people, and each of these relationships is unique in quality. My relation-ship with you is perfect, is it not?'

'I thought so,' she answered sadly.

'If you think so it is so. Is it spoilt if I have another relation-ship, much less intense, much less important, but also perfect in its way, with Albertine Marel? Be frank now. You didn't mind me being alone for hours with my grandmother; you wouldn't mind if I went to a club, or spent hours with some old school friend, a man. You are not sad because the hours are not spent with you, you realize we can't be together every minute of the day; you mind because Albertine is a still desirable woman. And yet we are old school friends – nursery friends, in fact, and we share a great interest and hobby, that of collecting. I will tell you something very seriously, Grace. If you don't empty your mind and heart of sexual jealousy, if you let yourself give way to that, you will never be happy with me. Because I really cannot help liking the company of women. Do you understand what I have said?'

'It sounds all right,' said Grace.

'Try and remember it then.'

'Yes, I'll try.'

'Are you happy again?'

98

'Yes. But, oh dear, how nice it would be if you had tea here with us every day.'

'In the nursery? With Nanny? Are you mad?'

Chapter Twelve

On Madame de Valhubert's birthday, in February, Charles-Edouard, Grace, and Sigismond went to the Père La Chaise with a bunch of spring flowers for her. It was beautiful weather, a respite between two particularly sharp spells of winter. The sun shone, the birds sang, and the blue gnomes who keep order in the streets of the dead were all beaming cheerfully. Even the floating widows looked as if they did not much object to being left alone a few more years above the ground.

'Have a good look at everything, Sigi,' said Charles-Edouard, 'you will be longer here than anywhere on earth.'

'Oh the funny little houses,' said the child, running from one to another and looking in, 'can I come and live in one?'

'All in good time. So, we'll pay some visits as we go.'

They climbed the long, steep hill, Charles-Edouard pulling Grace up by the hand.

'Many friends. Here are the Navarreins. The first ball I ever went to was in their house. M. de Navarrein was a link with the past, one of those things I never can remember. Let me see, his father was kissed by somebody whose great-great-grandfather had been held in the arms of *le grand Condé*. You know, it all depends on everyone concerned having children when they are ninety, really rather disgusting. There's the beautiful tomb of the Grandlieus – Madame de Grandlieu was my godmother, and she gave me the praying hands by Watteau which are over my bed.'

'Oh look,' said Grace, 'poor little Laetitia Hogg – younger than Sigi. What was she doing in Paris, and why did she die, I wonder?'

'One of those questions which are posed in graveyards. James and Mary Hogg must have loved her, since they bought her this tomb in perpetuity. Ha! the Politovskis, I'd not noticed them here before.' He went up to read the inscription, and began to laugh loudly. 'Oh no! This is too much! I've never heard such a thing! They've given themselves an S.A.R.! It's perfect, I can't wait to tell Tante Régine, what rubbish really. "*Il conquit Naples et resta pur.*" Maybe he did, though not very likely, but even that doesn't entitle him to be a Royal Highness. Langeais and his wife, so charming, Sauveterre (poor Fabrice, give me one flower for him, how he would have laughed to see me here with wife and child). We've already passed enough friends to collect a large dinner party, a large amusing dinner party. *Hélas*, where are they all now, I wonder?'

'Having large, amusing dinner parties somewhere else,' said Grace, suddenly seeing herself as doomed to eternal dinner parties, 'wishing you were there and wondering what I'm like.'

'Yes indeed. *L'Anglaise!* Intelligence Service. *Fille de franc-maçon*,' said Charles-Edouard with his inward laugh. 'Here we are, this is the Avenue of the Marshals of France, our future home. Sigismond will spend some melancholic moments here, I hope, before it is his turn. Is it not beautiful up on this cliff, are we not lucky to be so well placed? Mind you, it is not the smart set, but at least we are not among presidents of the Republic, actors, duellists, and English pederasts. We have this pretty view and we have *la gloire*. Not bad, is it?'

'I feel sad,' said Grace, 'it reminds me of your dear grandmother's funeral.'

'I was very sad. Tired, and very sad. But there is only one thing I clearly remember of that whole day, the look of terrible triumph on the face of Madame de la Bourlie.'

'Oh surely not, at her age?'

'Age cannot blunt the hatred of a lifetime.'

They put their flowers at the base of a stone pyramid. It was a fine Empire tomb with bas-reliefs of battles and battle trophies.

'Poor Grandmère, she can't be very much pleased with the neighbours – Masséna, Lefebvre, Moscowa, Davout – not at all for her, I'm afraid. Come here, Sigismond, can you read this?'

'*Famille* Valhubert,' he spelt it out.

'This is your little house.'

'Can't I have one with a lace table-cloth and a door?'

'No. You will lie here with Grandmère and all of us.'

'Yes, but supposing I am killed in a stratospheric battle with the Martians?'

'That I should applaud. You may or may not become a Marshal of France, but you should always die in battle if you can, or you may live to be shot by your fellow-countrymen, like poor Ney over there, who was not fortunate enough to be killed by the enemy like Essling and Valhubert. I hope you are paying attention to what I am telling you, Sigismond. And now who would you like to see? I can offer you painters, writers, musicians, cooks (Brillat-Savarin, the French Mrs Beeton, is here), and all the great bourgeois of Paris. The 19th-century Russians, *rastaquouères* of their day, with huge, extravagant tombs, Rumanian princes in miniature Saint Sophias, domed and frescoed. Auguste Comte, the founder of positivism, might interest Sigi? But you look very tired, my dearest, and I think we had better walk gently back to the motor.'

The following day Grace had a miscarriage. They said she had perhaps walked too fast up the hill. It was not serious, quite early in her pregnancy, but it pulled her down, depressed her spirits, and she was a long time in bed. This was not a bad place just then. Late snow had fallen, it lay in the garden, white and brown, under a low, dark sky.

But her room gave a sunny impression, yellow with spring flowers. The mimosa was changed three times a day so that it should be always fluffy. People were very kind; Ange-Victor said that Madame Auriol herself would not have had more inquiries, flowers and books poured into the house, and so, when she was well enough to receive them, did visitors. Among those who came, and found Grace by chance alone, was Albertine Marel-Desboulles.

'I never see you,' she said, smiling with all her great charm at Grace. 'Before Madame de Valhubert died I used to have the pleasure of that lovely face to look at over the dinner-table – those huge, boring dinners in the autumn. Now, though we live so near, you have vanished again. But I have met the entirely delightful Sigismond.'

'I know. He told me. He thought you were heavenly.'

'When I heard you were ill I decided to call on you. Charles-

Edouard and I are the oldest friends in the world – foster-brother and sister in a way, since we had the same nanny – well, to cut short all these explanations, here I am. How pretty you have made this room. I know it of old because here we used to put our coats when Madame de Valhubert gave her famous music parties.'

'I didn't know Madame de Valhubert was musical.'

'Oh well, music was not the only object of the parties, but the house has this music room and Régine Rocher had a Polish lover who played Chopin, so it all fitted in rather conveniently. As I was saying, then, we used to come up here with our coats – it was a hundred years ago – and in those days there was an Empire dressing-table with a marble top, very ugly, I can see it now, and on this slab of horrid grey marble there were hair-pins and safety-pins and *papier à poudre* for our shiny noses. I must explain that this was thought very old-fashioned and a great joke even then. I am old, but not so old that I have ever not owned a powder puff. It was freezing up here, agony to take off our coats, so we only stayed a moment, I don't suppose anybody ever used the *papier à poudre*. Then we would go to the music room, where the Polish lover was fiercely thumping away with passionate glances at Régine, and Charles-Edouard couldn't be stopped from talking. He would sit next the prettiest woman, which sometimes happened to be me, and talk at the top of his voice, while Régine got more and more furious. But dear Madame de Valhubert, who literally never knew one note from another, not that it would have made much difference if she had, was quite delighted to see him enjoying himself so much.

'So I've known this room a long time, but it's never been as pretty as now. I can see that you are one of those women with a talent for living in a house, which is quite different from the talent for arranging houses, and far more precious.'

Of course Grace was completely won over. Presently the door opened again and the pretty head of Juliette Novembre, in a sable hat with violets, peeped round it.

'I've brought you a camellia – can I come in, or are you talking secrets?' she said, like a child.

'Oh please please come in.'

'Just look at her, *la jolie*,' said Albertine, 'what a seasonable hat.'

'I love my little bit of rabbit. How are you?' she said to Grace. 'Isn't it horrid? I had one last year.'

Albertine said, 'I'm longing to hear about the ball, Juliette.'

'Yes, but why didn't you come? We were all wondering.'

'I was discouraged. My new dress wasn't ready, and I do hate autumn clothes in the spring. So after dinner I went home. But as soon as I had sent the motor away I longed very much for the ball. I couldn't go to bed, I sat in my dressing-room until three consumed by this longing to be at the ball. Isn't it absurd, really! But to me a ball is still a miracle of pleasure. I see it with the eyes of a Tolstoy and not at all those of a Marcel Proust, and really, I promise you, it is terrible for me to miss one, even at my age. So now, torture me, tell us exactly what it was like.'

'Divine, a *bal classique* – no fancies, no embroideries. The prettiest women, in their prettiest clothes, a very good band, sucking pig for supper, wonderful champagne, in that house where everybody always looks their best. I loved it; I stayed to the end, which was after six. But nothing dramatic, Albertine, no fight, no elopement, nothing to tell really, hours and hours of smiling politeness.

'I knew it, what I love the most. You have twisted a knife in my heart,' cried Albertine. 'Perhaps I ought to have gone, even in an old dress. But there – a ball to me is such a magical occasion that I cannot enjoy it wearing just anything. For days I have been seeing myself at that ball wearing my new dress, and when I found it couldn't be ready in time (nobody's fault, influenza in the workrooms), I didn't want to spoil the mental picture by going in another dress. Don't you understand?'

'Oh yes,' said Juliette. 'I'm just the same. I can't think of any occasion – a tea party even – without seeing an exact picture of how I shall look at it, down to shoes and stockings. I often wonder how social life – or life at all – can be much pleasure to people who don't care about dress. I'd hardly get myself out of bed in the morning if I hadn't something pretty and rather new to put on, and never get myself to a party. Now take all one's old relations, they love going out, but why? How can they enjoy it, really?'

'Oh their enjoyment comes from thinking of all the money they have saved by not dressing. They look at Régine Rocher and they add up what her clothes must have cost (you'll find they know, too, to a penny) and they feel as if somebody had given them a present of the amount.'

'Poor you, all that mourning,' Juliette said to Grace.

Like Albertine, she was out to please. They chatted away and Grace enjoyed herself. It was the enjoyment of frivolous, cosy, feminine company, of which she was very much starved. Carolyn, her only woman friend in Paris, could neither be described as frivolous nor cosy. She had many virtues, Grace knew that she was loyal and would be a rock in times of trouble, but she was not much fun, too restless and discontented. These two, rattling on with their nonsense, seemed to her perfectly fascinating, and she quite forgave Charles-Edouard for liking to be with them, it seemed so natural that he should.

Presently she sent for Sigi, who arrived hand in hand with his papa. Juliette became extremely animated, almost fidgety, making up to both father and son. Grace thought 'it's rather charming now, she's still only like a little girl, but at forty she will be terrible'. Albertine went to the chair on which she had put her things, produced a long, beautifully made wooden box, and gave it to Sigi.

'A present for you, darling. Open it.'

'What is it?' he said, pink and excited.

'It's called a kaleidoscope. Take it out. It was made for the poor little Dauphin,' she said to Grace.

'Oh you shouldn't! How good of you.'

Charles-Edouard took it from Sigi. 'You shut one eye, like Nelson, and see the stars. So.'

'Is it a telescope?'

'Better, you make your own stars as you go along. Venus – can you see? Shake it. Mars. Shake it. Jupiter as himself. Shake it. Jupiter as a swan.'

'Charles-Edouard, you'll muddle him.'

'Now here's another star you can see with the naked eye,' he said, pointing to Juliette. 'Doesn't she twinkle? She'll tell us all the gossip of the heavens. So, Juliette, tell.'

'Nothing to tell. I lead the life of a good little girl who does her lessons.'

'Ah yes? What lessons?'

'In the morning I sing, coloratura, "Hark, hark the lark"; in the afternoon I paint a snowy landscape; and when it is night I go to the Louvre and see the statues lit up.' She looked at Charles-Edouard with huge, innocent, blue eyes.

'Hm, hm,' he said, clearly rather annoyed. Grace felt again that horrid pang or twinge of jealous uneasiness that she had had on seeing Charles-Edouard outside Albertine's house in the rue de l'Université. Only that morning he had promised to take her, when she was well again, to see the statues lit up, saying how beautiful was the Winged Victory, white in the black shadows and then black against a white wall. She could not help noticing his present embarrassment, and was quite sure that he must have been to see the statues with Juliette. Her feeling of not being able to blame him for liking to be with this pretty wriggler, this flapper of eyelids and purser of lips, suddenly gave way to a feeling that she blamed him very much, and indeed could hardly bear it.

Meanwhile Sigi was entranced with the kaleidoscope.

'Please,' he said, 'can I take it to bed when I go?'

'But this child is his father over again,' cried Albertine. 'The moment he sees something pretty he wants to take it to bed with him.'

Two large tears rolled down Grace's cheeks. She felt, all of a sudden, most exceedingly tired.

Sir Conrad now came over to visit Grace, though he refused to stay with her, preferring the freedom of an hotel. When in Paris he liked to submit himself to the rather strenuous attentions of a certain Hungarian countess, an old friend of before the war; after visiting her establishment he needed a restful morning, and did not feel up to much family life before luncheon-time.

Charles-Edouard introduced him to Madame Rocher, and this was a stroke of genius, they could have been made for each other. She came out of mourning and gave a large dinner party for him, at which he charmed everybody. The rumours about the Allinghams not being people to know were now for ever scotched. He and Madame Rocher embarked upon a shameless flirtation, and were soon on such intimate terms that she even taxed him with being a Freemason. Sir Conrad, who was of course perfectly aware of the implications of this in France, roared with laughter, did not make any definite statement but let it be understood that his daughter had, of course, been joking, and a very good joke too. Madame Rocher, who was no fool, began to see that Charles-Edouard must have been quite right in what he had said about English Freemasons. Henceforward she addressed Sir Conrad as *Vénérable*, referred to him as *le Grand Maître*, and all was merry as a marriage bell.

He liked Charles-Edouard more than ever. It would have surprised and gratified Grace to know that they had long, interesting discussions on political subjects when they were alone together, during which Charles-Edouard showed himself quite as serious, if not quite as long-winded, as Hector Dexter. One evening Charles-Edouard, though protesting that he himself only cared for society women, took his father-in-law round the brothels. These, having lately been driven underground by the ill-considered action of a woman Deputy, had become rather difficult for a foreigner to find.

Sir Conrad, who had never had many topics on which he could converse with his daughter, now found fewer even than when she was living with him.

'Are you happy?' he asked her, before leaving.

'Very happy.'

'Take care of yourself, darling. You don't look well.'

'I was quite ill. I shall be all right in a week or two.'

'Nanny hasn't changed much.'

'Oh dear, no.'

'Well, sooner Charles-Edouard than me is all I can say. Must you keep her? Couldn't you get a governess soon, or a tutor or something?'

'Papa! Nanny! – I couldn't possibly do without her.'

'No, no, I suppose not. And as she seems to have the secret of eternal youth (sold her soul to the devil, no doubt) I suppose

Sigi's children won't be able to do without her either. If we were savages she would undoubtedly be the chieftainess of the tribe.'

Back in London, Sir Conrad went straight off to see Mrs O'Donovan and recount his visit.

'It's such a pity you didn't come,' he said, 'next time you really must. Grace would love to put you up, she asked me to tell you.'

'I don't believe I shall ever go back to Paris,' she said. 'I've known it too well and loved it too much. I couldn't bear to find all my friends old and poor and down at heels.'

'If it's only that,' he said with a short laugh, 'I've never seen them so prosperous, all living in their own huge houses, thousands of servants, guzzle, guzzle, guzzle, swig, swig, swig, just like old days.'

'Are they really so rich? But why?' she said querulously, as if they ought not to be.

'I suppose I don't have to enter into the economic reasons with you. You know as well as I do why it is.'

'In any case you can't deny they are all ten years older.'

'But the point is you'd think they were twenty years younger. They've all had Bogomoletz. That is something we must look into, you know. You get the liver of a newly killed young man (killed on the roads, of course, not on purpose) pumped into your liver, and the result is quite amazing.'

'My dear Conrad —'

'Or if you jib at that you can press unborn chickens on to your face before going out.'

'Thank you very much if by you, you mean me. *I* get one Polish egg a week on my ration.'

'Remarkable what your cook manages to do with that one Polish egg, I must say. Hens must lay enormous eggs in Poland, or are they ostriches? But to go back to your friends, none of them looks a day more than forty. I can't think why you're not pleased; you're supposed to love the French so much.'

'I think it's frightfully annoying, after all they've been through. Now I want to hear a great deal about other things. What is the exact situation at present.'

'Situation?'

Sir Conrad had come back in a very uppish mood, she thought, like a child after a treat.

'The political situation, of course. What does Blondin say, for instance?'

'My dear Meg, I didn't see Blondin, or any of them. I was entirely given over to pleasure and fun. But you know what the silly fool says as well as I do, since I am well aware that, like me, you see all the French papers.'

Mrs O'Donovan sighed. She did wish her English political friends could be a little more serious about the terrible state of the world. Sir Conrad, she thought, might well take a leaf out of the book of that important, well-informed Mr Hector Dexter whom she had met the day before at a dinner party, and who had told her some interesting, if rather lowering, facts about present-day French mentality.

Sir Conrad was not unconscious of these critical thoughts, he knew Mrs O'Donovan too well for that, but he was still a little drunk with all the pleasure and fun he had been having, so he went carelessly on,

'I want you to help me give a big, amusing dinner for Madame Rocher des Innouïs next month if she comes, as I hope she will, to stay at the French Embassy.'

'Régine Rocher,' said Mrs O'Donovan, faintly, 'don't tell me she's got the liver of a newly run-over young man.'

'I should think she's got everything she can lay her hands on. Anyhow she's remarkably pretty for what Charles-Edouard says is her age. He says she spends £8,000 a year on clothes, and the result, I'm obliged to tell you, is top-hole.'

'Simply ridiculous, I should imagine.'

Mrs O'Donovan, who was generally the driest of blankets, was proving such a wet one on this occasion that Sir Conrad took himself off to the House. Here he had a sensational success with all his traveller's tales about Bogomoletz and embryo chickens, not to mention detailed descriptions, unfit for the ears of a lady, of the goings-on *chez* Countess Arraczi.

Chapter Thirteen

'OUR visit to London,' said Hector Dexter, 'was an integral success. I went to learn about the present or peace-time conditions there and to sense the present or peace-time mood of you Britishers, and I think that I fully achieved both these aims.'

The Dexters and Hughie Palgrave were dining with Grace. Charles-Edouard had told her earlier in the week that he was obliged to dine alone with Madame de la Ferté to talk family business.

'My uncle is so old now, he really makes no sense at all, and Jean is no use to her either. Nobody knows whether he is a case of arrested development or premature senile decay; she is having him injected for both, and the only result so far has been a poisoned arm. Why don't you ask some friends here to keep you company?'

Grace jumped at the idea of having the Dexters without Charles-Edouard. Although he never said they bored him, and indeed professed to admire Carolyn, whom he always referred to as *la belle Lesbienne,* she could somehow never bring herself to suggest inviting them again when he was there. As for Hughie, there would clearly be an awkwardness if he were to meet Charles-Edouard. She herself saw him quite often at the Dexters, and once a certain embarrassment between them was over they had become good friends again. They had never been much more than that, never passionate lovers.

'It's not the first time you've seen London, is it?' Grace said.

'No, Grace, it is not. I was in London during World War II and I will not pause now to say what I felt then about the effort which every class of you Britishers was putting forward at that time because what I felt then is expressed in my well-known and best-selling book *Global Vortex.* This time I found a very different atmosphere, much more relaxed and therefore much more difficult to sense, harder to describe.'

'Whom did you see?'

'We saw a very representative cross-section of your British

life. We were in London and had a good time there, many very pleasant lunch parties and dinner parties and cocktail parties being given for us. We spent some nights with Carolyn's relatives in the North and had a good time there and some nights with some other relatives of Carolyn's near Oxford and had a good time there too.'

'So now what was your general impression, Heck?'

Hughie revered Hector, who seemed to him quite the cleverest man he had ever met. His own ambition was to go into politics as soon as he could get a seat to contest, and he liked picking Hector's brains on international subjects, or rather, allowing Hector's brains to flow over him in a glowing lava of thought.

'I must be honest with you, Hughie, my impression is not quite satisfactory.'

'Oh dear, that's bad. In what way?'

'An impression, I am sorry to say, of a great deal of misplaced levity.'

'Levity? I never see much levity at home; nothing much to levitate about, I shouldn't have said.'

'I must explain a little further. My government expects and gets, reports from me on the political equilibrium, stability, and soundness of the various countries I visit. At first sight this stability, equilibrium, and soundness seem very great in Britain. At first sight. But there is a worm, a canker in this seemingly sound and perfect fruit which I for one find profoundly disquieting. I refer to the frivolous attitude you Britishers have adopted, just as it has been adopted here (the difference being that nobody expects the French to be serious whereas we do most certainly expect it of you Britishers), the frivolous attitude towards – we are all grown-up and I guess I can speak without embarrassing anybody – sexual perversion.'

'Have we adopted a frivolous attitude?' said Hughie. 'The poor old dears are always being run in, you know.'

'I think I will put it this way. I think it cannot be generally understood and realized in Britain, as we understand and realize it in the States, that morally and politically these people are lepers. They are sickly, morbose, healthless, chlorotic, unbraced, flagging, peccant, vitiated and contaminated, and when I use the word contaminated I use it very specifically in the political sense.

But I think you British have absolutely no conception of the danger in your midst, of the harm these perverts can do to the state of which they are citizens. You seem to regard them as a subject for joking rather than as the object of a deep-seated, far-reaching purge.'

'But they're not in politics, Heck – hardly any, at least.'

'Not openly, no. That's their cunning. They work behind the scenes.'

'If you can call it work.'

'For the cause of Communism. The point I am trying to make is that they are dangerous because politically contaminated, a political contamination that can, in every traceable case, be traced to Moscow.'

'I say, hold on, Heck,' said Hughie. 'All the old queens I know are terrific old Tories.'

'I am bound to contradict you, Hughie, or rather I am bound to put forward my argument, and you are going to see that it is a powerful argument, to persuade you of the exact opposite of what you have just said and to persuade you that what you have just said is the exact opposite of the truth as known to my government. We Americans, you may know, have certain very very sure and reliable, I would even say infallible, sources of information. We have our Un-American Activities Committee sections, we have our F.B.I. agents, we have countless very very brilliant newspaper men and business men all over the world (men like Charlie Jungfleisch and Asp Jorgmann); we have also other sources which I am not at liberty to disclose to you, even off the record. And our sources of information inform us that nine out of every ten, and some say ninety-nine out of every hundred, of these morally sick persons are not only in the very closest sympathy but in actual contact with Moscow. And I for one entirely believe these sources.'

Hughie was unconvinced. 'But my dear Heck, in Russia you go to Siberia for that. I've got a friend of mine who's awfully worried about it in case they come —'

'Maybe you do, maybe you don't. There are some very curious anomalies, things you would hardly credit, Hughie, but of which our agents are cognizant, going on in that great amorphous blob of a country today. But I am not concerned with the pervert in

Russia, my concern is with the pervert in Western Europe because my professional concern at the moment is with Western Europe, more especially in its moral and ethical aspect.'

'Then what about the pervert in America?' said Hughie.

'And I am very very glad to say that this very unpleasant problem does not exist in the States. We have no pederasts.'

'How funny,' said Grace, 'all the Americans here are.'

She was thinking of various gay, light-hearted fellows whom she met with Charles-Edouard and his friends. Mr Dexter was displeased with this remark and did not reply, but Hughie said,

'Perhaps they have a bad time at home and all come here, like before the war one used to think all Germans were Jews. But honestly you know, Heck, what you've just said makes no sense, and the more one thinks of it the less sense it makes.'

'I will make one more attempt to explain my meaning to you, Hughie, and then we must go. If a man is morally sick, Hughie, he is morally sick, if he is sick in one sense he will be sick in another, and if he is sexually sick he will be politically sick as well.'

'But, poor old things, they're not sick,' said Hughie, 'they just happen to like boys better than girls. You can't blame them for that, it's awfully inconvenient, and they'd give anything to be different if they could. But I don't see that it's any reason for calling them Bolshevists. I probably know more about them than you do, having been at Eton and Oxford, and if there's one thing they're not it's Bolshevists. Anything for a quiet life is their motto. I'm afraid, old man, you've got the wrong end of the stick there, and if this is what your infallible sources are telling you, I should advise a comb-out of the sources.'

The Dexters now got up to leave. The Jungfleisches, they explained, were giving a party for important people, and they had promised to be there early.

'Poor old Heck,' said Hughie when they had gone. 'He does see things in black and white. Funny, really, for such a clever man. I can't help remembering how all over the Russians he used to be, in Italy. He bit my head off the other day for reminding him, but it's true.'

'Like Carolyn,' Grace said, laughing, 'she used to be our school Communist. I know it was she, though now she pretends I've been mixing her up with another girl. She gets furious when I tease her about it.'

Hughie said, 'Let's go and have a glass of wine somewhere before bed-time, shall we?'

Grace felt tired, as she often did now, but it seemed rather a shame to send him away so early, and she consented.

'Just for an hour then,' she said.

They went to a White Russian night club, a stuffy, dark, enclosed room with music from the Steppes. Cossacks, in boots and white blouses, have keened here night after night for thirty years over a life that has gone for ever. The hours of darkness seem too short for them to express the whole burden of their desolation, so that any reveller who will sit up and listen to the wails and whimpers of their violins until late into the next day becomes their brother and their best beloved. Whereas in other night places the band may be anxious to catch the last metro and go home, these Russians would rather anything than that a lack of customers should drive them out to the first metro. The little room has come to represent Holy Russia to them, and when they leave it in the morning exile begins again. It is really a place designed for lovers or for drunkards, people who like to sit all night engulfed in sound rather than for those who want an hour of sober chat.

Hughie had come to unburden himself about Albertine, and he had to talk very loud so as to be heard over the scream of the violins. From time to time the noise suddenly dropped to a dramatic hush, intended to represent the lull in a storm, and then Hughie's powerful English voice would ring out into the silence so that he was embarrassed, and Grace wanted to giggle. As soon as he had lowered it a gusty crescendo would swallow up his next sentence. It was a very fidgety way of confiding.

'Of course she'll never want to marry me, I know. I don't allow myself to think of it. She is far above me, far too clever and wonderful. She knows everything, not only all French literature but English and German too – she has even read Mrs Henry Wood, for instance. I wish you could hear her reciting – by the hour, it's extraordinary. When I think of all the years I've wasted – but I never guessed there was somebody like that just round the corner or I would have tried to educate myself a bit.

You can't be surprised she rather looks down on me, as it is. So now I'm trying terribly hard to make up for lost time, just in case one day she might think of marrying me. Not very likely, I know, but in life things do sometimes happen. For instance she might be ruined and need a home, or have a fearful accident and be disfigured, or lose a leg —'

The words 'lose a leg', falling into one of the pools of sudden silence, echoed round the room so that Grace could not help laughing.

'Lose a leg?' she said.

Hughie laughed himself, saying, 'Oh well, of course it sounds ridiculous; it's one of those things which I sometimes think of. After all Sarah Bernhardt did, it can happen, and then she'd need somebody to push her about. The worst of it is such hundreds of people do want to marry her, she'd be unlikely to choose me. There's another terrible worry. She talks of going into a convent. I wake up in the night and think about it. Supposing one day I were to call at her house only to be told "Madame Marel-Desboulles is no more. Pray for Soeur Angélique"?'

Grace laughed again, and said, 'You've been reading Henry James – so do I, in the hopes of understanding them all better. But I don't think Albertine is another Madame de Cintré, nor do I think she'll ever marry again. I guess you'll be able to go on like this for years, if it's any consolation to you.'

'It's very much better than nothing, of course. So, as I say, I read a lot to try to educate myself, but I must have let my mind go badly and it's an awful strain. Have you ever tried the *Mémoires* of Saint-Simon? Heavy weather, I can tell you. Then I try and see as many clever people as I can. That's why I go such a lot to the Dexters.'

'D'you think them so very clever?'

'Carolyn is brilliant of course, she takes me sight-seeing and we go to lectures. As for old Heck, well, if he is a bit muddle-headed about some things, he's got the gift of the gab, hasn't he? I wish I could talk like that, on and on.'

'I always think he talks as if he doesn't quite know English.

'Really, Grace, what an idea. All those words – I'm English, but I don't know what half of them mean. Albertine would like me much better if I could put on an act like Hector, I'm sure she would. But when I'm with her I seem to get so tongue-tied.'

At this moment a large party of people got up to go. The violinists came forward, still playing, to try and persuade them to stay. They surrounded them, playing with all their souls. But the people, though smiling, were firm, and made a passage through the deeply bowing, still playing Cossacks. When they had gone, and the violinists had returned to the band, Grace suddenly perceived, in a very dark corner, hitherto obscured by these other people, the figures of Charles-Edouard and Juliette. Their backs were turned, but she could see their faces in a looking-glass. They were evidently enjoying themselves enormously, heads close together, laughing and chattering sixteen to the dozen. Grace was particularly struck, stricken to the heart indeed, by Charles-Edouard's look, a happy, tender, and amused expression, which, she thought, she herself used to evoke at Bellandargues but which she had not seen of late.

She felt weak, as if she were bleeding to death. 'I'm so sorry,' she said, 'but I think I might faint. Could we go home please, Hughie?'

'Goodness,' he said, 'you are white, Grace.' He hurried her to the motor, full of self-reproach. 'I should never have suggested this, you're not strong enough yet.'

'Don't worry, it's nothing, I promise. I feel better already. I'm just a little tired, that's all. Don't come in,' she said, when they arrived at her house. 'My maid always waits for me – she's old-fashioned; I'm so lucky. Good night, Hughie.'

When Charles-Edouard got back, not very late, she was in bed, crying dreadfully.

'Why do you weep?' he said, with great solicitude.

'Because you're in love.'

'I am in love?'

'With Juliette.'

'Why do you say this?'

'I was at the Russian place. I saw you.'

Charles-Edouard looked very much taken aback. 'But you never go to night places.'

'I know. I hate them, but Hughie wanted to —'

'Ha! You've been out with Hughie?'

'I told you we were all going to dine here, me and Hughie and the Dexters. Well the Dexters went on to a party after dinner so Hughie and I — Oh Charles Edouard, you're in love with her?'

He raised his hand, shook his head, and replied, 'Not at all.'

'Then why were you looking so happy?'

'Would I look happy if I were in love with Juliette? It would be very inconvenient, after all she is my cousin's wife. No, I look happy because I am happy – happy in my life and with you, and then I do love to go out with a pretty woman.'

'Why did you pretend you were going to dine with Tante Edmonde?'

'But my dear Grace, it was no pretence at all. I did dine there. It so happens that Juliette also was dining with her mother-in-law. Jean has gone to Picardy; she was alone in her flat so she dined downstairs. When I had finished talking with my aunt I took her out for half an hour before bedtime. I didn't want to come back here and find your dinner still going on.'

'Oh!' This sounded so reasonable. 'Oh dear, I'm sorry to make a scene and I do apologize.'

'For what? The rights of passion have been proclaimed once and for all in the French Revolution.'

'The worst part of the whole thing,' said Grace, tears beginning to well into her eyes again, 'is that what I minded so terribly was your look of happiness. I am supposed to love you and yet I mind you looking happy. When you were sad, when your grandmother died, I was sorry, of course, but I could easily bear it – now I find that what I can't bear is for you to look happy. What can it mean, it doesn't make sense.'

'That, I'm afraid,' said Charles-Edouard, 'is love.'

'But what can I do! I can't live with somebody whom I would rather see sad than happy. Perhaps I'd better go back to England?'

'No. Do stay.'

Grace laughed. 'You say that as if you were asking me for a week-end.'

'Do stay, for good.'

'I can't bear to make scenes, I'm ashamed of myself, it is dreadful.'

'You won't have to very often.'

'I shall begin to imagine all sorts of things whenever you go out.'

'That would be the greatest pity – imaginative women are terrible. Now let's calmly consider what did happen this evening. What did you actually see? Juliette and me, sitting quite properly at a table in a perfectly proper establishment. I was not looking unhappy, but then I have no reason to, I'm not a White Russian violinist. So! That is what you saw. Then your imagination got to work, and what did you imagine? That I had told you a lie, sneaked off to dine in a loving intimacy with Juliette and then taken her to a night club. Knowing me as you do, you might have thought it more probable that, if I were in love with Juliette, I would go straight to bed with her, but no! We choose the night club where we can be seen by all and sundry, and where in fact you see us, staying perhaps an hour, not more. I take her home, but only to the door. My aunt's concierge, like ours, has to get out of bed to let people in, so there could be no question of me going upstairs with Jean's wife; the whole of Paris would know it tomorrow if I did. I say good night in the street and come back here – it is still not one o'clock. I don't think any of this indicates the existence of a great and guilty passion for Juliette. You must be more reasonable, dearest. Shall I give you a piece of advice, quite as useful in love as in warfare? Save your ammunition, and only shoot when you see the whites of their eyes. Now in this particular case I would have you observe that I spent exactly the same sort of evening as you did. We both dined with a few rather dull people, and then went out with the least dull of them for an hour or so before bed.'

'Hughie isn't as pretty as Juliette.'

'Hughie is very handsome, and you know it. But I haven't come near to seeing the white of his eyes yet. I shan't shoot this time, and nor must you.'

Grace was completely reassured. She went happily to sleep.

Chapter Fourteen

A FEW days later Grace lunched with Carolyn, and the talk was all of a certain guide who took personally conducted tours into the private houses of Paris. Carolyn said that she had followed one of these tours every day that week.

'I've been into such wonderful houses, which I would never have seen otherwise,' she said. 'He gets permission to visit anything that is "*classé*", and of course that means anything worth seeing. His lectures, too, are good and informative. Yesterday we went to Mansard's own house in the Marais.'

She described it to Grace. Carolyn was at her best on the subject of old Paris and really knew a great deal about it. She liked the monuments of the town better than its denizens who still threw her into a fever of irritation.

'Now I asked you not to be late,' she said, 'because this afternoon M. de la Tour is taking us to see a very famous private house, one of the hardest to get into, the Hôtel de Hauteserre in the rue de Varenne. I simply must go, and you'd better come too, Grace. It's a chance we shan't have again for ages, and I believe the *boiseries* are unique.'

Grace had nothing much to do and was, like Hughie, for ever trying to scrape up a little culture. Besides, she thought, it might be something for Charles-Edouard with his perpetual 'What are the news?' She never had enough to tell him about her day. 'So, what did *la belle Lesbienne* recount? Or did you sit, as usual, gazing at each other in silence?' As her talk with Carolyn was never anything that could possibly interest him, being all about nannies, the Parc Monceau, and mutual friends at home, and as Grace had no talent for cooking up such plain food with either the spice of malice or the sauce of funniness, she was always obliged to leave it that they had gazed in silence. 'Very strange, this dumbness.'

After luncheon Carolyn drove her across the river to the rue de Varenne. Her exasperation with the French always reached boiling-point when she was driving a motor. As they went she told Grace about a dishonest mechanic who had put back her spare wheel unmended (she was never happier than when some little thing of this sort occurred, another stick with which to beat them), and punctuated her story with, 'Look at that! Did you ever see such driving? I shan't give way; I'm in my rights and he knows it. Disgusting. Oh get on. What a place to park. What people, really!'

It was one of those Paris afternoons when, by some trick of the light, the buildings look as if they are made of opaque, blue glass. Grace wondered how much Carolyn really did love the stones of Paris. She seemed not to notice, as they went by, the blue glass façade of the Invalides surmounted by its dome powdered with gold, but only the bad driving in the Esplanade.

Now when they arrived at their destination Grace saw that it was none other than the Ferté house. She had never known that its old name was Hôtel de Hauteserre, to her it had always been 83 rue de Varenne or the house of Tante Edmonde. She laughed, and said to Carolyn, 'But I know this house by heart – it belongs to Charles-Edouard's old great-uncle; we lunch or dine here every week of our lives. I don't think there's much point in me going in.'

'Nonsense,' said Carolyn, 'you'd better come along as you're here. M. de la Tour will tell you all about it, and very likely show you lots of things you hadn't ever suspected.'

Grace thought again that it would be something funny to tell Charles-Edouard, and that the idea of her sight-seeing in that house would be sure to amuse him. So she paid 100 francs at the door and went in with Carolyn. There was quite a crowd of people, and the guide was just beginning his lecture.

'This house,' he said, 'was built in 1713 by Boffrand for the famous – I should perhaps say notorious – Marquise de Hauteserre, who created a record by keeping the Régent as her lover for eighteen weeks. He was by no means her only lover, and they were, in fact, numberless. I am glad to be able to announce that when we have seen the state rooms, which are of an extraordinary beauty, we are to be allowed the great privilege, hardly ever accorded to tourists, of seeing Madame de Hauteserre's own bedroom. Madame la Duchesse has given me the key; she knows that we are all serious students of French art and not mere gaping sightseers.'

'Have you seen it?' whispered Carolyn to Grace.

'No.'

'There – what did I tell you?'

'This bedroom,' the guide continued, 'has an erotic ceiling, a thing rare in France though not uncommon in Italy, by Le Moine; a Régence bed of wonderful quality, and *boiseries* by Robert de Cotte. When I tell you that all this is quite unrestored, you will easily realize that what you are about to see is unique, of its sort, in Paris.'

They went upstairs into the reception rooms of the first floor which Grace knew so well, gold and white, blue and white, gold and blue with painted ceilings. The lecturer went at length into the history of every detail; they were nearly an hour examining these three rooms, and Grace began to feel tired. At last, in the Salon de Jupiter, where the Fertés usually sat after dinner, the lecturer went to a little door in the wall, which Grace had never noticed there. Taking a large key from his pocket he unlocked this door, saying, 'And now for the famous bedroom of Madame de Hauteserre.'

Grace happened to be standing beside him, and together they looked in. It was a tiny room decorated with a gold and white trellis; an alcove contained a bed, and on the bed, in a considerable state of disarray, were Juliette and Charles-Edouard.

The guide quickly slammed and relocked the door. He turned to the crowd, saying, 'Excuse me, I had quite forgotten, but of course the *boiseries* and the ceiling have gone to the Beaux Arts for repair.'

Nobody but Grace and the guide had seen into the room; greatly to her relief the tourists accepted his statement without dispute, if rather crossly. They had certainly had their money's worth in this beautiful house, although they had been looking forward to the erotic ceiling as a final titbit. Carolyn, still gazing at a panel in the Jupiter room, said, 'Oh never mind, we've really seen enough for one day. Shall I give you a lift home, Grace?'

Grace got into the motor, talked away quite naturally, thanked Carolyn for the afternoon, and went into her house as if nothing had happened. She lay on the day bed in her library, saying to herself, 'This is the end.' But, as with some physical blow, she had not yet begun to feel any pain.

Presently Charles-Edouard came in.

'I looked for you in the nursery,' he said.

'Aren't you having tea with Madame Marel?'

'Not today. I never do on Wednesday, it's her day for receiving. Where do we dine? Oh yes, of course, I remember, Tante Régine. That's sure to be great fun. So, what are the news? Don't tell me, I can guess. You lunched, in an impenetrable silence, with la Dexter. Such a curious friendship, I find.'

'And after luncheon we went sight-seeing.'

'Indeed? Where?'

'The Hôtel de Hauteserre.'

Charles-Edouard looked at her, startled, and then said, quite angrily for him, 'Really, Grace, you are too extravagant. What could have induced you to pay 100 francs to see the house of your uncle, which you know perfectly well already? No – this is not sensible, and I'm very cross with you. Why, 100 francs was a dowry when my grandmother was young.'

'You pay for the lecturer. He shows all sorts of unexpected things.'

'I will take you over it one day. I know much more about it than any lecturer.'

'You would never show me what he did, this afternoon.'

'Ha!' said Charles-Edouard. He went to the window and looked out of it.

'This is very annoying,' he said presently.

'I thought so too. I've seen the whites of their eyes, Charles-Edouard.'

'Imbecile of a lecturer. He should know better than to come bursting into bedrooms like that.'

'Yes. Being French you'd think he would.'

'Perhaps I'll give up Juliette.'

'You needn't bother. I'm going back to England.'

'Do stay,' said Charles-Edouard.

'For the week-end?'

'No. For ever.'

'It's no good, Charles-Edouard. I'm too English; your behaviour makes me too miserable, and I can't bear it any more.'

'But my dear, that's nothing to do with being English. All women are the same; indeed if you were Spanish I daresay you would have killed me by now, or Juliette, or both. No, we've been particularly unlucky. This unspeakable lecturer, paid 100 francs to open bedroom doors in the middle of the afternoon! What could have induced Tante Edmonde to let him, she is out of her mind. I know what it is of course, she hopes to get off taxes by allowing the public into her house, but what a short-sighted action! Half that crowd must have been Treasury spies, nosing about to see how many signed pieces she owns, and the rest of course were burglars making out lists of all the objects in the glass cases. I blame her terribly. Then I'm bound to say it was a little bit your own fault, wasting 100 francs and a whole afternoon in a house where you dine at least once a week. Bad luck, and bad management.'

'In fact everybody's fault but yours.'

'No, no, I blame myself most, for being so careless.'

'Oh dear! How cynical you are.'

'Not at all. I see things in the light of reality.'

'Yes. Well I also must try to be a realist. After this I could never again be happy with you because I should never again have an easy moment when you were out of my sight, never. You are wonderful at explaining things away until one happens to have seen with one's own eyes, but from now on the explanations won't be any good. So I shall go back to Papa.'

'And when do you leave?'

'Tomorrow. I shall take Sigi.'

'Yes, you must. And Nanny, too, perhaps?'

'And Nanny, too. And please excuse me to Tante Régine. I've got a headache, and there's a great deal of packing to be done.'

'Nanny, we're going home to England tomorrow.'

'What, all of us?'

'You and me and Sigismond.'

'Mm.' The tone was one of disapproval. 'Tomorrow, dear? And what about the packing?'

'The train isn't till 12.30 and there's Marie to help you. You must manage somehow, darling, please.'

'But how long are we going for?'

'For good. Now don't look sad, it will be London, not Bunbury. So think – Hyde Park every day, Daniel Neal, steam puddings, Irish stew —'

'Irish stew indeed. My sister says you never see a nice neck, these days. And Sigi's Papa?'

'He's not coming.'

'Mm.'

'Do be pleased, darling. I thought at least somebody would be.'

'Well dear, I've always said little boys ought to have a mummy and a daddy.'

'That can't be helped. And think of the hundreds who don't.'

'I'm wondering how I'm ever to get all his toys packed up in the time. Funny thing, one never gets any notice of these journeys.'

'Send Marie out to buy an extra hamper if there's no room.'

Next day there had to be a special motor to take Sigi's luggage; he had exactly twice as many items as his mother.

'Anybody would suppose that he was a famous cocotte,' said Charles-Edouard, who went to the station exactly as if he were seeing them off for a little change. Sigi skipped about on the platform, getting in everybody's way and saying, 'Can I ride on the engine, please, Papa?'

'Certainly not. And I hope you'll have learnt to read before I see you again.'

'Will you give me a prize if I can?'

'Perhaps. If you can read everything, and not only the little bit out of the *Journal des Voyages* you already know by heart.'

'What sort of prize?'

'A good sort.'

'Can I ride on the *chevaux de Marly* for my prize?'

'You can only ride on the *chevaux de Marly* when you know *A la voix du vainqueur d'Austerlitz* by heart.'

'How can I learn it, in England?'

'I can't imagine. Anyhow you can learn to read. Shall I tell you what will become of you if you can't read when you are grown up?'

'All grown-up people can read,' said the child, conclusively.

'Good-bye, Grace,' said Charles-Edouard. 'Do come back soon.'

'For a week-end?'

'No. For good.'

He kissed her hand and left them. He was quite surprised at how much he minded their departure.

Chapter Fifteen

'What's all this about?' said Sir Conrad when Sigi, Nanny, and their baggage had been deposited in the nursery and he had Grace to himself. 'I'm delighted to see you, it goes without saying, but why such short notice? Is it not rather hysterical?'

'Yes, well, you may call it so. I've left Charles-Edouard.'

'You've left your husband?'

'Yes.'

Sir Conrad was not surprised, since this sudden run for home could hardly, he knew, mean anything else.

'And are you going to tell me why?'

He did not doubt what the reason would be, broadly speaking, but was curious as to the details.

Grace told him at some length about her life in Paris.

'I could bear it when he went to tea every day with Madame Marel, though I didn't like it; I could even bear his terribly open flirtation at every party we went to, with Juliette Novembre, but what happened yesterday afternoon at the Hôtel de Hauteserre is more than I can endure or forgive.'

'What did happen?'

But when she told him Sir Conrad annoyed her very much indeed by bursting into a hearty laugh.

'I say, what bad luck! Now don't look so cross and prim, darling, I quite see it was horrible for you, and I'm very sorry, but I can't help thinking of Charles-Edouard too. You must admit it was bad luck on him, poor chap.'

'Perhaps it was. But lives can't be built entirely on luck.'

'No good saying that, as they always are. Luck, my darling, makes the world we live in. After all, it was by luck you met

124

Charles-Edouard in the first place (bad luck for Hughie); by luck that he came back from the war safe and sound; by luck that you had that clever little Sigi – by luck, indeed, that you got your mother's large blue eyes and lovely legs and not my small green eyes and bow legs. Luck is a thing you can never discount. It may be unfair, it generally is, but you can't discount it. And if Charles-Edouard is having, as he seems to be, a run of bad luck you ought to be there, sympathizing with the poor chap. It doesn't seem right to go off and leave him all alone. I hoped I'd brought you up better than that.'

'You're talking as if he had lost all his money at the races.'

'Oh well, not quite so bad, thank goodness.'

'And as if you're on his side.'

'We must try and see his side of the question, I suppose.'

'I don't think you need, you're my father.'

'Now listen, my darling child. I love you, as you know, and only desire your happiness. This is your home, available for you whenever you need it. You can always come here, and even bring Nanny if you must, so please don't think I want to send you away. Quite the contrary, I like to have you here, it's a great pleasure. But it's my plain duty, as your father, to try to make you see things as they are, and, above all, to try and make you see Charles-Edouard as he is. I'm very fond of Charles-Edouard, and I presume that you are too, as you married him.

'Now he is a man who likes women in the French way of liking them, that is he likes everything about them, including hours of their company and going to bed with them. I suppose you would admit that this is part of his charm for you. But you hardly ever find a man, or anyhow a young man, with his liking for women who can be faithful to one woman. It's most exceedingly rare.'

'Yes, Papa, all this may be true about Charles-Edouard. But with me it's a question of how much I can stand, and I can't stand a life of constant suspicion and jealousy. Juliette, Albertine, the women he looks at in the street, the way he flirts with everybody, everybody, even Tante Régine, the way he kisses their hands, the way he answers the telephone when they ring up – oh no, it's too much for me, I can't.'

'My dear child, I always thought you had a healthy outlook

on life, but this is positively morbid. You really must pull yourself together or I foresee great unhappiness for you in the future.'

'I shan't be unhappy a bit if I can marry an ordinary, faithful, English husband.'

Grace had been sustained during her journey by the mental picture of an idealized anglicized Charles-Edouard, whom she was to meet and marry in an incredibly short space of time. This vision had come to her when the light airiness of Northern France, with its young wheat, pink roads and large, white, rolling clouds, had been exchanged for the little, dark, enclosed Kentish landscape, safe and reassuring – home, in fact. She had looked out of the window at the iron grey sky pressing upon wasteful agriculture, coppices untouched by hand of woodman, tangles of blackberry and gorse, all so familiar to her eyes, and she was comforted by the thought that she could be an English countrywoman once more, gardening, going for walks, playing bridge with neighbours, a faithful English Charles-Edouard, tweeded and hearty, by her side. She would be quite happy, she thought, living in an oast-house, or a cottage with a twist of smoke on the edge of Mousehold Heath, or a little red villa with glass veranda in the Isle of Wight – anything, anywhere, so long as it was safe in England and she safely married to this tower of strength and reliability, this English Charles-Edouard.

'I'm afraid an ordinary faithful English husband will seem very plain pudding after the extraordinarily fascinating French one you are throwing away so carelessly,' said her father. 'People like Charles-Edouard don't grow on every tree, you know. The fact is women must choose in life what sort of a man it is that they do want – whether what is called a good husband, faithful to his wife but seldom seeing her, going off to the club and so on for his relaxation, or one that really loves women, loves his wife, probably, best and longest, but who also and inevitably feels the need for other relationships with other women.'

'Is that the sort of husband you were, Papa?'

'Yes, I'm afraid so. And as I never had a quarter the bad luck of poor Charles-Edouard, and as your mother was either entirely unsuspicious or else very very clever, it was a perfect success, and we were happy. But I didn't care to risk it again after her death, so here I am unmarried.'

'Don't you feel lonely sometimes?'

'Often. That's why I can't help being pleased to see you and the little boy back again, though I suppose if I had any moral sense whatever I'd send you off with a flea in your ear. May I ask what you are planning next?'

'Really, Papa, I hadn't thought.'

'You should try to think before you act, my dear child. Do you want a divorce?'

'Don't let's talk about it now, I'm so tired. Divorce sounds so horrible.'

'Yes, well, leaving your husband is rather horrible.'

'But I suppose it will come to that.'

Sigi now put in an appearance, to say 'Grandfather —'

'Yes, Sigi?'

'You know adultery —?'

Sir Conrad raised an eyebrow and Grace quickly intervened, saying, 'Really Nanny is too naughty, she will teach him these dreadful words out of the Bible. Adultery is for when you're older, darling.'

'Oh I see. A sort of *pas devant* thing?'

'Yes, that's just it. So Nanny must be pleased to be back in her own old nursery again?'

'Not a bit. Fluff under the carpet — she doesn't know what the girls are coming to these days. One thing she will say for Páris, the housemaids there did know their work. And she's just rung up her sister — offal is a thing you never see in London now. So Nanny's in a terrible dump. Grandfather —'

'Now what?'

'Are there cartridges again, and can I learn to shoot?'

'We'll have to talk to Black about that, when we go to Bunbury.'

'Oh good. Can you have a word with Nanny before dinner, Mum?'

Grace, who had been expecting this summons, sighed deeply and went upstairs.

PART II

Chapter One

THE days of 'run along, Sigismond' were now in the past; no-body ever said it to him again. Grace, lonely and wretched, con-centrated herself on the little boy, he was with her from first thing in the morning to his bedtime. He would arrive with her breakfast tray, open her letters, answer her telephone, and play with the things on her dressing-table. From time to time, in a desultory manner, she gave him reading lessons.

'You simply must be able to read books by the time you see Papa again,' she said.

'And when shall I see him again?'

'I expect it will be after the summer holidays.'

'Shall I go and stay with him?'

'I expect so.'

'In Paris, or Bellandargues?'

'Paris. He's not going to Bellandargues this year.'

'And you too?'

'We'll see when the time comes.'

'I say, Mummy, are you divorced?'

'Certainly not, darling. What do you know about divorce?'

'Well I've told you about Georgie in the Park? His mummy and daddy are divorced and he says it's an awfully good idea – you have a much better time all round, he says, when they are.'

'Goodness, darling —!'

'Actually his Mummy and Daddy have both married again, so he's got two of each now, and he says the new ones are smashing, really better than the original ones. You ought to see the things they give him, they're so lovely and rich. So shall you be marrying again, Mummy?'

'You seem to forget that I'm married already, to Papa.'

'Nanny told her sister she thought perhaps Mr Palgrave. She always thought it would have been better, in the first place.'

'Don't fidget with that necklace, Sigi, you'll wear out the string.'

'Do you know what Mr Palgrave gave me last time I saw him?'

'No, what?'

'Eleven bob.'

'What a funny sum.'

'Yes, well, Nanny always takes 10 per cent for her old lepers. I told him that and he very nicely made it up. I need a lot of money.'

'Why do you?'

'Because I'm saving up for a space ship when it's invented. Mum, when can I have a bike?'

'When we go to the country perhaps.'

'And why don't you marry Mr Palgrave?'

'Because not.'

'Nanny says it's nicer for little boys to have a mummy and a daddy, but I expect it's best of all when they have two mummies and two daddies.'

'Shall we get on with the reading?'

They went for the summer holidays to Bunbury. At first Grace thought she would find it unbearable to be in the place so impregnated now with memories of Charles-Edouard, where they had spent their honeymoon, where she had lived all those years dreaming of him, and where he had come to find her after the war. But her father wanted to go there, it would be good for Sigismond, and it was, after all, her home, the home of her ancestors; it would belong to her when Sir Conrad died. Memories of Charles-Edouard were not the only ones connected with it. And, in any case, her thoughts were of him all day, wherever she was.

'One thing I must ask you,' she said to Sir Conrad. 'Will you give orders for the Archduke to be taken out of my room?'

'Certainly I will,' he replied. 'The proper place for that Archduke is the hall – I never could understand what he was doing upstairs. And while we are on the subject, I should very much like to see my Boucher back in the drawing-room, if you don't mind.'

In the end Grace's room became less like a corner of the Wallace Collection and more like an ordinary country-house bedroom. It was really more convenient.

Nanny, in so far as she was ever pleased by anything, was pleased to be back at Bunbury. Just as Grace had spent the war years dreaming of Charles-Edouard, so Nanny had spent them dreaming of Hyde Park and what fun it would be, now she had a baby once more, taking him there. But when at last, on their return from Paris, she had achieved this objective, the dream, as dreams so often do, had turned to ashes. The Park, she found, had lost its old character. Not only had the railings disappeared, the beautiful fleur-de-lis railings which used to surround it, the stout stumps of Rotten Row, the elegant Regency railings of the flower beds, and the railings on which children loved to walk a tight-rope at the edges of the paths, but so, to a very great extent, had the nannies. Increasing numbers of little boys, it seemed, while they had a multiplicity of mummies and daddies, had no nannies at all. They were no longer wheeled about in prams, morning and afternoon, as a matter of course, but when they needed fresh air they were hung out of windows in meat safes. As soon as they could toddle they toddled off to nursery schools, where they were taught to sing little songs, given a great deal of milk to drink, and kept strictly out of the way of their harassed parents. So Park society was not what it had been. There was no wide range of choice, as in the past, and the few nannies who were left clung together, a sad little bunch, like the survivors in an autumnal poultry yard, most of whose fellows had already gone to the pot. Nanny had few friends among them and pronounced them to be, on the whole, a very inferior type of person. But at Bunbury she had congenial gossips, the old housekeeper, the groom's wife, Mrs Atkin the butler's wife, and Mrs Black, to whom she was able to boast and brag about her year in France until they stretched their eyes. Anybody who knew how terribly she had complained during the whole of her sojourn there, or who could have heard her comments to Nanny Dexter on every aspect of French civilization, would have been amazed by the attitude she now assumed over the clanking cups of tea with her cronies.

'Say what you choose, France is a wonderful country – oh it is wonderful. Take the shops, dear, they groan with food, just like pre-war. I only wish you could see the meat, great carcasses for anybody to buy – the offal brimming over on to the pavement

– animals like elephants. They could have suet every day if they knew how to make a nice suet pudding. But there is one drawback, nobody there can cook. They've got all the materials in the world but they cannot serve up a decent meal – funny, isn't it? It's the one thing I'm glad to be back for, you never saw such unsuitable food for a child – well I ended with a spirit lamp in the nursery, cooking for ourselves. There now – I wish you could have seen our nursery, a huge great room looking out over the garden, with a real English fireplace. Then I wish you could have seen the château, it is different from Bunbury – oh it is. Abroad, and no mistake. Like a castle in a book, at the top of a mountain, you quite expect to see knights in armour coming up on their horses. And warm! Well, imagine the worst heat wave you ever knew in your life, the summer of 1911 for instance, and double that. No, I didn't mind a bit, it simply didn't affect me, though the poor mite got rather peaky. You don't know what heat can be, in this country.'

Sir Conrad gave Sigi a little gun, and with it a great talking to on the handling of guns in general and the manners of a sportsman in particular.

'And just remember this,' he said in conclusion, 'never never let your gun pointed be at anyone. That it may unloaded be matters not a rap to me! And Black is going to keep it for you in the gun-room; he'll teach you to clean it and so on, and you may only use it when you are with him.'

So Sigi never left Black's side all the long summer days, trotting happily about the woods and pooping off at magpies and other vermin.

'There's something I do regret,' he remarked to his mother. 'I would like to show my gun to Canari. It's small, but you could kill a man with it if you got the vital spot. Now Canari isn't a silly little baby mollycoddle, like dear little Foster Dexter, or dear little Georgie in the Park. Canari is a *maquisard*, a brave, a dragon, and he would never sack me out of his *bande* again if I had this gun. They're terribly short of equipment in Canari's maquis, it's a shame.'

Grace could hardly bear to think of lovely Bellandargues shut up and empty all the summer and that, for the first time in living memory, the big salon would no longer be the scene of a conversation piece like that which was discovered when Charles-Edouard had first held open the door for her to walk in, and repeated thereafter every day of her visit; Madame Rocher at the piano, M. de la Bourlie at his canvas, and Madame de Valhubert deep in earnest talk with M. le Curé.

She had an uneasy feeling of guilt, exactly as if it were all her own fault and not that of Charles-Edouard.

Also she longed very much for the heat and light of Provence. They had come home to a typical English summer. Rain poured all day on to the high trees out of the low clouds, clouds which lifted and parted towards nightfall so that a pallid ray of north-western sunshine illumined the soaking landscape, a pallid ray of hope for the morrow.

'It's lovely now – we must go out. Don't you think the weather may have turned at last?'

The next morning those who, suffering in their bodies, or, like poor Grace, in their hearts, and who therefore slept little at a time, would awake with the birds to such a glorious glitter of sunshine from cloudless sky upon wet leaves that summer, it would seem, must be there at last. This happened nearly every morning to Grace, who would presently doze off again, rather happier. But long before breakfast the rain would be blowing in fine white sheets across her window, the promise of early morning quite forgotten. She would go down, later on, to the drawing-room, glad to find a little fire.

Charles-Edouard, she knew, had gone to Venice this year. He had taken a palazzo on the Grand Canal and was entertaining many Paris friends, among others Madame Rocher, the Novembre de la Fertés, and Albertine Marel-Desboulles. This had been a great blow to poor Hughie. He had cherished a hope all the summer that Albertine might have gone with him for a motor tour in Sweden. But as soon as the Venetian party offered itself, with Charles-Edouard and all her friends, the motor tour became, for various good reasons, impossible. Furthermore she discouraged Hughie from following her to Venice, saying vaguely that she would be taken up with the film festival. So he often came now to spend a day or two at Bunbury. He was trying to stand for Parliament, but had had no luck so far with the Selection Committees, partly of course, he said, because he was so stupid, and partly because he had no wife. He longed more than ever to be married to Albertine, even though he felt sure that in that case it would be her they would want as candidate and not him. He could just imagine the kind of speech she would make, bringing her point of view, inspired, sensible, and well expressed, to bear on all the problems under discussion.

'I, the soul of the French bourgeoisie, my solid legs planted on the solid earth, I Albertine Labé, descended from generations of timber merchants, who have always given good measure for good money, I have the gift of seeing things clearly and truthfully as they are. I cannot pretend. I feel the truth, I feel it here in my heart and here in my bowels as well as knowing it here in my brain. It is a power, this seeing and feeling and knowing truth, and it has been bred in me by my ancestors the merchants.'

'And I tell you, I, Albertine Labé, bourgeoise, that it is this power of truthfulness and of knowing truth which is needed if we are to rebuild your England, rebuild my France, and rebuild our Europe.'

Just the stuff for the Selection Committees, he thought. There was another line of talk which ran, 'I who loathe the bourgeoisie, I who would rather burn charcoal in the woods than buy or sell anything whatever it might be, I who would rather freeze to death out of doors in the cruel winter of my native Lorraine than sit over a warm fire in a back shop, I, Albertine Labé de Lespay, aristocrat, child of knight and warrior, whose ancestors never touched money or even carried it on their persons because they thought it the dirtiest of dirt, I tell you that I know the truth, I know it here and here and here, and it is this truth, this virtue, this hatred of gold that is needed if we are to rebuild etc. etc.'

The second statement, actually, had more foundation in fact, since Albertine did not possess one drop of bourgeois blood, and her ancestors, a line of powerful princes, had only been timber merchants to the extent of owning vast forests in Lorraine. But the trend of the modern world had not escaped her notice, and the timber merchants were ever increasingly brought into play. Hughie was much too much dazzled by her to notice any discrepancy; both these statements had, at different times, bowled him over, as he assumed that they would bowl over the

Selection Committees. He was unable to imagine anybody, even an English Conservative, standing up against the charm and brilliance of this extraordinary woman. With her by his side, to inspire and teach him, it seemed that no goal in the world would be unobtainable.

'Of course I'm glad to think of her in Venice,' he said, not gladly though, to Grace, as they sat over the little drawing-room fire, summer rain fiercely beating on the windows. 'She loves Italy so much, she needs the beauty. Then there is the important work she does there, with the films.'

'What work? She's frightfully rich, she doesn't need to work.'

'She doesn't need to, she does it for her country, for France. She is a moving power in the French film industry with her taste and knowledge and influence. No film is ever made there without first being submitted to her, you know. She has an infallible instinct. Yes, I love to think of her in Venice, but I do wish she would write to me. She won't, of course. "What is writing?" she said once. "Just a scratch of metal upon paper." Well, look at it that way and what is it?'

Grace, whose heart was also in Venice, and who would also have welcomed a scratch of metal upon paper, or even upon a post-card, sympathized with Hughie, but did not quite enjoy his interminable eulogies of Albertine, who seemed to her one of the many causes of her own wretchedness. She wondered if he was aware that Charles-Edouard went to tea with her every day, but was too polite and tactful to mention it.

'Don't you think young people nowadays manage their lives much worse than we used to?' Sir Conrad said to Mrs O'Donovan, who had come down for a little country air. 'Surely you and I would have been more competent than either of those two in the same circumstances, and less gloomy? I'm tired of all the despondency in this house; it's getting me down. Why on earth don't they pack up and go off to Venice and have it out finally with these frogs?'

'Just imagine having anything out finally with Madame Marel,' she replied. 'As for Grace, you mustn't be too hard on her. I think she has received a terrible shock, and is still suffering from it. To see a thing like that with your own eyes can have really grave results, psychologically.'

'Oh, nonsense, Meg. She ought to have another baby, that's all.'

'Having a baby is not a sovereign cure for everything, although all men, I know, think it is.'

'Anyhow, she's in a thoroughly tiresome state of mind. I can't find out what it is she does want – divorce or what. She says one thing one day and another the next, and it's time something was settled, in my view.'

'What does he think, do you know?'

'Yes, I do. I've had a long letter from him. As I've often told you, I never understood why he wanted to marry her in the first place, but whatever the reason may have been it still seems to hold good, and he wants her back again.'

'Have you told her?'

'It wouldn't be any use me telling her in her present mood; he must come and tell her himself. But meanwhile she goes on havering and wavering about shall she or shan't she divorce until I'm tired of discussing it with her. She's grown up, and she must decide for herself which it is to be.'

'It really doesn't make a pin of difference,' said Mrs O'Donovan. 'They weren't married in church, and therefore neither Charles-Edouard nor anybody else in Paris counts them as being properly married at all.'

'I suppose it would only make a difference if one of them wanted to marry again. The whole thing is thoroughly tiresome and annoying. Well, after the holidays I'll run over to Paris and have a word with Charles-Edouard, that will be best. I'll tell him he must come and fetch her back if he wants her – I don't believe she'd ever resist him in flesh and blood. She'd much better stick to him, this fidgeting about with husbands is no good for women, it doesn't suit them. Hullo, Sigi, I didn't know you were there —'

'It's too wet to go out and too early for Dick Barton, and Mummy and Mr Palgrave are talking about Madame Marel, as usual. If you go to Paris I wish you'd take me.'

'Why?'

'Because I want to learn the words of *A la voix du vainqueur d'Austerlitz,* and nobody knows them here.'

'Oh I do,' said Mrs O'Donovan. 'I used to read them every

morning of my life when I was a little girl with a hoop in the Tuileries Gardens. I'll teach them to you if you come along to my bedroom before dinner.'

Chapter Two

THAT night Sigi was woken up by a tinkle of breaking glass under his open window. He nipped out of bed and looked down. The pantry window was underneath his and he saw a bit of broken glass shining on the gravel beside it; there seemed to be a light on in the pantry. Nanny was snoring away undisturbed in the next room, so it must be very late he knew; well after midnight. He crept out of his room and down the back stairs, feeling his way by the banisters. Sure enough there was a light shining under the pantry door. He put his eye to the keyhole and saw a man examining the door of the silver cupboard, big and heavy like that of a safe. Now Sigi, owing to a great friendship formed in early babyhood with Atkin the butler, knew all the little ways of this silver cupboard. He opened the pantry door and walked in. The burglar, a small, fair young man, turned quickly round and pointed a revolver at him.

'I don't care for these manners,' said Sigi, in a very governessy voice. 'Surely you know that never never should your gun pointed be at anyone. That it may unloaded be matters not a rap to me.'

'It's not only unloaded,' said the burglar, 'but it's not a gun at all. It's a dummy. You get into a terrible mess, in my trade, if you go carrying guns about.'

'Are you a burglar?'

'Yes, I try to be.'

'I think it's very careless of you not to wear gloves. What about the finger-prints?'

'I know. I simply cannot work in gloves – never could – can't drive a car in them, either. I'm not very good at my work as it is – look at this wretched door, I don't know how you'd open it.'

'Why do you do it then?'

'The hours suit me – can't get up in the morning, and every-

137

thing you earn, such as it is, is tax free, with no overheads. There's a good deal to be said for it. I expect I shall improve.'

'How about prison?'

'Haven't had any yet. I'm so fearfully amateurish that nobody ever thinks I can be serious, and when I get caught they simply think it must be a joke.'

'Where I live it's not a joke at all, burgling. They come with machine-guns and wearing masks and they generally kill off the whole family and the concierge before they begin.'

'That must make it much easier.'

'Yes. Sometimes they only sausage them.'

'They what?'

'Tie them up like sausages, brr round and round, and gag them and put them in a cupboard, where they are found next day more dead than alive.'

'Where do you live then?'

'Paris. I'm a French boy.'

'You talk pretty good English for a French boy.'

'Yes, and I talk pretty good French for an English boy. Would you like me to open the silver cupboard for you?'

'Why? Do you know how to?'

'Of course I do. Mr Atkin showed me. You blow on it, see. Like that.' The door swung slowly open. 'I always feel on the side of burglars because of Garth. So you go on and I'll keep *cave*.'

The burglar looked at him uncertainly. 'I suppose I'd better make sure,' he said, half to himself, and before Sigi realized what was happening he found himself gagged and trussed up.

'There you see. English burglars sausage people too sometimes,' said the young man, putting Sigi gently on the floor. 'I'm sorry, old fellow, it won't be for long, but really to leave you keeping *cave* would be carrying amateurishness too far.'

Sigi was perfectly outraged. 'All right then,' he said to himself.

The burglar went into the cupboard and began to examine its contents. Sigi waited a moment, then he rolled under the pantry table and kicked a certain catch he knew of. The cupboard door clanged to, and the burglar was trapped. Then Sigi began to roll and wriggle through the green baize swing-door into the dining-room, through the dining-room door, which luckily was open, into the hall, where he lay kicking the big gong until Sir Conrad appeared at the top of the stairs.

'Good gracious,' he said, when he saw Sigi rolling and wriggling like a little eel. 'My dear child,' he said, untying him, 'whatever have you been up to?'

'Ugh! That tasted awful. Grandfather, grandfather, I've got a burglar, in the silver cupboard.'

'What do you mean?'

'Yes, I promise. I did it with Mr Atkin's patent catch – he's in there now. Come and see.'

'I say! Good boy!'

'And he's got a dummy gun.'

'Never mind. He won't dare use that. Go and get Atkin for me, will you?'

'Mr Atkin – Mr Atkin – Grandfather wants you – I've got a burglar in the silver cupboard! Mummy, Mummy, I've caught a burglar! Nanny, Nanny, I've got a burglar. I did it all by myself.'

Nanny, hurrying into her dressing-gown, said, 'Tut-tut, all this excitement in the middle of the night is very bad for little boys. You're coming straight back to bed, my child.'

But Sigi was off again in a flash, down to the pantry, where Sir Conrad was sitting on the edge of the table talking to the burglar and surrounded by quite a little crowd. Hughie now put in an appearance.

'Hullo, Hughie,' said the burglar.

'Oh! Hullo, Ozzie. It's you, is it?'

'That your nipper?'

'No. I wish he were.'

'Wouldn't mind having him for a partner. The child's an expert.'

'I was your partner till you sausaged me,' Sigi said furiously.

'The milk train,' said Sir Conrad, looking at the pantry clock, 'leaves at 6.15. Perhaps you'd better be off, it's more than an hour's walk. Or would you suggest that I should send you in the motor?'

'I wouldn't hear of it,' said the burglar. 'Good-bye,' he said, rather in the manner of one who, leaving a party first, says a general good-bye in order not to break it up. He climbed out through the open window and was gone.

'Grandfather! He was my burglar – I caught him, and now you've let him go. It is unfair.'

'Yes, well you couldn't keep him as a pet, you know.'

'I wanted to see the coppers put the bracelets on and drag him off in a Black Maria.'

'Sigismond, will you come back to bed this instant, please?'

'You were a very good, clever boy,' said Sir Conrad, 'and to-morrow I'll get you a bike with three speeds.'

'I don't want any old bike at all.'

'There you are, these high jinks always end in tears. Now come along, and look sharp about it.'

'Really Papa,' said Grace, when a dejected Sigi had padded off with Nanny, 'I'm not sure you ought to have turned him loose on the community like that, you know.'

'Oh, my dear child, he hadn't done any harm. On the contrary, he spoke very nicely of my article on Turenne in the *Cornhill*, before you came down.'

Chapter Three

THE long, cold, light summer came to an end. As soon as autumn began, warm, mellow, and golden, the Bunbury household removed itself to Queen Anne's Gate.

It was now agreed between Charles-Edouard and Grace, through the medium of Sir Conrad, that they had better be divorced. Sir Conrad told Grace that the situation must be regularized one way or the other.

'You must choose,' he said, 'between going back to France and living with your husband – far the best solution, in my view – or divorcing the poor chap. It's too unsatisfactory to spend the rest of your lives married and yet not married, impossible, really. Besides, I want to make certain financial arrangements for you. I know you never think about money, you've never had to, so far, but you might as well know that I can't live on my income any more. I'm eating up my capital like everybody else, and before it's all gone I propose to make some over to you and some to Sigismond, in the hopes that you'll be able to keep Bunbury when I am dead. Now I must have a word with Charles-Edouard about all this. We had better arrange the divorce at the same time.'

'Oh – oh — !'

'Darling Grace, you know what I think about it, don't you? But if you really can't live with him you'll have to make up your mind to it, I'm afraid. It has to be one thing or the other.'

'Papa, I couldn't just go back like that, it's not so easy. For one thing he hasn't asked me to.'

'He didn't ask you to go away. He assumes that you will go back when you feel like it. He wants you to, I know.'

'It was he who made it impossible for me to stay. If he really wants me he must come over and ask me, beg me, in fact, show that he is serious, and promise —'

'Promise what?' Sir Conrad gave her a very unsympathetic look. How could Charles-Edouard promise what she would want him to? He thought his daughter was being utterly unreasonable.

Grace burst into tears and left the room.

Sir Conrad went to Paris. Charles-Edouard was most friendly, and they had long talks on many subjects of interest to them both, including the future of Sigi.

'One can't tell, of course, what things will be like by the time he inherits,' said Sir Conrad, 'but it seems to become increasingly difficult for anybody to live in two countries. I wonder if he'll ever be able to keep Bellandargues and Bunbury. Oh dear, the ideal thing would have been if Grace had had this other child and I could have settled Bunbury on him, or her. Now I suppose I must wait and see if she marries again, or what happens. I would so much like to have it all tied up before I get too old. I'm quite against leaving these decisions to a woman, specially Grace, who is so unpractical.'

'That wretched miscarriage was the beginning of all our troubles,' said Charles-Edouard. 'She was set on having that child; disappointment I think more than the actual illness pulled her down and made her nervous. Really so unlucky. Pregnant women, after all, don't have this tiresome mania for sight-seeing.'

'She is in a very nervous state indeed now,' said her father.

'Shall I go to London and see what I can do?'

'You can try, it would be the only way, and I suppose you'll succeed if she consents to see you. But I'm not at all sure, in her present mood, that she will. It's as if the whole thing had been too much for her, though presumably, in time, she'll become more reasonable.'

'Very well, I'll try. I'll say I've come to fetch the boy for a visit, then it will be quite natural to have a word with her between two trains. It won't be like a formal interview, which might put her off. I think I ought to be able to persuade her of how very much I long for her, as it's quite true.'

'I'm sure she longs for you. What an idiotic situation, really.'

'But in case this all goes wrong, and since you are here, perhaps we'd better begin to arrange about a divorce. It means nothing whatever to me, as I've certainly no intention of marrying again, but if we are to live apart I'd rather be divorced, I'm tired of people asking where my wife is. So perhaps we'll visit my lawyer. I've had to make a change, such a nuisance, but the old one of all my life was a terrible collaborator and you don't realize what that means. Two hours of self-justification before one can get down to any business. There's no bore like a collabo in all the wide world. So, this afternoon then?

'By the way, Tante Régine is coming to luncheon. When I told her you were here she screamed like a peacock and rushed off to buy a new hat.'

The hat was very pretty, and Madame Rocher was in a cheerful bustle between, she said, the autumn collections, which were simply perfect this season (for some forty-five seasons now they had appeared simply perfect in her eyes) and the Bal des Innouïs. This was a famous charity ball which she organized every other year in aid, not to put too fine a point on it, of her late husband's relations. The Rocher des Innouïs were an enormous tribe, as fabulously poor as she was fabulously rich, and she had devised this way of assisting them at a minimum cost to herself. With the proceeds of the ball she had built, and now maintained, the Hospice des Innouïs which, situated on a salubrious slope of the Pyrenees, not only provided a delightful setting for the old age of the Rocher relations, but also kept them far away from the Hôtel des Innouïs. 'If I must entertain them,' she would say, 'I'd much rather do so at the Hospice than at home.' So strong are family ties in France that, had they lived within reach of Paris, Madame Rocher would have received visits from all at least once a week; as it was she descended upon them every summer laden with boxes of chocolates, kissed them tremendously several times on each cheek, and vanished away again in a cloud of dust and goodwill.

The ball was always great fun, an intensely elegant occasion, and Madame Rocher would cut the photographs of it out of *Match* and papers of that sort and send them to be pinned up on the walls of the Hospice. She often said how much she wished her dear cousins could have been there to see for themselves what they were missing.

'We have been in despair,' she said to Charles-Edouard and Sir Conrad, 'to know what to have as our motif this year. We've already had birds, flowers, masks, wigs, moustaches, sunshades, kings, and queens. Now that darling, clever Albertine has got an entirely new idea; everybody is to suggest their own *bête noir*; not to be her, you understand, but to wear something that suggests her. It is very subtle – nobody but Albertine could have conceived it.'

'What a pretty idea,' said Charles-Edouard. 'Who is your *bête noir*, Tante Régine?'

'That I keep as a secret weapon. I said to M. Dior this morning "If my dress is not delivered tomorrow, Dior, it will be you". Most efficacious. And the lovely Grace – will she be back in time for it?'

All Paris was eaten with curiosity as to the situation between Charles-Edouard and Grace. He had given out that she was paying a long visit to her father, and had never dropped the smallest hint, even to his most intimate friends, even to Albertine, that there was any sort of a breach. She was always said to be expected back in a week or two. So rumours were rife, some saying that she had eloped, and others that she had a disfiguring illness, but the great majority headed by the Tournons maintained that she must have gone into a home for persons of retarded intellect. 'A bit late,' they said, 'but modern science can do wonders. And,' they said, 'it will need to.'

Charles-Edouard was getting tired of this 'coming back soon', which made him look a fool, and he knew that Sir Conrad's visit would already have set tongues wagging. 'The lovely Grace,' he now told Madame Rocher, 'wishes to divorce.'

'Very English, and all in the best Freemason tradition,' she said. 'So now you will have her tied to your apron strings once more, *mon cher Vénérable*.'

Having made this excellent joke she could hardly wait to get home to her telephone and scatter the news that Charles-Edouard was a marriageable unit once more. She was going to have great fun. The little girls of all her friends and relations would have to be lined up and looked over, an occupation she would very much enjoy. Like horses, their pedigrees would have to be carefully considered; certain strains were better avoided altogether, Bourlie blood, for instance, had never been know to do a family much good, while certain others always seemed fatal in combination. A substantial dowry, while not absolutely necessary, never spoilt anything. She imagined the excitement of the various mammas, and thought how amusing it was going to be to see the discomfiture of those who had recently married their daughters to less eligible husbands. In short, Madame Rocher foresaw some very agreeable hours ahead of her.

'Good-bye, *cher Vénérable,* all my best wishes to the Grand Orient,' she cried, waving a pink glove from the window of her motor.

*

'Well, Papa?'

'Well, darling. Charles-Edouard was most reasonable, as I knew he would be. I like him more every time I see him.'

Grace thought her father looked old and sad, and she had a pang of conscience. This was all her fault.

'You look tired, Papa.'

'Yes, I am. The fact is we had a bit of a night out, last night.'

'I see.' Really it was too bad, at this moment of crisis in her life, that her father should regard the man she was going to divorce merely as a dog to go hunting with.

'Naturally you never spoke about me, at all!'

'Oh, indeed we did. We spent hours with the lawyer, we arranged all about the divorce, the money, and Sigi, every detail.'

Grace realized that she must have been entertaining, sub-consciously, a hope which these words laid low, though what hope, exactly, she did not feel quite sure.

'Sigi? What about him?'

'You are each to have him six months of the year, to be divided up as seems most convenient, until he is ten, when he will live with his father during the term and with you during the holidays.'

'He's to go to school in France?'

'He's a French boy, my dear. I've got a letter for you from Charles-Edouard.'

She took it with, once more, a feeling, a flicker of hope. It was the first time she had seen Charles-Edouard's writing on an envelope since she left him. It was very formal, ending up *affectueusement et respectueusement,* and was merely to ask whether the little boy could now go to Paris for a while. She handed it to Sir Conrad, who said, 'Yes. If you consent, Charles-Edouard will come over himself next week to fetch him.'

'Oh of course I do. Only I won't see Charles-Edouard, Papa.'

'That's entirely for you to say, my love.'

'No, no, no – it wouldn't do at all.'

But she knew that if Charles-Edouard really wanted her back he would insist on seeing her, and that if he did so his cause was won. Everything would be different once they had seen each other. Life without him, here in London, had become so grey and meaningless that she was beginning to feel she would put up with almost anything, even the constant jealousy and suspicion she so much dreaded, to be with him once more in Paris. Surely, she thought, he would not bother to come himself for Sigi unless he wanted to see her, and if he wanted to see her it could only be for one reason.

The days went by. Charles-Edouard was definitely expected, Nanny's opposition to another move had been overcome, and Grace's will to resist was evaporating. She kept up a façade of resistance, she did not pack her things, or prepare to leave in any practical way, but the citadel was ready to surrender.

He came over in the ferry, and was to return, an hour or so

later, by Golden Arrow. When he arrived at Queen Anne's Gate, Grace (it was the last remaining gesture of independence) was still in bed. She never got up early, and, in case by some horrible chance Charles-Edouard did not ask her to go with them after all, she did not want to look as if prepared there and then to step into the train. In fact she calculated that she could easily be ready in time; her maid could bring the luggage later. She had had her bath, and was very carefully made up.

Sir Conrad's motor had gone to the station to meet Charles-Edouard. She heard it arrive; she heard his voice, and heard the front door slam. 'There's Papa,' she said to Sigismond. 'You run downstairs and ask him if he'd like a cup of coffee in here before you go. Hurry — !'

Sigi was off in a flash. 'Papa – Papa – are we going on the boat? Is there a storm? Can I stay on deck all the time?'

'Very likely you can. Where's your mummy? I want to see her.'

But Sigismond did not favour this idea at all. He wanted to travel, as he had been told he would, alone with his papa, attention concentrated on him, Sigi. If Papa went upstairs, if he saw Mummy, that daft kissing stuff would begin, 'Run along, Sigi', and who knows? Grown-up people are so unaccountable, Mummy might quite well decide to come back to Paris with them, and it would be 'Go to Nanny, darling' all day and every day as of old. Life had become considerably more fun with Mummy and without Papa; it would be considerably more fun to go back to Paris with Papa but without Mummy.

'Mummy's in bed and asleep,' he said.

'Asleep – so late – are you sure?'

'Quite quite sure. She went out dancing last night – she expected to be out till any hour, and strict orders are she is not to be called.'

'And your grandfather?'

But Sir Conrad was away, shooting in the North.

Charles-Edouard considered what he should do.

Nanny appeared on the stairs, the footman was sent to fetch a taxi, Sigi's luggage being far too much for one motor, and the footman and Nanny went off to Victoria to register the heavy things.

'Now listen, Sigi,' said Charles-Edouard when they had gone, 'you run up to your mummy's room, say I'm here (wake her up if she's asleep) and ask if I can see her for a moment.'

'All right.' Sigi ran up, but not to his mother's room. He waited on the landing for a minute and then skipped downstairs again, curling up bits of his hair with one hand, as he always did when telling lies though nobody had ever noticed the fact, and saying, 'No good. The door's locked and she's written up "don't disturb". I tell you, she wants to sleep till luncheon.'

'Come on then,' said Charles-Edouard, taking Sigi by the hand, 'we'll walk to the station. I need a little air.' He felt furious with Grace, deeply hurt and deeply disappointed.

The front door slammed again and Grace was left alone in the house, Sigi had not even said good-bye to her.

'Well,' said Charles-Edouard, settled in the train with a large English breakfast before him and Sigi opposite. 'Come on now, what are the news? What have you been doing in England?'

'Oh, Papa, I've had the whizz of a time. I caught a burglar all by myself – I cunningly trapped him in the silver cupboard – and I've saved up nearly £5 out of tips, and Grandfather is investing it at 2½ per cent compound interest, and I've got a gun and I shot an ill thrush, it was kinder really, and I've got a bike wot fair mops it up.'

'You've got a what which does what?'

'*Un vélo qui marche à toute vitesse*,' he kindly explained.

'Good gracious! And I have to compete with all this?'

'Yes, you have. But it's quite easy – I only want to ride on the *chevaux de Marly*.'

'Is that all. Which one?'

'I don't mind.'

'Ah! But do you know the words?'

The little boy shut his mouth tight and laughed at his father with shining black eyes.

'Sigismond. Do you?'

'I shall say the words when I am on the horse, and not before.'

'Then I fear,' said Charles-Edouard, 'that these words will remain for ever unspoken.'

In the Customs shed at Dover there was quite an excitement.

The woman next to them was asked to hand over a coat she was carrying on her arm. From its pockets the Customs officer drew several pound notes. He then began to search her luggage, and produced pound notes from everything he touched, like a conjurer; from books and sponge bag and hot-water-bottle cover and bags and pockets and shoes, everything capable of containing a pound note seemed to do so. The poor lady, white and sad, was then led away. Sigismond looked on, perfectly fascinated.

'She won't catch the boat,' said Charles-Edouard with the smugness of one who, having an English father-in-law, was under no necessity to conduct any illicit currency operations.

'Won't she really, Papa? Why?'

'She's a silly fool, breaking a silly law in a very silly way.'

'So will she go to prison?'

'No, not for pound notes. Gold would have been more serious. I expect she'll miss the boat, that's about all,' said Charles-Edouard. 'Come come, up that gangway with you.'

Chapter Four

As soon as Madame Marel was back in the rue de l'Université from her summer holiday, which had included a long visit to Vienna after Charles-Edouard's Venetian party had broken up, Hughie rushed over to Paris. He only stayed there two days, returning to London in a thoughtful frame of mind, the very day that Sigi left with his father.

Grace rather wondered what could have happened, but she said nothing and she was not a woman to ask for confidences. As she now felt lonely without her little boy, and as Hughie seemed to be at a loose end, they began to see a great deal of each other. Nearly every week he drove her down to his country house for a few days.

This house, Yeotown Manor, in Hertfordshire, was like a large, rambling cottage. Part of it was really old, a little old manor, but most of the low, dark, inconvenient rooms, the huge beams, the oak doors with wooden bolts and latches, the linen-fold panelling and inglenooks, while quite genuine of their sort, had a certain false air owing to the fact that they had been added to the structure by Hughie's mother out of old cottages which she had bought and carved up to serve her purpose. It had no beauty but a certain cosy charm, to which Grace was susceptible at that time since it was so completely English, so much the antithesis of anything she had known in France. Nothing in it reminded her of either of her French homes, or of Charles-Edouard. She was dreadfully saddened now by such memories, and only longed to put them from her.

Hughie always had a few people at week-ends, and perpetual games of bridge went on day and night. Thump thump thump went the radiogram, thumping its way through great heaps of jazz records from breakfast to bedtime, while Hughie and his guests sat by electric light at green baize tables, drink at their elbows, ash-trays filling all round them, shuffling, dealing, playing, and scoring.

At this time Grace was happier there than anywhere. She had always liked gambling, and now she flew to it as to a drug. Also she missed Charles-Edouard less acutely when she was with Hughie, whose masculine presence calmed her nerves. He had become very much more attentive to her of late; indeed, had she not known about Albertine, she would have supposed that he was courting her again. Onlookers, Mrs O'Donovan for instance, and Carolyn Dexter, assumed that it would only be a matter of months before they married.

Time passed, and a morning came when Grace woke up at Yeotown feeling, if not quite happy, at least without a stifling blanket of unhappiness. This blanket had hitherto weighed upon her like something physical, so that there had been days when she had hardly been able to rise from under it and get out of bed. But on this particular morning it seemed to have gone. Through latticed windows the sun shone on a bank of beeches and on the few golden leaves which still clung to their branches. The sky was very blue, her room was warm, her bed intensely comfortable. When she rang the bell Hughie's housekeeper herself came in with the breakfast tray, followed by a housemaid with all the Sunday papers. The servants there were very fond of Grace and spoilt her as much as they could, hoping that she would marry Hughie. The breakfast was a delight, as it always was in that

149

house, pretty to look at, piping hot, and carefully presented. Grace thought, not for the first time, that it would be difficult for somebody who led such an intensely comfortable life as she did to be quite submerged in unhappiness. There were too many daily pleasures, of which breakfast in bed was by no means the least. Perhaps too, she thought, this English life, so much more suitable for her than a French one, would in the end bring her more happiness. Here she was within her depth, she could do the things which were expected of her, and was not always having to try to learn and understand and do new things. It would have taken her years, she knew, to be able to tell at a glance whether an object was Louis XV or Louis Philippe, First or Third Empire; years before she could bring out suitable quotations from Racine or Apollinaire, write phrases in the manner of Gide and Proust, or even make, in good French, the kind of joke, naïve and yet penetrating, that is expected from an English person. Accomplishments of this sort seemed to be a necessity in France, the small change of daily intercourse. It had all been, quite frankly, a most terrible effort. The English, on the other hand, take people as they are, they don't expect that the last ounce of energy will be expended on them in the natural order of things, and are, indeed, pleased and flattered at the slightest attempt to entertain them.

She often had these moments of thinking that what had happened was really all for the best, but they never lasted very long. Today the reaction came as soon as she went downstairs. Thump thump thump went the radiogram, gobbling its waxen meal. Hughie was already shuffling the cards, the Dexters, who made up the party, already had glasses in their hands, and tedium loomed. The only hope was to get quickly to the game, but even that magic did not always work.

Hector Dexter had just made a tour of the Industrial North, and was telling, with his usual wealth of word and detail but with an unusual note of humanity, of life as it is lived in the factories. In these terrible, dark, Victorian buildings, he said, where daylight is never seen, the people sit at the same table going through the same motions hour after hour, day after day, with music while you work in the background. As Grace dealt the cards it occurred to her that week-ends at Yeotown were not unlike that. You sat by electric light at the same table hour after hour, going through the same motions, with music while you work, thump thump thumping in the background, life passed by, the things of the mind neglected, the beautiful weather out of doors unfelt, unseen. 'One club, two no trumps. Three spades. Four spades. Game and rubber. I make that one a rubber of 16 – pass me the washing book, old boy.'

'Luncheon is served,' said the butler.

A break, while you go to the canteen. Her life in Paris may have been difficult and exacting, she may have been a flustered witness ever in the box, ever trying not to give the game away to a ruthless cross-examining counsel, but it may also have been a more satisfactory existence than this. At least she had felt alive, she had been made to use whatever mind she possessed, and there had seemed to be point and purpose to each day. It had never merely been a question of getting through such hours as remain before the grave finally closes.

During luncheon Hector Dexter went on talking about his tour. 'I'm afraid I must be perfectly frank,' he said, 'and tell you that in my opinion this little old island of yours is just like some little old grandfather clock that is running down, and if you ask me why is it running down I must reply because the machinery is worn out, deteriorated, degenerated and decayed, while the men who work this machinery are demoralized, vitiated, and corrupt, and if you ask me why this should be so I will give you my viewpoint on the history of Britain during the past fifty years.' His viewpoint on this subject was then exposed, in great detail. Hughie listened to him with rapturous interest, wondering how anybody could achieve so much knowledge and such a flow of words – oh would that he could pour out its like before the Selection Committees. He had another in front of him that week. Grace felt more than ever as if she were a factory hand, in the kind of factory where people come and chat to the workers on subjects of general interest. 'We are lucky enough to have here today the important Mr Hector Dexter, who is going to talk to us about some of our problems, their roots in the past, and how they may be solved in the future.'

By the time they were drinking their coffee he had more or less finished with the roots, which were very dull and into which the word 'vision' came a great deal, and was warming up to the remedy.

'Now you will ask me if I can see a remedy for this state of things, a state of things, mind, which I do not only observe and take cognizance of in your country but which I have observed and taken cognizance of in all the European countries, that is to say all those countries in Europe west of the so-called Iron Curtain, to which I am sent by my government in order to form my views in order to acquaint my government of those views which I have formed. Now what you need in this little old island, and what is needed in all the countries of Europe west of the so-called Iron Curtain, and even more I imagine, though I do not speak with personal experience, in all the countries of Europe east of the so-called Iron Curtain as well as in the backward lands of the Far East and the backward lands of Africa, is some greater precognition of and practice of (but practice cannot come without knowledge) our American way of living. I should like to see a bottle of Coca Cola on every table in England, on every table in France, on every —'

'But isn't it terribly nasty?' said Grace.

'No, ma'am, it most certainly is not. It tastes good. But that, if I may say so, is entirely beside the point which I am trying, if I can, to make. When I say a bottle of Coca Cola I mean it metaphorically speaking, I mean it as an outward and visible sign of something inward and spiritual, I mean it as if each Coca Cola bottle contained a djinn, and as if that djinn was our great American civilization ready to spring out of each bottle and cover the whole global universe with its great wide wings. That is what I mean.'

'Goodness!' said Hughie.

'I say,' said Grace, who was getting rather fidgety, 'oughtn't we to have another rubber before tea?'

Grace did all she could to avoid being left alone with Carolyn, but to no avail. Carolyn came into her bedroom while she was dressing for dinner and was quite extraordinarily tactless; she seemed not to have any consideration whatever for her friend's feelings.

'Well,' she began. 'So what happened, exactly? Didn't I tell you, it's not possible for an English girl to settle down with a

French husband and be happy. What finally drove you away?'

'Nothing, Carolyn. I'm not finally driven away. I haven't been very well since my miscarriage, so I've been quietly at home with Papa.'

'Oh bunkum! I know you're going to divorce, Madame Rocher has told everyone so. I don't blame you, Grace, on the contrary, you're quite right. But now there's the problem of Sigi. You really must try and get him away from his father. I think it's my duty to tell you that Charles-Edouard is ruining that child. They're never apart, according to Nanny; he takes him to visit all his mistresses, has him down to dinner, keeps him up far too late and gives him wine. Nanny is quite in despair. You ought to see a lawyer and try and get a court injunction to stop it, you know.'

'But Sigi is a French boy. It's only right for him to be brought up at least half in France; Charles-Edouard won't do anything that's bad for him.'

'My dear Grace! I think it's your positive duty to get him away and bring him up yourself. Don't you lie down under it, show a little backbone.'

'I don't want to bring him up entirely myself. A boy needs his father.'

'Yes well, I'm coming to that. What we all hope is that you'll do as you ought to have done in the first place, marry Hughie. You're made for each other. Then he'll be a father to the boy, who couldn't have a better one. Hughie is through with the frogs for ever, he told Heck, no more sand in his eyes. He'll arrange for Sigi to go to Eton, and make a man of him.'

'Charles-Edouard used to be rather in favour of Eton – more than I was in fact.'

'Rather in favour! What a way to talk about Eton.' Carolyn's family, the Boreleys, were passionate Etonians.

'You're sending Foss there?' said Grace, hoping to change the subject. She couldn't bear discussing Sigi and Charles-Edouard, who were so much in her heart at the moment, with Carolyn. She had been half pleased and half tormented to hear from Nanny of Charles-Edouard's odd new passion for the child.

'It's a little different for us,' said Carolyn. 'Foss is an American boy and Heck thinks an Eton accent would do him a lot of harm when the time comes for him to get a job.'

'I wouldn't lie down under that,' said Grace. 'Show a little backbone, Carolyn.'

'Simply absurd, Grace. You don't seem to realize the unique position of the Union of States to which Hector and I belong. You can't compare them with any other country, because in a very few years they will be the absolute rulers of the world.'

'Oh. So we're going to be ruled by Foss, are we?'

'Yes, in a way. It's a privilege for a young man to be brought up there, as Foster will be. But France is finished and done for, and that's the difference.'

'It may be finished and done for, but it's far the most agreeable country to live in.'

'Well I notice you didn't stay there very long,' said Carolyn, triumphantly having the last word.

There was a tinkle of cowbells, meaning that dinner was ready, and they went downstairs.

Early on Monday morning the Dexters drove away in their huge, sick-coloured motor from which issued puffs of heat and high strains of coloratura. They were to visit some more factories on their way to London.

Hughie said he would motor Grace up in time for dinner. He took her for a long walk and asked her to marry him.

'But what about Albertine?' she said, in great surprise. 'I don't think I want another husband who goes to tea at the rue de l'Université every day. Charles-Edouard always did, you know; how I hated it.'

'You needn't worry about that. I shall never see her again as long as I live.'

'Why? Has something happened?'

'Yes. When I went over to Paris in October she played me a thoroughly low and dirty trick which I shall never forgive. But it did have one good result, it showed me quite clearly that you and I ought never to have got mixed up with all these foreigners; we ought to have married in the first place. The sooner we do so now, forget all about these people and settle down to an ordinary English life, the better.'

'I often think that,' said Grace. 'What was it, Hughie?'

'I haven't told you before because it involves your husband, Grace, but now I hear you are divorcing anyhow, so I can. Well. I hadn't seen her since the summer, as you know; she was away for ages, first Venice and then Vienna. I spoke to her on the telephone as soon as I arrived. She was terrifically loving, I was to go round at six, take her to a varnishing, and then dine with her.

'I was there on the stroke of six, as you can imagine, and Pierre showed me into the little salon there is under her dressing-room, saying she was changing and would be down at once. I could hear her upstairs, getting ready as I supposed, walking to and fro. I imagined her at her dressing-table, going over to the cupboard, trying on one hat, changing it, perhaps changing her dress again. I'd so often seen it – she takes hours to get ready, and then she changes everything again, and so on. I was feeling most awfully romantic, so I got a bit of paper and wrote a little poem about her in her dressing-room and hearing the tap tap of her heels overhead. Fearful rot, of course, but I began longing to show it to her, and finally I thought "why not, I'll go upstairs and find her."

'I went into the dressing-room, but it was Maria, her Italian maid, who was walking up and down. I didn't think much of this, I thought Albertine must be in her bedroom and I went through, and sure enough there she was – in bed with your husband. Never had such a shock in my life. She must have told Maria to walk to and fro to keep me quiet downstairs. You see? Not very nice, was it? But I think that kills two birds with one stone; it kills Albertine for me and it ought to kill Valhubert for you.'

Grace tried not to laugh. The story did not upset her at all. Could she possibly, she thought, be coming round to the point of view of her father and Charles-Edouard on these matters?

'Very French,' she said.

'Yes, and I wish you could have heard her trying to explain it away on the telephone afterwards – very French too. "Come now, Hughie, Charles-Edouard is my foster-brother, we had the same nurse and drank the same milk, how could there be anything between him and me? We were having a little rest after luncheon." 'Course I just rang off.'

'Poor Hughie!'

'Funny thing is I honestly didn't mind, in fact it was really, after the first shock, a great relief. You see, I'm too English, just as you are, Grace, to cope with people like that. It's unsuitable, we shouldn't attempt it. And it showed me something else too, that it's you I love, Grace. What I felt for Albertine was simply infatuation.'

'I always wish I knew the difference between infatuation and love,' said Grace.

'You are infatuated with your husband, but it can't last, it's not built on anything solid and very soon you'll begin to love me again. You like this place, don't you, and our life here, it suits you, and you like being with me. Then if I take up politics you'll like that; you're used to it, with your father, and you'll be a great help to me. You loved me all right before you met Valhubert, and I'm sure you will again, and you'll like having some real English children with blue eyes and things, more natural for you. Besides, we've both had the same experience now, it makes us understand each other as an outside person never would. So, when the divorce is over, Grace —?'

'Let's wait a bit,' said Grace. 'No hurry, is there? I'm pleased and touched to have been asked, but I can't say, yet. It all depends, very much, on Sigismond.'

'He'll be all for it, you'll see,' said Hughie with confidence. 'I'll think of every sort of amusing thing for him to do when he gets back.'

Chapter Five

IT did not take Sigi very long to notice that life in Paris alone with Charles-Edouard was a very different matter from family life there with a mummy you only saw at tea-time and a daddy you hardly ever saw at all. It was much more fun. He was with his father morning, noon, and night, and all the things they did together were delightful. They went to the antique shops and museums; Sigi learnt about marquetry and china and pictures and bronzes and was given a small cabinet to house an ivory collection of his own. They went to the Jockey Club, and though Sigi was left sitting, like a dog, in the hall, he didn't mind that because he collected small, but regular, sums in tips from various members who thought he looked bored and wanted to see him smile.

'Shall I belong to the Jockey Club when I'm grown up?'

'If I remember to do for you what my father did for me,' said Charles-Edouard, 'and get you in before you've made too many enemies among husbands. Husbands can be most terrible black-ballers. But it's very dull.'

'Then why do we come so often?'

'I don't know.'

On the rare occasions when Charles-Edouard was at home in the evening Sigi dined downstairs with him, and this was the greatest treat of all. He was given a glass of wine, like his father, and made to guess the vintage. When he got it right Charles-Edouard gave him 100 francs.

'In England,' said Sigi, 'little boys don't have dinner.'

'No dinner?'

'Supper. And sometimes only high tea.'

'What is this, high tea?'

'Yes well, it's tea, you know, with cocoa and scones, and eggs if you've got hens and bacon if you've killed a pig, and marma-lade and Bovril and kippers, and you have it late for tea, about six.'

'How terrible this must be!'

'Oh no – high tea is absolutely smashing. Until you come to supper-time, and then I must say you do rather long for supper.'

Nanny sat talking with the Dexter Nanny, who had come round for her evening off. They had been obliged to put Sigi to bed in the middle of their nice chat, which they both con-sidered an outrageous bore. He now lay in the next room, on the verge of sleep but not quite off, and a certain amount of what they were saying penetrated his consciousness. It was all mixed up with noise from the B.B.C., which ran on in that nursery whatever the programme. Young, polite, rather breathy English voices were playing some sort of paper game; their owners hardly seemed to belong to the same race as the two Nannies, so dim their personalities, so indefinite their statements.

'The Marquee never used to look at him when Mummy was with us. Funny, isn't it? It's as much as I can do now to get him up here for the time it takes to change his shoes – thoroughly spoilt he's getting – out of hand. More tea, dear?'

'Thanks, dear. But it's always like that with separated couples, in my opinion. I've seen it over and over. Because, you know, each one is trying to give the child a better time than the other.' At these words Sigi woke right up and began listening with all his ears. 'Nothing can be worse for the children.'

'I know. Shame, really. Well I told Mummy – I don't care for these youths on the wireless much, do you?'

'Not at all. There seems to be nothing else nowadays, youth this and youth that. Nobody thought of it when I was young.'

'Yes well, as we were saying. If you ask me I rather expect they'll come together again, and I'm sure it's to be hoped they will. I know Mummy was awfully upset about something, but I don't suppose he's worse than most men, except for being foreign of course, and I think it's their plain duty to make it up for the sake of the poor little mite. That's what I shall tell Mummy when I see her again, and I shall warn her plainly that if he goes on like this, getting his own way with both of them as he does now, he'll become utterly spoilt and impossible. No use saying anything to the Marquee, he's always in such a tearing hurry, though I must say I'd like to give him a piece of my mind about these dinners – the poor little chap comes to bed half drunk if you ask me.'

It was while listening to this conversation that Sigismond first made up his mind, consciously, that his father and mother must never be allowed to come together again if there was anything he could do to prevent it.

Charles-Edouard always took Sigi with him now when he went, at five o'clock, to see Albertine. She gave them an enormous tea, after which Sigi would play with her collection of old toys and automata. The most fascinating, the one of which he never tired, was a toy guillotine. It really worked, and really chopped off the victim's head, to the accompaniment of sinister drums and the horrified gestures of the other dolls on the scaffold. Besides this there were many varieties of musical box, there were dancing bears, smoking monkeys, singing birds, and so on, and while Albertine told the cards Sigi was turned loose among them, with tremendous injunctions from Charles-Edouard to be very very careful as they were very very precious.

'Why are they more precious than other toys?'

'Because they are old.'

'Are old things always precious?'

'Yes.'

'In that case Nanny must be very precious.'

'Always this young man between you and the blonde lady you think about so much.'

'Could it be Hughie?' Charles-Edouard was very much puzzled. He knew that Grace was seeing a good deal of Hughie now, but had never given the matter a serious thought. 'Did he ever come back again, by the way, Albertine? What happened?'

'He was furious, I've never known a man so angry. I rang him up twice and explained everything, but each time he rang off without even saying good-bye. These English —!'

'How did you explain it?' said Charles-Edouard, very much amused.

'I told him the truth.'

'No wonder he rang off in a rage.'

'My dearest, you know as well as I do that there is never only one truth and always many truths. I told him that you, Charles-Edouard de Valhubert, and I, Albertine Labé de Lespay, had drunk the same milk when we were little, young babies.'

'What milk?'

'Come now, Charles-Edouard, we had the same nurse!'

'Old Nanny Perkins didn't have one drop of milk when I first knew her, and wasn't that amount younger when she was with you!'

'We had the same nurse, therefore, to all intents and purposes, we drank the same milk. We are foster-brother and sister – how could he think of us as anything else? The Anglo-Saxon mind reduces everything to sex, I've often noticed it. Cut three times. Very odd indeed – here is the young man again, keeping you apart. Surely surely she cannot love Hughie?'

'Oh yes she does,' Sigi piped up from his corner. 'He is the love of her life.'

'This is very strange,' said Charles-Edouard, genuinely surprised that anybody in a position to be in love with him could fancy Hughie.

Albertine was not displeased. 'Come here, Sigi, and tell us how you know.'

'When Mr Palgrave is coming to see her, she looks like this,' he said, and did a lifelike imitation of his mother as she had looked after the front door had slammed that morning when Charles-Edouard came to fetch him away. He opened enormous eyes and smiled as if something heavenly were about to happen. 'She thinks the world of Mr Palgrave, and so do I. He gives me pounds and pounds.' He was twisting his hair into curls as he spoke.

'Go on with the cards,' said Charles-Edouard, very much put out.

'Cut then. But why did you not have an explanation with her when you were in England?' she said in Italian, so that Sigi would not understand.

'She was in her room and refused to see me.'

'Unlike you not to gallop up the stairs.'

'In what way unlike me? I would have you observe, Albertine, that I have never forced my way into a woman's bedroom in my life.'

'Take four cards. What a curious thing – intrigues and misunderstandings, just like a Palais Royal farce, with this real old-fashioned villain plotting away in the background. Fancy Hughie being so wicked, it makes him more interesting, all of a sudden. I must send him a Christmas card. What do you want for Christmas, Sigi?'

'I want to ride on the *cheval de Marly*.'

'This child has an obsession.'

'And what else?'

'Nothing else.'

'Be very careful, Sigismond. Consider it well. Do you really want to wake up with an empty stocking, to find a tree loaded with no presents, to spend the whole day unpacking no parcels?'

'Well, what will you give me?'

'You must say what you want first. It's always like that. Then we have to consider whether we can afford it.'

Sigismond became very thoughtful and hardly spoke another word the rest of the evening.

'M.P.'s daughter divorces French Marquis,' Sigi, chanting this loudly, came into his father's bathroom. Charles-Edouard was shaving at the time.

'What do you know about this – who told you?'

'I heard Nanny clicking her tongue at the *Daily*, so I went and looked over her shoulder and saw it. I can read quite well now, you see, how about a prize?'

'You couldn't read a word of *Monte Cristo* last night.'

'I can only read if it's in English, and printed, and I want to. At first the marriage was a happy one – who are the other women, Papa? I know, Madame Marel and Madame Novembre.'

'Be quiet, Sigi. These are things you must not say.'

'*Pas devant?*'

'*Pas du tout.* If you do you'll be punished.'

'What sort of punishment?'

'A bad sort. And you'll never never be allowed to ride on the *chevaux de Marly*.'

'O.K. And if I don't speak, when can I ride?'

'I don't know.'

'So now you can't be married to Mummy again, can you?'

'Yes I can. Tomorrow, if she likes.'

'Oh !' His mouth went down at the corners.

'Why, Sigi? Don't you want us to be?'

'It wouldn't be the slightest good wanting, I'm afraid. My mummy is quite wrapped up in Hughie now.' His hand went to his hair and began twisting it.

'Mr Palgrave.'

'He lets me call him Hughie.'

'How very unsuitable. But is she?' said Charles-Edouard. 'Is she really, Sigi? He is very dull.'

'That's nothing. Look how dull is Mr Dexter, and yet Mrs Dexter is quite wrapped up in him, the Nannies always say so.'

'What is all this wrapping up, Sigi?'

'*Emballé.* Like you are with Madame Novembre.'

'Hm. Hm. Get ready to go out and I'll take you to see Pascal.'

'Well if I can't ride on you know what, I suppose that dreary old Pascal will have to do.'

Now that Charles-Edouard's divorce was in the papers, great efforts were made, in many directions, to marry him, and nobody tried harder than his two mistresses.

Albertine, shuffling the cards, said, 'I have been noticing a very different trend in your fate. It seems to become more definite, more inescapable, every time I take up the pack. You have turned a corner, as one sometimes does in life, and a new landscape lies at your feet. For some days the cards have left the atmosphere of Palais Royal and have pointed to a grave decision – two grave decisions in fact – which lead to extraordinary happiness, to a journey and to advancement. Anybody who knew the rudiments of fortune-telling would see these bare facts, they repeat and repeat themselves; it now remains to interpret them, and that, of course, is more difficult. Cut the cards. There now. It looks very much like service to your country in some foreign land.'

'Indo-China?' Charles-Edouard looked puzzled. 'I'm rather old, now, it's only the regular army they want. Still, I suppose there would be something for me, though I can't say I'm absolutely longing to go back.'

'Oh I don't mean that, not military service. All the same, have you never thought that now your marriage is over it might be a good thing to go away for a while? To change your ideas?'

'But Albertine, I never go away from Paris, you know that very well. I go to Bellandargues when I must, but otherwise I can't be got as far as St Cloud even. What are you thinking of?'

'Let me tell you, calmly and clearly, what I see. Cut the cards. I will lay out the whole pack. Now. I see you in a foreign land, a civilized one, among white people, and I see you negotiating, treating, making terms, and driving bargains, for France.

'There is a word for somebody who does all those things – ambassador. Why should you not, in fact, become an ambassador?'

'Me? Albertine, you must be mad!'

'So mad, my love? After all, you have been in the foreign service – there are still broken hearts in Copenhagen I believe.'

'Oh that Copenhagen – dinner at 6.30 – never shall I forget it.

But if you remember, I resigned because I can't bear to be away from Paris. I was away seven years during and after the war, and that is enough for my lifetime, thank you very much.'

'I don't believe it. I believe you would like to serve your country once more, to put this time at her disposal, as well as your great courage, your charm and eloquence, and gift for languages. You have extraordinary gifts, Charles-Edouard.'

'Well, but who is going to make me an ambassador all of a sudden?' he said, rather more favourably.

'I could help you there. I am on very good terms with the Foreign Minister, and, even more important, with Madame Salleté. I am practically certain it would be arranged. And that brings us back to the cards. You understand that you would need to be married for such an assignment; an unmarried ambassador (and especially if that ambassador were you, dear Charles-Edouard) is in a position to be gravely compromised. It wouldn't do at all. Salleté wouldn't consider it for a single moment. Now the cards, ever since they have taken on this new direction, as you might call it, have been pointing to re-marriage. An older wife, not only nearer your own age but older, mentally, than our poor dear Grace. A Frenchwoman, of course, who would be able to play her part; a widow, whom you could marry in church. Above all,' she said, lowering her voice, 'somebody who would be able to help you with the education of our beloved little Sigismond.'

Charles-Edouard saw just what she meant. 'Ah yes,' he said, 'but the fact is that I am obliged to remain in Paris precisely on Sigi's account. Presently he must go to the Condorcet as I did, while living here with me.'

'You don't feel that a cosmopolitan education is more precious for a boy of today?'

'Sigi will be bilingual whatever happens. I think he ought to go to school in France. And besides, I don't, I really don't, think I could accept any favour from Salleté.'

Albertine was much too clever to press her point. 'Think it over,' she said, calmly, 'and now, cut three times.'

Charles-Edouard did think it over, and soon began to feel that marriage with Albertine was perhaps not such a bad idea. He got on very well with her, old friend of all his life; she never failed to amuse him, they talked the same language, understood the fine shades of each other's character and behaviour; they knew the same people and had identical tastes. Albertine owned several pictures that Charles-Edouard had always coveted; he would give a great deal to see her big Claud Lorraine on his own walls, not to mention her Louis XIV commode in solid silver. No need for a quick decision, his divorce was not yet absolute, but some time, he thought, he might find out how Sigismond felt about it.

Juliette's approach was more direct. She rolled lazily over in Madame de Hauteserre's bed (the door now bolted as well as locked), her eyes, which always became as big as saucers after making love, upon the erotic ceiling, and said, 'So I hear you have your divorce at last. What now, Charles-Edouard?'

'I'm tired. Perhaps I'll sleep for a few minutes.'

'No. Don't sleep. I want to talk. What are your plans?'

'No plans.'

'Charles-Edouard! But you must marry again.'

'No more marriage.'

'But my dearest, you'll be lonely.'

'I'm never lonely. It's people who can't amuse themselves who feel lonely, another word for bored. I am never bored, either.'

'Shall I tell you what I think?'

'No. Tell me a story, to amuse me.'

'Presently. I think you and I ought to go and see M. le Maire together.'

'And what about poor Jean?'

'I'm perfectly sick of poor Jean. He's the dullest boy in Paris.'

'I thought you wanted to be a duchess?'

'I will renounce it for your sake. I will be divorced and give up being a duchess, Charles-Edouard, and all for you.'

'How would you get an annulment?'

'There may be grounds for that.'

'It would take years and years.'

'But I thought we might be married by M. le Maire, as you were with Grace.'

'Yes, and a terrible mistake too. I will never be married again, except in church. No,' he said sleepily, 'of all the women in the world you are the one I would soonest marry, but, alas, it cannot be.'

'Why not?'

'Because of Sigismond. From now on my life must be dedicated to him.'

'But the poor child needs a mother. And little sisters, Charles-Edouard, darling, pretty little girls, surely you'd like that?'

'Well now, perhaps I would,' said Charles-Edouard. He turned over, laid his head between Juliette's breasts and went to sleep.

As it became increasingly obvious that the key to Charles-Edouard's heart was held by his little boy both Albertine and Juliette now proceeded to pay their court to Sigismond. Juliette employed exactly the same technique of seduction and cajolery as with his father; Albertine's approach, while she never neglected the uses of sex, was rather more subtle.

Juliette gave the little boy treat after treat. She took him to all the various circuses, to musical plays, to the cinema, and even to see the clothes at Christian Dior. Greatest treat of all, and a tremendous secret, she would drive him out of Paris in her pretty little open motor, and when they came to the straight, empty, poplar-bordered roads which lead to the east she would change places with him and let him take over the controls.

'Look, look, Madame Novembre, *cent à l'heure*,' he would cry in ecstasy as the speedometer went up and up. She bore it unflinchingly, though sometimes very much frightened.

After one of these clandestine outings they were drinking hot chocolate with blobs of cream in her pretty, warm little boudoir at the rue de Varenne. The mixture of camaraderie and sex in Juliette's approach to Sigi made her almost irresistible and the little boy was fascinated by her, though rather sleepy now from the cold afternoon air. Presently she said, 'We do have a good time together, eh, Sigismond?'

'Oh we do!'

'You'd like it to go on for ever, wouldn't you?'

'Yes please, I would.'

'For ever and ever. It easily could, you know. I could become your *maman* and live in the same house – would you like that?'

'Mm,' he said, his nose in the chocolate.

'Then you could drive my motor every day, not only sometimes, like now. We'd do all sorts of other lovely things, specially in the summer.'

'Could we have a speed-boat on the river?'

'Yes, that would be great fun.'

'And a glider perhaps.'

'Surely.'

'And I very much long for a piebald rat.'

'Well —' she said with a slight shudder, 'why not?'

'And what else?'

'Let's see what would be nice. Perhaps – little brothers and sisters?'

Sigi took his nose out of the chocolate and gave her a very sharp and wide-awake look. He finished the cup, put it down on the table and said, 'I think it's time to go home.'

Juliette realized at once that she had made a blunder, though she did not know quite how fatal it was going to be to her ambitions, and nor could she know that her words would be underlined that very evening by the two Nannies.

'That Madam November,' Sigi overheard, from his bed, 'is a perfect menace. She gets hold of the child, and the things they do – thoroughly unsuitable – dress shows, and awful sorts of films, and he says (not that I quite believe it, mind you, but you never know) that she lets him drive her car. Anyway she fills his little head with rubbish and spoils him, oh she does spoil him. If you ask my opinion it's the Marquee she's after and that's the way she's setting about it, and quite likely it would be all for the best if she got him. Because then little Master Grown-up would be back in the nursery for good, sure as eggs is eggs, no more high jinks, and the young person occupied with her own children likely as not.

'That child's getting ruined between the lot of them, and I don't mind who knows it. I can't do a thing with him any more.'

'Yes well,' said Nanny Dexter, 'none of it's any surprise to me.'

'Papa,' said Sigi next morning.

'Hullo! You're early today.'

'Yes I've got something very important I want to talk about.'

'Well?'

'You know how you're wrapped up in Madame Novembre?'

'So you always tell me.'

'Were you thinking of marrying her?'

'Why, Sigismond?'

'Because she's not at all the type of person I would like to have as my *maman* – not at all.'

'Nothing,' said Charles-Edouard, 'could be further from my thoughts.'

But this was not perfectly true. The idea of marriage with Juliette had been occupying his mind of late, chiefly because, as he said to one of his men friends, it was so dreadfully tiresome always going to bed in the afternoon. However if Sigi felt like that about it the question would arise no more.

Chapter Six

ALBERTINE played upon the little boy's social sense, already very much developed.

'I have three invitations for you, darling, two parties and luncheon at the Ritz.'

'You know, Madame Marel, I'm very tired of parties. Always that silly old conjurer, he's getting on my nerves with his doves and rabbits. Can't I go to a ball?'

'You want to go to a ball now, do you? But for several reasons that is impossible. Firstly, how would you dress? Secondly, you are too small for dancing with grown-up people, and thirdly, as it is not the custom for boys of your age to go to balls you'd find that you would not enjoy yourself at it. You must wait for balls until you are older.'

Sigi's mouth went down at the corners and he looked very glum. He was not accustomed, now, to being refused things.

'What can we do?' Albertine said to Charles-Edouard when he had gone home. 'The poor little boy looked so sad. I must think this over.'

She thought it over, and presently had an idea of genius. She would give a ball for Sigi, a fancy-dress ball, 'Famous parents with their famous children', which would be the most sensational of the season. Her first intention was that parents with their children only would be allowed, no famous child admitted without a famous parent, and, far more testing, no famous parent without his or her own famous child. But this rule led to such shrieks down the telephone from Albertine's many bachelor friends that she was finally obliged to relax it in favour of uncles and aunts. Further she would not budge; nobody, she said, would be allowed in without either their own child or their own nephew or niece.

Never before had children been at such a premium. A great deal of sharing out took place in families. 'If I have Stanislas and you take Oriane that still leaves little Christophe to go with Jean'; fleets of aeroplanes were chartered to bring over nephews and nieces for the many bachelors from Chile, Bolivia, and the Argentine who live in France, while legal adoptions were hurried through at a rate never previously known in the department of the Seine. The Tournons, and others who, like them, had had several children in order to avoid taxation, now sent to the country for them, and these little strangers suddenly found themselves the very be-all and end-all of their parents' existence.

As was to be expected, the Tournons were positively dramatic in their approach to the ball; indeed one night, shortly before it was to take place, Madame de Tournon woke up screaming from a nightmare in which her nursery had caught fire before her very eyes and all her now priceless brood had perished in the flames. M. de Tournon calmed her with difficulty, promising to go out as soon as the shops opened and buy the latest form of fire-escape. Even so this dream, which had been a particularly vivid one, recurred to her at intervals for several days. She was dreadfully shaken by it, and never felt quite comfortable again until the ball had begun. Of course the great question was how should they go to it. What famous couple, fair husband dark wife, with three boys and one girl, was famous enough for the Tournon family? They racked their brains, they refused all their invitations in order to stay quietly at home, thinking. At last Eugène de Tournon said that they would never have any truly original idea in the hurly-burly of a town, and that the absolute peace and quiet of the country were essential to any such act of creation. So away they went. They had not seen the country, except through the windows of some fast-moving vehicle, for several years, and they came back to Paris saying that people ought to go there more, it really was rather pretty. Their friends were relieved to hear that the journey had been a success, the great inspiration having come to them as they walked down a forest glade – Henri II, Catherine de Medicis, the three little kings and la Reine Margot. Almost every other family of four children had had the same idea. Indeed there was very little originality in the choice of characters; parents with only sons were Napoleon, Eugénie, and the Prince Imperial; mothers with only daughters Madame de Sévigné and Madame de Grignan; uncles with only nephews (of which there seemed to be dozens) Jerome or Lucien with l'Aiglon; families of a boy and a girl Louis XVI, Marie Antoinette and their children, and so on. Charles-Edouard decided upon Talleyrand and Delacroix, chiefly because Sigismond looked so charming in the black velvet coat and big, floppy bow tie of the artist. Albertine, in a wonderfully elaborate dress made of fig leaves, was Eve the Mother of All.

Madame Rocher des Innouïs alone was allowed to break the hard and fast rule about blood relations, but then she was a law unto herself, nobody in Paris, not even Albertine, would think of giving a party without her. She sent for two little orphans from the Hospice des Innouïs. 'After all,' she said, 'I am Tante Régine to everybody at the Hospice.' Two ugly little boys arrived, one very fat and one very thin. After some thought she dressed them in deer-stalkers, white spats and beards as Edward VII and the Tsar of Russia, going herself as the Queen of Denmark, 'Mother-in-law of Europe'. When they arrived Albertine murmured rather feebly, 'I said aunts, not mothers-in-law,' but of course she let them pass.

She was not so lenient, however, to Madame Novembre. Juliette had no possible excuse for being asked, except a niece, the daughter of her only sister who had married a Czech and gone to live in South Africa. This wretched spoil-sport refused to deliver up her child, even on the receipt of several long, explanatory telegrams from Juliette. It must be said that the probability of such a refusal had been taken into the fullest consideration by Albertine when making her plans.

Juliette now became perfectly frantic, and told her husband there was nothing for it, they must adopt a child. But at this the worm turned. Jean Novembre may not have been very bright in the head, but he was impregnated with a deep respect for his own family tree. Never, he said, would he bestow the great name of Novembre de la Ferté, not to speak of the proportion of his income which, by the laws of adoption, he would be obliged to settle, on some little gutter-snipe, simply in order to allow Juliette to go to a ball. He said it was unreasonable of her to expect such a thing; he also pointed out that she was the one who had consistently refused to have children of their own, which he wanted very much.

'Everybody's doing it,' said Juliette.

'The *rastaquouères* and Israelites may be, and who cares? Paris can easily support the presence of a few more Montezumas and Montelevis, it makes no difference to anybody. But Novembre de la Ferté is quite another matter. It's entirely your own fault, Juliette. You have always mocked at Isabella de Tournon for having all those children – I tell you she's a clever woman, and now you see who has come best out of the affair.'

Finally Juliette was reduced to borrowing her concierge's child, a loathly specimen whom she hoped to pass off as the South African niece. Albertine was not deceived for a moment by this manoeuvre, and Madame Vigée Lebrun and her daughter entered the house only to make an ignominious exit. 'Take that hideous child away this instant, Juliette. I know perfectly well who it is – I see it picking its nose every time I come into your courtyard. Off with you both and no argument. A rule is a rule; I refuse to make any exceptions.'

Very fortunately, three (really) famous (real) musicians, all excellent mimics, happened to be arriving at this moment. For weeks afterwards they re-enacted the scene, in high falsetto, at every Paris gathering. It became longer and more dramatic every time they did it, and was finally set to music and immortalized in the ballet 'Novembre approche'.

A pair of young mothers now became the centre of interest. They had risen from their lying-in much sooner than the doctors would otherwise have allowed. (French doctors are always very good about recognizing the importance of social events, and certainly in this case had the patients been forbidden the ball they might easily have fretted themselves to death.) One came as the Duchesse de Berri with l'Enfant du Miracle, and the other as Madame de Montespan and the Duc du Maine. The two husbands, the ghost of the Duc de Berri, a dagger sticking out of his evening dress, and Louis XIV, were rather embarrassed really by the horrible screams of their so very young heirs, and hurried to the bar together. The noise was indeed terrific, and Albertine said crossly that had she been consulted she would, in this case, have permitted and even encouraged the substitution of dolls. The infants were then dumped down to cry themselves to sleep among the coats on her bed, whence they were presently collected by their mothers' monthly nurses. Nobody thereafter could feel quite sure that the noble families of Bregendir and Belestat were not hopelessly and for ever interchanged. As their initials and coronets were, unfortunately, the same, and their baby linen came from the same shop, it was impossible to identify the children for certain. The mothers were sent for, but the pleasures of society rediscovered having greatly befogged their maternal instincts, they were obliged to admit that they had no idea which was which. With a tremendous amount of guilty giggling they spun a coin for the prettier of the two babies and left it at that.

The famous parents and their famous children were now lined up for the entrée. Each group, heralded by a roll of drums, entered the ballroom by a small stage. Here they posed a few moments for the photographers, after which they joined the crowd on the ballroom floor. Very soon the famous parents dumped their famous offspring at the buffet and left them there while they went off to dance, flirt, gamble, or gossip with other famous parents. The children happily stuffed away with cream and cake and champagne, all of which very soon combined with the lateness of the hour to produce a drowsy numbness. Every available sofa, chair, and settee now bore its load of sleeping babies; they lay on the floor round the edges of the rooms, under the buffet, and behind the window curtains. The grown-ups, all set for a jolly evening, waltzed carelessly among their bodies.

Presently two incongruous, iron-clad figures appeared, clicking their tongues, the Dexter and Valhubert nannies in search of their charges. They peered about, turning over an occasional body, and looking like nothing so much as two tragic mothers after some massacre of innocents. Sigi was found in the arms of the Reine Margot; Foss had crept into a corner and been terribly sick. Of course Carolyn knew that she ought never to have allowed him to come, she felt most extremely guilty about it; but the fact was that this ball had had the effect, in Paris, of a bull-fight in some small Spanish town – that is to say, disapprove of it as you might, the atmosphere it produced was such that it was really impossible to resist going to it. Bearing away the little bodies, their faces glowing with a just indignation, the two English Nannies vanished into the night.

Charles-Edouard spent most of his evening with Madame de Tournon, whom he had always rather fancied but whom he had never so far courted because she was Juliette's greatest friend. He detested scenes and drama in his private life, and would go to almost any lengths, within reason, to avoid them.

Madame Rocher set her cap at Hector Dexter. She was organizing a gala at the Opéra in June, to provide the Hospice des Innouïs with some new bath-chairs and other little comforts for the aged.

The Dexters were just the people to rope in for this gala, a big box, she thought, and possibly a row of stalls as well. Having been told that one certain way to the heart of every American was through his mother, she said,

'Your mother was a Whale, I believe, Mr Dexter?'

'Why yes, indeed, Madame des Innouïs, that is so.'

'My late husband, who knew America, was entertained there by the Whales; he has often and often told me that their house was an exact copy, but ten times the size, of – let me see – was it Courances or Château d'O? – one of those houses entirely surrounded by water anyhow.'

'This is another branch of the Whale family, Madame Innouïs. There are hundreds of Whales in the States since this family is a very very large and extensive one and I have a perfect multiplicity of aunts and uncles and cousins and other more distant relatives, spread over the whole extent of the U.S.A. and all originating as Whales.'

'How delightful.' Madame Rocher's attention was wandering. She longed to join the group round Janvier, Cocquelin and Daudet, the musicians, who were doing their imitation of Juliette's gate-crashing, Janvier leading in Daudet, Cocquelin as the outraged Albertine – not the polished affair it afterwards became but none the less funny for that – to the accompaniment of happy shrieks from their audience. First things first, however. She turned again to Mr Dexter, saying, 'And have you any children yourself?'

'I am glad to be able to tell you yes, Mrs Innouïs. I have a son and a daughter by my first wife, the first Mrs Dexter, and a son by my second wife, and a son, who is here this evening costumed as George Washington, by my third wife, who is also here, costumed as George Washington's mother, I myself being costumed as you can see, as George Washington's father. My eldest son, Heck junior, is not perhaps quite brilliant, but he is a very very well-integrated, human person. My daughter, Aylmer, is married, and happily married I am glad to say, to a young technician in a very prominent and important electrical concern. My son by my second wife is now at Yale, having a good time. In the States, Madame Innouïs, we believe in all young folk being happy, and we do all we humanly can to further their happiness.

'Now here in Europe a very different point of view seems to prevail. Here so many of the entertainments and parties seem to be given by old people for other old people. Now I am over forty, Madame Innouïs, but many and many's the time, in French houses, when I have been the youngest person present, and I've never yet, at any parties, seen really young folks, college boys and girls or teen-agers. How do your French teen-agers amuse themselves, Madame Innouïs?'

'They are young, surely that is enough,' she said indignantly. 'Surely they don't need to amuse themselves as well.'

'But in the States, Madame Innouïs, we think it our duty to make sure that precisely while they are young they are having the best years of their lives. Now in what way do the young folks here spend these best years of their lives, Madame Innouïs?'

'I believe they are entirely nourished on *porto*,' said Madame Rocher enigmatically. She decided that she must get away from Mr Dexter come what might, and even if it had to be at the expense of that big box and two rows of stalls. She made a sign of command to Eugène de Tournon, who sprang forward, gave her his arm, and took her to supper.

'Many people don't realize at all,' she said, 'what I go through in order to support those dear good creatures at the Hospice. Champagne please, at once. He called me Madame Innouïs.'

'But everybody knows, Tante Régine, that you are a saint, an absolute, literal saint.'

'Yes indeed, Tante Régine,' said Charles-Edouard, at whose table they sat down, 'we shall find you on the ceiling one of these days, I've always thought that.'

'And where is our adorable little Sigi?' she asked, as a very tipsy Grand Dauphin tottered past the table, followed by Mademoiselle de Blois who, with that high whine peculiar to French children, was demanding another glass of champagne. The innocents were beginning to come to life again.

'That old dragon of a Nanny came and took him away. So stupid. As if one night out would do him any harm.'

'Poor little things.' Madame Rocher surveyed them through her lorgnette. 'I'm glad it's not me growing up now. What a world for them! Atom bombs, and no brothels. What will their parents do about that – after all you can't very well ask your own friends, can you? I suppose they'll all end up as pederasts.'

'Far the best thing to be, if you can fancy it,' said Charles-Edouard. 'Just imagine – no jealous husbands, what, Eugène? None of the terrible worries that make our lives so distracting. No pregnancies, no abortions, no divorce – I envy them.'

'Blackmail?'

'Blackmail indeed! They've only got to write a journal clearly stating what they are. You can't blackmail a man by threatening to tell the world what he has told the world already.

'Now supposing I were to write a journal making it quite plain how much I have loved women – to begin with nobody would buy it, and to go on with it would have a terrible effect on the husbands and I should be in worse odour than ever before. It's really most unfair.'

Charles-Edouard got up to shake hands with Mr and Mrs Dexter, saying, since they were clearly going to, anyhow, 'Do come and sit here. We are talking about brothels, pederasts, and blackmail.'

'You don't surprise me at all,' said Carolyn.

The Dexters, having now lived two years in Paris, had become quite accepted as part of French society, and were asked everywhere. But Carolyn still could not get to like, or be in the least amused by, the French.

'I am very very happy to be able to tell you,' said Mr Dexter, settling into his chair, 'that when our ancestors left little old Europe and shook its dust off their feet in order to found our great United States of America, those three things are three of the things they left behind them here on your continent.'

'Well then, perhaps you can tell us,' said Madame Rocher, 'how, in a country where there are no brothels, do the young men ever learn?'

'I am very very happy to be able to tell you, Madame Innouïs, that the young American male is brimming over with strong and lustful, but clean desire. He is not worn out, old, and complicated before his time, no ma'am, he does not need any education sentimentarl, it all comes to him naturally, as it ought to come, like some great force of nature. He dates up young, he marries young, he raises his first family young and by the time he is ready to re-marry he is still young. And I am now going to give you a little apercoo of our American outlook on sex and marriage.

'We, in the States, are entirely opposed to physical relations between the sexes outside the cadre of married life. Now in the States it is usual for the male to marry at least four, or three times. He marries first straight from college in order to canalize his sexual desires, he marries a second time with more material ends in view – maybe the sister or the daughter of his employer – and much later on, when he has reached the full stature of his maturity, he finds his life's mate and marries her. Finally it may be, though it does not always happen, that when he has raised this last family with his life's mate and when she has ceased to feel an entire concentrated interest in him, but is sublimating her sexual instincts into other channels such as card games and literature, he may satisfy a longing, sometimes more paternal than sexual, for some younger element in his home, by marrying the friend of one of his children, or, as has occurred in certain cases known to me personally, of one of his grandchildren.

'In the States we just worship youth, Madame Innouïs, it seems to us that human beings were put on this earth to be young; youth seems to us the most desirable of all human attributes.'

'In that case I very much advise you to go in for Bogomoletz. The wonders it has done for me! Why, my hair, which was quite red, has positively begun to go black at the roots.'

'My faith, Madame Innouïs, is pinned to this diet I follow. Perhaps you would care to hear of it. Well it was entirely invented by a very very good friend of mine and its basis is germ of wheat oil, milk fortified with powdered milk and molasses, and meat fortified with yoghourt. Now in my case this diet, very carefully followed over a period of months, has succeeded in strengthening, beyond belief, the tissues of certain very very important organs —'

'The usual conversation of the over-forties, I see,' said Albertine, joining them. 'Let me just warn you all not to brush your faces. Little Lambesé was told to brush his face, to induce circulation or some rubbish, and he is still in his room, poor boy, marked as if he had encountered a savage beast.'

'After all, the face is not a suède shoe,' said Madame de Tournon. 'Is that why he's not here? He told me he was coming as a famous aunt.'

'Yes, and he wouldn't have been the only one.'

'I think it's very hard luck, and I'm sorry,' said Madame Rocher. 'Now supposing I make more money than I expect to at the Gala des Innouïs I will try and give Lambesé a Bogo; if anybody deserves one it is he.'

'I thought the lift had been such a great success, and if so why did he brush?'

'He thought nothing of it,' said Madame Marel. 'If you want that extra radiance, he was told, brush – brush. He did have some particular reason for wanting it – he brushed – and there he was looking like Paul in *Les Malheurs de Sophie*.'

It was past six when the ball ended. The famous parents gathered up their famous children, wilting and dishevelled, as accessories to fancy dress always are by the time a party is over, and carried them away. The last to leave was Henri II, with the three little Valois kings and la Reine Margot, but without Catherine de Medicis.

'Where is my wife?' he said to everybody he saw.

'And where,' said Albertine, more in sorrow than surprise, 'is Charles-Edouard?'

Chapter Seven

THE next day, after luncheon, Charles-Edouard and Sigi set out to walk to the Jockey Club, both feeling the need for a little fresh air after their various excesses of the previous night. They crossed the Place de la Concorde as only Frenchmen can, that is to say they sauntered through the traffic, chatting away, looking neither to right nor to left and assuming that the vehicles whizzing by would miss them, even if only by inches. (A miss is as good as a mile might be taken as their motto by French pedestrians.) The skirts of their coats were sometimes blown up by passing motors, but they were, in fact, missed, and reached the other side in safety.

'So what did the Reine Margot tell you?'

'She isn't really the Reine Margot, she's Jeanne-Marie de Tournon.'

'And what did she tell you?'

'Nothing at all – it's easy.'

Sigi was sometimes quite as obstinate as his mother when it came to 'What are the news'.

'Ha!' said Charles-Edouard. 'So you lay together on that sofa, hour after hour, gazing into each other's eyes and saying nothing at all. How very strange!'

'She lives in the country all the year round. She is dull. I was dull when you first knew me and I lived always in the country.'

'Are you not dull now?'

'I am not. I can read and write and do difficult sums and I'm excellent company. I know all about the Emperor and I can say the words of – oh Papa, Papa, do look —'

Some workmen were engaged upon Coustou's horses. The right-hand one was being cleaned and the other, with the arm of its groom over its back, still had a long ladder poised against the stone mane.

'Papa! Can I?'

Charles-Edouard looked round. There was nobody very near them, and no policeman nearer than the Concorde bridge.

'Do you know the words?'

'Yes. You'll hear, when I'm up there.'

'On your honour, Sigi?'

'*Honneur,*' he cried, taking off his coat, '*à la Grande Armée!*'

He nipped up the ladder and, clambering with the agility of a monkey on to the horse's back, began to chant: '*A la voix du vainqueur d'Austerlitz l'empire d'Allemagne tombe. La confédération du Rhin commence. Les royaumes de Wurtembourg et de Bavière sont crées. Venise se réunit a la couronne de fer, et l'Italie toute entière se range sous les lois de son libérateur. Honneur à la Grande Armée.*'

The motors in the Champs Elysées and Place de la Concorde began to draw into the side and stop while their occupants got out to have a better view of the charming sight.

'It must be for the cinema,' they said to each other. '*C'est trop joli.*'

And indeed the little boy, with his blue trousers, yellow jersey, and mop of bright black hair on the white horse, outlined against a dappled sky, made a fascinating picture. Charles-Edouard laughed out loud as he looked. Then, as several whistling policemen arrived on the spot, he decided to allow Sigismond to deal alone with the situation as it developed. He hailed a taxi and went home. It was quite another half-hour before Sigi dashed into the house with a very great deal to tell.

Photographers, it seemed, had appeared; a man with a megaphone had told him to stay where he was. The crowd, led by Sigi, had begun to sing his favourite song, *Les voyez-vous, les hussars, les dragons, la garde.* The firemen had arrived in a shrieking red car, had swarmed up more ladders to the horse, had carried him down and borne him home in triumph, shooting across red lights in the boulevard.

'So these words have not remained unsaid after all, Papa, you see.'

'If his mummy had been here,' come floating into the night nursery, 'none of this would ever have happened. That Madam Marel would never have given that wicked ball (poor little mites, I can't get them out of my head lying about in great heaps all over the shop), and the Marquee would never have taken him for a walk – once in a blue moon was how often we saw the

178

Marquee when Mummy was here. Allowing him to ride up on that horse indeed; it's a mercy he didn't fall off and crack his little skull.'

Next morning Charles-Edouard drank the several cups of black coffee and ate the several slices of ham which constituted his so-called English breakfast, with Sigi, on the floor beside him, busily cutting photographs of himself out of half a dozen newspapers brought in by Ange-Victor.

'Now guess what I'm going to do,' said Charles-Edouard. 'Ring up Mummy and tell her all about it and see if she'd like to have you over there for a bit.'

'Oh good,' said Sigi. 'Can I go tomorrow?' He was longing to see his mother, boast to her about what Nanny called the high jinks of the last two days, and see what she could do, now, to amuse him.

'Yes, unless you think she'd like to come over and pay us a visit instead? What do you say, Sigismond? We can always try to persuade her, can't we?'

If Charles-Edouard had seen the look Sigi gave him he might have interpreted it correctly, but he had already taken up the telephone (he seldom sat out of reach of this instrument) and was dialling the foreign exchange number.

'I want a personal call to London,' he said, giving Grace's name and number. He then went off to have his bath. 'Sit by the telephone, Sigismond, and call me at once if it rings.'

Sigi perched on his father's bed, reflecting.

As soon as the water began to run loudly in the bathroom next door he lifted the receiver and cancelled the call to London. When the water stopped running Charles-Edouard heard 'That you, Mummy? We're coming back tomorrow. Yes, Nanny and me, on the Arrow. Yes. Unless you'd like to pay us a visit here, Papa says? Oh! Mum!' a tragic, reproachful note in the voice. 'Won't you even speak to him? Here he is, out of his bath – oh! She's cut off,' he said, handing the receiver to Charles-Edouard, who, indeed, only heard a dialling tone. He slammed it down furiously and went back to his bath, saying 'Go and tell Nanny to pack, will you?'

Sigi went slowly off, twisting his hair until it was a mass of tangles.

In London Grace cried over her coffee. 'Paris wants you' to her had meant that in a minute or two she might hear the voice of Charles-Edouard. But when her telephone bell rang again and she answered it with beating heart it was only to hear : 'Sorry you have been troubled. Paris has now cancelled the call.'

Chapter Eight

GRACE now had two suitors, Hughie Palgrave, and a new friend, Ed Spain. Ed Spain was a leading London intellectual, known to his contemporaries as the Captain or the Old Salt, which names he had first received at Eton, on account, no doubt, of some long-forgotten joke. He had a sort of seafaring aspect, accentuated later in life by a neat beard; his build was that of a sailor, short and slight, and his keen blue eyes looked as if they had been concentrated for many years on a vanishing horizon. In fact he was a charming, lazy character who had had from his schooldays but one idea, to make a great deal of money with little or no effort, so that he could lead the life for which nature had suited him, that of a rich dilettante. When he left Oxford somebody had told him that one sure road to a quick fortune was the theatre. With his small capital he had bought an old suburban playhouse called, suitably enough, the Royal George, and had then sat back awaiting the success which was to make him rich. It never came. The Captain had too much intellectual honesty to pander to his audiences by putting on plays which might have amused them but which did not come up to his own idea of perfection. He gained prestige, he was said to have written a new chapter in theatrical history, but certainly never made his coveted fortune.

However he soon attracted to himself a band of faithful followers, clever young women all more or less connected with the stage and all more or less in love with the Captain, and these followers, by their energy and devotion, kept the Royal George afloat. He called them My Crew, and left the management of his theatre more and more in their hands as the years went on, a perfect arrangement for such a lazy man. The Crew were relentlessly highbrow, much more so, really, than the Captain, whose own tastes, within the limits of what was first-class of its kind, were catholic and jolly. The Crew only liked plays written by sad young foreigners with the sort of titles (*This Way to the Womb, Iscariot Interperson*) which never seem to attract family parties out for a cheerful evening. Unfortunately these are the mainstay of the theatre world. The Crew, however, cared nothing for so contemptible a public. Their criterion of a play was that it should be worthy of the Captain, and when they found such a work they did not rest until they had translated, adapted, and produced it at the Royal George.

They took charge, too, of the financial side of the venture, which they ran rather successfully on a system of intellectual blackmail. Nobody in a certain set in London at that time, no clever Oxford or Cambridge undergraduate, would dare to claim that he was abreast of contemporary thought unless he paid his annual subscription, entitling him to two stalls a month, to the Royal George. These subscriptions, payable through Heywood Hill's bookshop, ensured a good, regular income for the theatre, but would not necessarily have brought in an audience but for the Captain's own exertions. Nobody minded forking out a few pounds a year to feel that they were in the swim, but the agony of sitting through most of the plays was hardly endurable. However, if the theatre was quite empty for too many performances the Crew was apt to get very cross; it was the Captain's job to see that this did not happen. He let it be understood that those who wished to keep in his good graces must put in an occasional appearance at the Royal George.

As he was one of the most amusing people in London, as his presence was a talisman that ensured the success of any party (so long as he was well fed and given what he considered his due in the way of superior French wines, otherwise he had been known to sulk outrageously) this exacting tribute was paid from time to time by his friends and acquaintances. There was no special virtue, however, in going to a first night, since the house was always full on these occasions. First nights at the Royal George were very interesting affairs, and the Captain himself allocated all the seats for them. M. de Tournon's anguish over the placing of dukes at his dinner-table found its London counterpart in the Captain's anguish over the placing, on these first nights, of the grand young men of literature and the arts. His own, or Royal box, only held four. Neither he nor the Crew were ever likely to forget the first night of *Factory 46* when Jiři Mucha, Nanos Valaoritis, Umbro Apollonio, Chun Chan Yeh, and Odysseus Sikelberg had all graciously announced their intention of being present. The situation was saved by Sikelberg getting mumps, but only at the very last minute.

Grace and her father went with Mrs O'Donovan, who was what she called '*abonnée*', to the first night of *Sir Theseus*. Naturally they were not in the Royal box, full, on this occasion, of darkies, but they were well placed, in the second row of the stalls. The Captain, who often saw Sir Conrad at White's, came and sat with them for part of the time, a signal honour. *Sir Theseus* was, in fact, *Phèdre*, written with a new slant, under the inspiration of modern psychological knowledge, by a young Indian. Phaedra was the oldest member of the Crew and really rather a terror, only kept on by the Captain because she was such an excellent cook. She was got up to look, as Sir Conrad said, like a gracious American hostess, with crimped blue hair and a housecoat. When she bore down upon Hyppolitus, whose disgust at her approach, as he cowered against the backcloth, had nothing to do with histrionic art, Sir Conrad said in his loud, politician's voice, 'She's got young Woodley on the ropes this time.' The Captain loved to laugh, as he did at this, though really he half-hated the sort of joke which implied that art might not be sacred. He half-loved and half-hated, too, the sort of person represented by Sir Conrad. If the Captain had known in which direction he wanted to set his compass, life would have been that much easier for him. However on this occasion, attracted by the beauty and elegance of Grace, he invited her father to bring her and Mrs O'Donovan back to his house for supper after the play.

The Captain lived in a large, rambling, early 19th-century house, built to be an hotel or lodging-house, on the river, hard by the Royal George. This he shared with such members of the Crew who were able and willing to do housework. They lived in attics and cellars which no servant would have considered for a single moment, but which the clever Captain had invested with romance. *'Les toits de Paris'* he would murmur, craning through a leaky skylight and squinting at *les toits de Hammersmith,* while the cellars, damp and dripping, were supposed to be the foundations of a famous convent, 'the English Port Royal'. He reserved for himself big, sunny rooms on the first floor furnished in the later manner (much later, some said) of Jacob. Here an excellent supper, withdrawn from oven and hay-box by Phaedra with the assistance of Oenone, was served to quite a large party, consisting mostly of critics and fellow highbrows, such as the editors of *Depth* and *Neoterism.* The Indian author of *Sir Theseus* lay on the floor reading a book and never spoke to anybody.

'What really wonderful champagne,' said Sir Conrad.

'I'm so glad you like it.' The Captain was pouring out two sorts of wine, a Krug 1928 for some and an Ayala for others. This had nothing to do with meanness; he really could not bear to see the bright, delicious drops disappear into a throat that would as soon receive any other form of intoxicant. There were many such throats among them on this occasion.

Presently those members of the Crew who had been engaged upon the more mechanical jobs at the theatre began to arrive. They looked very much alike, and might have been a large family of sisters; their faces were partially hidden behind curtains of dusty, blonde hair, features more or less obscured from view, and they were all dressed alike in duffle coats and short trousers, with bare feet, blue and rather large, loosely connected to unnaturally thin ankles. Their demeanour was that of an extreme sulkiness, and indeed they looked as if they might be on the verge of mutiny. But this appearance was quite misleading, the Captain had them well in hand; they hopped to it at the merest glance from him, emptying ash-trays and bringing more bottles off the ice. The Royal George, if not always a happy ship, was an intensely disciplined one. Like the Indian, however, the Crew added but little to the gaiety of the party. They sat in silent groups combing the dusty veils over their faces and thinking clever thoughts about *The Book of the It, The Sheldonian Synthesis, The Literature of Extreme Situations* and other neglected masterpieces.

The Captain was very much struck by Grace with her French name and Paris clothes, a year old, but all the easier for that on an English eye. He knew about the General de Valhubert killed at Friedland because this General had been a great friend, indeed one of the few known friends, of General Chaderlos de Laclos. He took Grace to his library and showed her what he said was his greatest treasure, General de Valhubert's own copy of *Les Liaisons dangereuses*. It was bound in red morocco with the Valhubert coat of arms, a stag and a rose tree, and the General had written a sort of journal, or series of notes, during one of his campaigns, all over the margins. It was a collector's piece of rare interest. That coat of arms, so familiar to Grace, who during her short and happy life in France had seen it every day on china, silver, carpets, books, and linen, gave her a dreadful pang.

'How strange. It must have been stolen from Bellandargues,' she said, looking sadly at the book.

'Thrown away, more likely. No respectable French family would have cared to have *Les Liaisons dangereuses* lying about their house, in the 19th century.'

'Oh yes, that's it, of course. And then my husband always said they were really ashamed of the Marshal, though in another way pleased to have had a Marshal of France in the family. All very complicated.'

'French people are complicated. Did you like the play?' he asked.

'Yes, though I like the real *Phèdre* better.' It was Charles-Edouard's favourite play, she remembered.

'The real *Phèdre* is wonderful poetry, but, as my friend Baggarat has shown us this evening, it is psychologically quite unsound. Racine's *Phèdre* has two psychological weaknesses – the first is that we can never believe in Hyppolite's love for Aracie, and the second we cannot understand why he should recoil in such horror from this fascinating woman who loves him.'

'Except that she was as old as the hills.'

'How do you know? My guess is that she was half-way between the ages of Thésée and Hyppolite, and still very attractive. But if Hyppolite was homosexual, everything is explained – he adores Hara-See the dancing boy, he loathes the idea of making love to a woman. I think my friend Baggarat has done a very fine piece of work, valuable for the future of the theatre.'

Grace was impressed. She liked the Captain very much, she liked his jolly, careless, piratical look, she thought his house most original and charming, and she was quite prepared to like the Crew. But the Crew despised her and made no effort to conceal the fact. They could not be the clever girls they were without seeing life a little bit through Marx-coloured spectacles, and to them Grace was the very personification of the rich bourgeoisie. They despised the rich bourgeoisie. Her presence in the house made them uneasy, superstitious, it was as though Jonah had come aboard the Royal George.

They sat in a sulky, silent group, combed their hair over their faces and watched the Captain through it. To their distress they saw that he was putting himself out to be as agreeable to Grace as if she had been Panayotis Canellopoulos in person. Why? What could he see in this spineless creature, who, unable to get on with her husband, had run back to her father like a spoilt child? When the various members of the Crew had been unable to get on with their husbands they had struck proudly out on their own, taken rooms near the Deux Magots, hitch-hiked to Lithuania, or stowed away to the Caribbean. She was the sort of woman, with no self-respect, whom they positively execrated. They combed and watched, but if they harboured mutinous thoughts, they still hopped to it at a look from the Captain. In those days it seemed unthinkable that actual rebellion should ever break out on that ship while the Captain was at the helm.

The Captain soon fell in love with Grace, if that can be called love which has nothing physical in its composition. He was not attracted to her physically, she was too clean, too tidy, and too reserved for him; impossible to conceive of cuddling or rumpling Grace. Her stiff Paris dresses, lined with buckram and padded petticoats, in themselves precluded such cosy goings on. He could not even imagine her sitting on his lap. But in every other way he loved her; he loved her elegance, her sad, romantic look, and the serious attention which she bestowed upon everything he said. Above all he loved his own mental picture of what life with her would be like if they were to marry. He imagined a small

18th-century villa not too far from London, where great luxury would prevail. Large, delicious, regular meals would arrive with no effort to himself, none of the expense of spirit which it cost him to keep Phaedra up to the mark; he would have a gentleman's library, a first-class cellar, intellectual friends would come and stay, he would be able to chuck the Royal George and write a masterpiece. Later, when Sir Conrad was dead, they would live at beautiful Bunbury. Sex would not play much part in all this. The French husband, it was to be hoped, would have satisfied her in that respect for ever, and after all people could live together very happily without it. He knew many cases. They would just have to sublimate their sexual desires, it was really quite easy.

Grace, too, had made a mental picture of what marriage with the Captain would be like, as women always do when they become aware that a man's thoughts have turned in that direction. Her picture was not so very different from his. As with his, sex was left out. They would live together like brother and sister, she thought, a long, quiet, cultivated life. She saw them as the Wordsworths, in a larger, warmer house, nearer to London and without Coleridge; as Charles and Mary Lamb without the madness; as Mr and Mrs Carlyle without the liver attacks. Visits to Paris came into this picture, since she could not imagine life always away from France, and revenge of some sort on Charles-Edouard for making her so very unhappy. She began to see a great deal of the Captain, whose intentions became increasingly clear.

Sir Conrad was not enthusiastic about either of his possible sons-in-law as such. Hughie was a nice, good creature, of course, but so boring, with his political pretensions. Sir Conrad thought that politics should be transacted, lightly, by clever men, and not ponderously by stupid ones. The Captain, whose company he very much enjoyed, seemed to him altogether too bohemian for marriage.

'Don't you think,' he said to Mrs O'Donovan, 'that there may still be a chance of her marrying Charles-Edouard again? They both adore the boy, surely it's only reasonable to think that they ought to make some sacrifices on his account. After all, so little is wanted – a little discretion from Charles-Edouard and a little toleration from Grace. Mind you, it all depends on Grace. I happen to know that Charles-Edouard would take her back tomorrow, he still wants her.'

'It all depends,' said Mrs O'Donovan rather severely, 'on Grace taking a more Christian view of the duties of a wife. I have been able to forgive her behaviour up to now on account of the shock she must have received, but she has got over that. She is certainly planning to marry again, and is making up her mind whether it shall be Hughie or the Captain. This ceremony, if you can call it that, in a registry office naturally meant nothing to her and marriage as a sacrament is quite outside her experience.'

'Yes, well, you're a Papist, Meg, so that's how you look at it. I think it all comes from a sort of silly pride. Anyhow it's most exceedingly tiresome. That wretched Carolyn with her mania for sight-seeing. I never could stand her, even as a child. The sort of woman who always manages to put her foot in it. Well she managed that time to some tune, it's enough to make you cry. Just when everything was going like a marriage bell. Grace was so happy with Charles-Edouard, and furthermore so happy, which is rare for an Englishwoman, living in Paris. She loved it.'

'Is that rare?' she said with a sigh. 'I know I should love it.'

'Most English people hate living in France. I always think it's got a great deal to do with French silver. They don't realize it's another alloy, they think that dark look means that it hasn't been properly cleaned, and that makes them hate the French. You know what the English are about silver, it's a fetish with them. I've so often noticed it. In the other war the silver at Bombon used to put up the backs of all our generals; they never could talk about anything else after a meal there with old Foch.'

'I like that rich, dark silver,' said Mrs O'Donovan.

But then she liked everything French, indiscriminately and unreasonably, and her life in England, though it was all she had ever known, seemed to her a perpetual exile, so insistent was the beckoning from over the Channel.

Chapter Nine

GRACE, called to the telephone in the middle of a rubber of bridge at Yeotown, came back and said to Hughie, 'Most mysterious – Sigi and Nanny have arrived in London. I think I must go back.'

'Don't do that. I'll send the motor for them. They'll be here by dinner-time.'

Dinner had begun when the little boy burst into the room and threw himself into his mother's arms, saying 'D'you know what, Mum – I rode on a *cheval de Marly*.'

'No!'

'Yes I did – look!' He fished some very tattered newspaper cuttings out of one pocket, but somehow forgot to fish a letter from Charles-Edouard out of another. Charles-Edouard had written coldly but clearly stating that, in his view, it was their absolute duty to their child to re-marry as soon as possible. He had done so without much hope of moving Grace, but he wanted her to know quite definitely, to read in black and white, his views on the subject, and to make it clear that their continued estrangement was her own responsibility.

'My darling Sigi – however did you get up there? But first say how d'you do please to Mr and Mrs Fawcett and Hughie, and thank Hughie very very much for sending his motor. No – you don't kiss people's hands in England.'

'Please always kiss mine,' said Mrs Fawcett, 'I love it, Sigismond.'

'Don't muddle him, Virginia, he must learn the difference.'

'Well, Mummy, I got up a ladder the workmen had left. Papa allowed me to and then he went home and left me there, and I rode for ages, it was so lovely up in the sky, and there was an enormous crowd to see me and I recited to them. Well first I said the words, that was for Papa, then we had *Waterloo, morne plaine,* then we all sang *Les voyez-vous,* and then the pompiers came and we had the *Marseillaise,* all the verses, then they carried me down and took me home.'

'I never heard such a thing,' said Grace, with a look at Hughie which clearly said 'Now what? We can never compete with this.' 'Ask Hughie if you may dine here with us as a great great treat.'

'Wouldn't be any treat at all in Paris, I always dine with Papa and have a glass of Bordeaux and 100 francs if I can tell the vintage.'

'You can have a glass of Bordeaux here,' said Hughie, 'only we call it claret, and half a crown if you can tell the vintage.'

He poured it out.

'Quite an honourable wine,' said Sigi, 'but not *grand cru*. I can only tell when it's *grand cru*.'

This remark having gone down, he saw, rather badly, Sigismond settled to a hearty meal.

Presently Hughie said to him, 'What do you do all day in Paris, Sigi?'

'In Paris,' said Sigi, 'I have two great friends. One is Madame Novembre de la Ferté, who gives me treats, allows me to drive her motor, and so on, and the other is Madame Marel, who gives me my lessons. They both give me very very expensive presents.'

'But doesn't M. l'Abbé give you your lessons any more?'

'He did for a while, but he's gone away. So now I have lessons with Madame Marel. I like it far better. I know masses of poetry by heart and we go to the *jardin des plantes*.' Sigi was curling up bits of hair with one hand. 'And what d'you think we saw the turtles doing? Yes, but it wasn't her fault, they only do it once every three years – bad luck really. You ought to have heard them bellowing.'

'Well,' said Hughie, 'that doesn't amount to much. You've ridden a stone horse and driven a car – which you'll do every day of your life when you're grown up – and learnt poetry and heard turtles bellowing.'

'They weren't only bellowing,' said Sigi. 'Expensive presents, too – and a ball.'

He spoke very crossly. He was tired after the journey, more than half asleep, and felt that he had not done himself justice or made it sufficiently clear that nobody in Paris could think of anything from morning till night but how best to keep him amused. However he was reassured by Hughie's next words.

'What about learning to ride a real horse so that you can go hunting next winter?'

'O.K. Can I begin tomorrow?'

'No. Tomorrow is Sunday. You can begin on Monday.'

Grace left Sigi in the dining-room and went up to see Nanny.

'High time we did get back, in my opinion. Such goings on, dear. The Marquee does spoil him – oh he does, lets him do anything he says. That Madam November too and that Madam Marel – they fill his head with the most unsuitable ideas between them. Did he tell you about the ball?'

'He did say something. He's half-asleep, I think.'

'You'll hear it all, no doubt. I never saw such an exhibition in my life, those poor little mites, in ridiculous clothes for children (though I must say Sigi looked sweet) kept up I believe, some of them, till six in the morning. Nanny Dexter and I – the servants didn't want to let us in, but we weren't having any of that – we went and fetched our two away quite early on. Sigi was sound asleep, but poor little Foss, oh he was sick. I wish you could have seen the stuff he kept on bringing up. She hasn't got his little tummy right yet. The usual rush over the packing, of course, and nobody to meet us at Victoria, dear.'

'But Nanny, nobody knew you were coming.'

'There now. The Marquee said he'd rung up and everything was arranged – oh well, French you know!'

Sigismond was very sleepy indeed, but not too sleepy to burn his father's letter to his mother in the empty nursery grate, with a match he had brought upstairs with him on purpose, while Nanny was running his bath.

The fact that Hughie now began to pay court to Sigismond just as, in Paris, Albertine and Juliette had paid court, and with the same end in view, that of becoming his step-parent, was clear as daylight to the little boy. Like his mother he had been quite doubtful whether the high level of amusement to which he had lately become accustomed could be maintained in England. Greatly to his surprise he found that it was positively surpassed. It so happened that Sigi had a natural aptitude for all forms of sport, and therefore very much enjoyed practising them. Hughie, an excellent athlete, gave up hours a day to coaching him; he played tennis, squash, and cricket with him, and taught him to ride. So of course Sigi loved being at Yeotown and very much approved of Hughie, whose stock, in consequence, soared with Grace. Visits to Yeotown became more and more frequent and prolonged, and very soon Sigi was quite ready to consider Hughie as an auxiliary papa. He realized that his mother could never have put on such a good show by herself.

Hughie said to Grace, 'This child must go to Eton – I'm sure they'd make a cricketer of him. Seems waste of excellent material for him to go to some French school where they do nothing but lessons.'

'But he was never put down for it,' said Grace.

'I can fix that, I'm sure. A word with Woodford. The boy is exceptional, you see.'

'Oh dear, I wonder whether Charles-Edouard would allow it. He did once seem to think of it, I remember.'

'It's my opinion that child can do anything he likes with his father. If he wants to go he'll go, it all depends on that.'

Hughie was one of those to whom Eton is bathed retrospectively in a light that never was on land or sea. He talked much of it to Sigi, who began to imagine himself as Captain and Keeper of this and that, and inclined very favourably to the idea. At last Hughie suggested that the three of them might go down for the day, take out his own nephew, Miles Boreley, and let Sigismond have a look round.

'We'll go down next Thursday, I'll ring up Miles's tutor now and arrange it. Once the child has seen it for himself the thing's a foregone conclusion – there'll be no holding him – he'll be as good as there.'

Miles Boreley was a sad little boy. He stood waiting for them at the Burning Bush, top hat crammed on to large red ears, mouth slightly open, large, red hands hanging down. Though very plain, he had a disquieting look of his handsome uncle Hughie. They left the motor and walked with him towards Windsor. He said he had engaged a table for luncheon at a restaurant there.

It was one of those summer days when the cold of the Thames valley eats into the very bone, though the boys who slouched about the street with no apparent aim in view, looking like refu-

gees in a foreign town, did not seem to notice it. Sigi's bright
little eyes, which missed nothing, darted from one to another. He
was amazed by their archaic black clothes and general air of ill-
being. Hughie, bathed in the light that never was, glanced at
him from time to time, wondering if the magic had already
begun to work. Had he known his Sigi better he would have
been quite well aware that it had not. The corners of the mouth
were drooping in a very tell-tale way.

They were shown their table in the restaurant and were
settling themselves round it when Miles, looking with disfavour
at the seat of his chair, asked if he could have a cushion. The
waitress quite understood, and went off to get him one.

'Been in trouble, old boy?' said Hughie.

'Only been beaten by the library.'

'Bad luck. What for?'

'Changing the times sheet, as usual.'

'Oh I say, you shouldn't do that, you know.'

'You're telling me.'

'Beaten?' said Sigi. His blood ran cold.

'Yes, of course. Aren't you ever beaten?'

'Certainly not. I'm a French boy – I wouldn't allow such a
thing.'

'What a sissy!'

'But do you like being beaten?'

'Not specially. But I shall like it all right when it's my turn to
beat the others.'

Hughie said, 'When I got into the library I used to lay about
me like Captain Bligh. I had a lot of leeway to make up – we
had an awful time at m'tutor's from a brute called Kroesig. But
I got my own back. How's the food this half, Miles?'

'Well you literally can't see it, there's so little. We buy everything at the sock shop now. M'tutor is married,' he explained
for the benefit of Grace and Sigi, 'and Mrs Woodford has got
three children and a fur coat, all paid for by the housebooks, of
course, and is saving up for more.'

'More children or more fur coats?'

'More of everything. She's literally the meanest miser you ever
saw.'

'Yes, married tutors can be the devil,' said Hughie. 'Mine was a bachelor and I'm bound to say he never starved us, but m'dame used to steal our money.'

'Steal it!' said Grace. 'What a shame.'

'Well that's what we used to say. Rather like Miles and the fur coats, you know. These Eton rumours shouldn't be taken too seriously, they would none of them stand up to scientific investigation.'

Sigi looked relieved. 'What about the beating?' he said. 'Is that a rumour too?'

'Just take a look at my behind,' said Miles. 'I'll show you after. That will stand up to any amount of scientific examination, as you'll see.'

A family party now came in. A woman, looking incredibly old to be the mother of children in their teens, was followed by two little girls and a stocky boy with a square of pink elastoplast on the back of his neck. They hurried through the restaurant and went upstairs.

Miles's mouth opened wider; he turned quite pink.

'Badger-Skeffington,' he said.

'No!' said Hughie, craning round to look. But they had disappeared.

'Badger-Skeffington!' said Grace, laughing hysterically. She was thinking that, wonderful as it seemed, some man must have gone to bed with that old lady only a few years before, since the youngest little girl was not more than twelve.

'What are you laughing at?' said Hughie.

'Such a funny name.'

'It may seem funny to you, but I can tell you, you haven't heard it for the last time. That boy is an extraordinary athlete; it's years since they've had such a boy here. Tell them, Miles.'

'Keeper of the Field, Keeper of Boxing, Captain of the XI. They'll be having a black-market lunch up there,' he said enviously. 'Badger-Skeffington's mother is a most famous black-marketeer.'

'Are you sure? She doesn't look a bit like that.'

'Didn't you notice how they were all weighed down with baskets and things? Tons of beefsteak, I expect, pots of cream, pounds of butter. That's why they go upstairs, so that nobody shall see what they are unpacking. They bribe the police with huge sums, it's well known.'

'Miles! I expect they have a farm.'

'So likely, in Ennismore Gardens. That's why Badger-Skeffington always wins everything – Daddy says he's literally full of food, like a French racehorse. They're *nouveaux riches*, you know.'

'Now hold on, Miles, that's not true. I often see Bobby Badger at my club, he's frightfully poor, it was a fearful effort to send the boy here at all, I believe.'

'Yes, I know, Uncle Hughie, the point is they are *nouveaux riches* and frightfully poor as well. There are lots like that here. Their fathers and mothers give up literally everything to send them.'

'Oh dear, how poor everybody seems to be, in England,' said Grace. 'It's too terrible when even the *nouveaux riches* are poor.'

'Yes, and while we are on the subject I would like to know exactly why it is they are all so stinking rich in France,' said Hughie, stuffily. He was rich himself, but his capital seemed to be melting away at an alarming rate. 'It seems quite sinister to me.'

'Quite easy really. The French have always looked after their estates. They have foresters in their forests, not just gamekeepers, and their vineyards are a gold mine. In England, when I was a child anyhow, landed estates simply drained away the money – I remember quite well how my father and uncles used to talk as if it was a most tremendous luxury, owning land. There was never any idea of making it pay.'

'H'm,' said Hughie. Were he clever, like Albertine, had he the gift of the gab, like Heck, he would have been able, he thought bitterly, to prove to Grace the undoubted fact that the French are rich because they are wicked, while the English are poor because they are good. As he was neither clever nor gabby he was obliged to leave the last word with her. It was most annoying.

Some friends of Grace's now came in, accompanied by two charming little boys. They said 'hullo', looked with interest at Sigi, and went through to another room. 'See you later, perhaps.'

'They look rather nice,' said Grace to Miles. 'Do you know them?'

'Who, Stocker?'

'Yes.'

'Yes, he's in my house.'

'Is he nice?' she persevered.

'He's just a boy.'

'Yes, I see. And the other?'

'The other one is a tug. We must only hope Badger-Skeffington doesn't see him. Badger-Skeffington is the scourge of the tugs.'

'What is a tug?' said Sigi.

'Somebody a bit brighter in the head than the rest,' said Grace, to tease Hughie. He was suddenly very much on her nerves. They had been too much lately at Yeotown, she thought, and decided they must have a few days in London, though no doubt Sigi would complain dreadfully at being dragged away from his riding and all the games.

After luncheon they went with Miles to his house, and there they followed him through a rabbit warren of passages and up and down little dark staircases. A deathly silence reigned.

'How empty it all seems,' said Grace. 'Where's everybody?'

'Having boys' dinner.'

'Very late.'

'Yes, well, it doesn't make much difference. Late or early there's literally nothing to eat.'

Miles's room, when they finally got to it, was extraordinarily bare and bleak. The walls were beige, the window curtains orange, and a black curtain hung from ceiling to floor in one corner. Over the empty fireplace there was a valedictory poem, illuminated and framed, on the closing of the Derby racecourse.

> There'll be no more racing at Derby
> It rings indeed like a knell, etc., etc.

It was terribly cold, colder than winter. Grace sat on the only chair, huddling into her fur coat, and the others stood round her as if she were a stove.

'Is this your bedroom?' Sigi said, taking in every detail.

'Yes, of course.'

'Is there a bed?' If he had been told that Miles slept on a heap of rags on the floor, like the concierges in Poland, he would not have been at all surprised.

'Here, of course,' said Miles scornfully. He lifted the black curtain to disclose an iron instrument against the wall. 'You pull it down at night, and the boys' maid makes it. And now, Uncle Hughie, if you'll excuse me, I must go off and do my time. Will you wait here or what?'

'I'm so terribly cold,' Grace said imploringly to Hughie. 'Couldn't we go home?'

'Well, rather bad luck on Miles when we've come to take him out. His time won't last more than three-quarters of an hour, you know.'

'Give him two pounds, he won't mind a bit,' she whispered.

'Oh I say, Uncle Hughie, thanks very much. Are you going, then?' he said, in tones of undisguised relief. 'Good-bye. Will you excuse me? – I shall be late.' He clattered away down the passage.

'Really, Grace – two pounds! I usually give him ten bob.'

'I'll go shares,' she said, 'put it on the bridge book. Worth it to me, I was dying of cold simply.'

The visit to Eton finished off Hughie's chances of marrying Grace for ever. Sigismond had seen a red light, and immediately took action.

'Mummy!'

'Hullo – you're early this morning!'

'Well yes, I've got something rather important to say. You know Hughie?'

'Yes.'

'Were you thinking of marrying him?'

'Why, darling?'

'The Nannies always say you will.'

'Would you like me to?'

'That's just the point. I would not.'

'Oh – Sigi —!'

'No use pretending, I would not.'

'Very well, darling. I promise I'll never marry anybody you

don't like. And now just go and tell Nanny to pack, will you? We're going up to London after luncheon.'

Sigi gave his mother a nice hug and trotted off. He was not at all dissatisfied to find himself later in the day on the road back to London. The riding and the games had been great fun, but if they were to lead to the prison house, whose shades he had now seen for himself, they simply were not worth it.

Chapter Ten

ALL this time the Captain had been going on with his pursuit of Grace, and of course he too had seen that, if there were a way to her heart, that heart so curiously absent, it would be through Sigismond.

'Bring him to *Sir Theseus* on Thursday afternoon,' he said.

'My dear Captain – is *Phèdre* very suitable for little boys?'

'*Exquise* Marquise, what about the Matinée Classique at the Français – is it not full of little boys seeing *Phèdre*?'

'All right then,' she said. It was a comfort to her to be with somebody who knew about the Matinée Classique and other features of French life. Hughie, in spite of all his efforts to educate himself in the Albertine days, had never really got much further than the Ritz bar, and now his love for everything French had turned to unreasonable hatred. Whenever Grace spoke to him of France he would say horrid little things which annoyed her. Like many large, bluff, and apparently good-natured men, Hughie had a malevolent side to his character, and knew exactly how to stick a pin where it hurt. He was always exceedingly catty about the Captain, who spoke, however, rather charmingly of him.

'Why does he hate her so much?' asked Sigi, as Hyppolitus recoiled in homosexual horror before the advancing Phaedra.

'Because she's his stepmother.'

'Oh. If Papa married Madame Marel would she be my stepmother and would I hate her?'

'Sh – darling, don't talk so loud, it's rude to the actors.'

She couldn't very well have said it was disturbing to the

audience. A beautiful, hot day, one of the very few that summer, had not been helpful in filling the Matinée Classique with little scholars of modern psychological drama, and the theatre was empty. Three or four members of the Crew sat about, balefully watching Grace through their hair; the Captain, who always said he preferred to see his plays from the back of the gallery, an excellent alibi, was having a guilty sun-bath on the roof of his house.

'Mum?' Sigi was wriggling about, bored.

'Yes?'

'Where's Hyppolitus's own mummy?'

'I'm not sure, I think she's dead, we must ask the Captain.'

'Mummy? Sir Theseus what?'

'You must ask the Captain that too.'

'Well – what's happened to Hyppolitus now?'

'Darling, try and pay attention. Didn't you hear Theramenus saying how he had fallen off his bicycle and been run over by a lorry?'

'Coo! Phaedra is upset and no mistake.'

'Don't say coo. I'm always telling you.'

'Mummy, why has Sir Theseus adopted Hara-See?'

'I suppose he feels rather lonely, now everybody seems to be dead.'

'Will he have to make over some of his money to Hara-See?'

'I don't know. Here's the Captain, you must ask him.'

The Captain took them backstage and showed them the machinery, switchboard, and so on, all of which interested Sigi a great deal more than the play. After this he was allowed the run of the Royal George, to the displeasure of the younger members of the Crew, who had seen through their hair exactly how the land lay. Phaedra, however, took a great fancy to Sigi and spoilt him.

The Captain's courtship, meanwhile, was not making much real progress. He was hampered in it by Grace's failure to attract him sexually, by a shyness and feeling of discomfort in her presence that he never seemed to get over. While it may be possible to do without sex in married life, he began to realize that it is very difficult to propose to a beautiful young woman without ever having had any physical contact with her. A little rumpling and cuddling bridges many an awkward gulf. In fact it now seemed to him as if the impossibility of cuddling Grace was endangering his whole heavenly scheme. He blamed her bitterly for it. Why should she be so stiff and remote? Why not unbend, make things easier for him? It was very hard. He had thought so much, during many a wakeful night, of all that marriage with her would bring. The laurels of Madame Victoire, the griffins and castles of Madame de Pompadour, the dolphins and the fleur-de-lis; Château Yquem, Chambolle-Musigny, Mouton Rothschild. He could feel, he could see, he could taste them. Sometimes he thought that he would break down and cry like a child if all this and much more were to elude his grasp, simply because of his inability to grasp the waist of Grace.

Nothing was going well for the Captain at this time. Subscriptions to the Royal George were falling off at a disquieting rate, various creditors were pressing their claims, Sir Theseus could obviously not be made to run much longer, and, worst of all, the Crew was in a chronic bad temper. Only old Phaedra was nice to him now, but her varicose veins had got worse and the doctor said she must give up the kitchen while she was playing this long and arduous role. So he was at the mercy of the others for his comforts, and they gave expression to their feelings through the medium of housework. Smash and burn were the order of the day. His home life had never been so wretched.

It now became imperative to find another play with which to replace Sir Theseus. The Crew pushed their hair out of their eyes and read quantities of manuscripts, many of them in the original Catalan, Finnish, or Bantu, and wrote résumés of them for the Captain to see. He had told them, and indeed in their hearts they knew it, that this time they must put on something which would sell a few seats. 'For once,' he said, 'try and find a play with a plot. I believe that would help. Something, for once, that the critics could understand.'

One bright spot in the Captain's life just then was how well he was getting on with Sigismond. The little boy hung about the theatre, thoroughly stage-struck, and told his mother, who of course repeated it, that he revered the Captain second only to M. l'Abbé.

The Captain, on his side, was entranced. Knowing as he did

no children of that age, Sigi appeared to him a perfect miracle of grace and intelligence. He kept begging to be given a part in a play, and the Captain thought that, if something suitable could be found, it would be from every point of view a good idea. The child had received a great deal of publicity for having ridden the *cheval de Marly,* he was very pretty, possibly very talented, and the whole thing would bring the Captain into continual contact with Grace. Sitting with her in his box on the first night, both feeling rather emotional, it might suddenly become possible for him to take her hand, to press her knee, even to implant a kiss on a naked shoulder when nobody was looking.

Now it so happened that a certain member of the Crew had been teasing the Captain for quite a long time to put on a play she had translated from some Bratislavian dialect, and of which the protagonist was a little boy of ten. The Captain had read her translation, which, he thought, probably failed to convey the fiery poetry and political subtleties of the original. In English it seemed rather dreary. But now this play was being very much discussed on the Continent. It was put on in Paris, where it had a mixed reception, and was said to have run clandestinely for several months in Lvov. The Captain, with Sigi in mind, decided to have another look at it.

It was called *The Younker.* An old Communist, whose days had been spent wringing a livelihood from the bitter marsh land round his home, lay on his bed, ageing. He lay alone because, so ungovernable was his temper, no human dared approach him. His dog, a famous mangler, lay snarling by the empty hearth. His only son had married a foreign Fascist woman; for this he had turned him out. The son had gone to the foreign Fascist woman's land and there had died. The old man kept his savings in gold in a pot under his bed, and it came upon him that he would like to give this pot, before he died and before the Party got it, to his son's son, and that he would like to see this child before his old eyes failed. The younker arrived. He was a manly little fellow, not at all awed by his grandfather's ungovernable rages, or by his grandfather's dog, the mangler. Indeed he went everywhere with his little hand resting on its head. He brought love into that house, and presently he brought his mother, the Fascist woman, and she made the bed, which had never been made before. And by degrees this child, this innocent, loving little creature, bridged even the great political gap between his mother and his grandfather. They joined a middle-of-the-road party and all ended in happiness.

The Captain began to see possibilities in this play if it could be altered and adapted according to an idea he had, and put on with Sigi in the name part. The great difficulty would be to get round the Crew; if only he could achieve that he foresaw a box-office success at last.

He called a conference on the stage after the Saturday matinée. The Crew sat about in high-necked sweaters, shorts, and bare, blue feet, their heads bowed and their faces entirely obscured by the curtain of hair. Though he did not know it, they were in a dangerous mood. They had hardly set eyes on the Captain of late, either at home or in his theatre; he had been, they knew, to many parties, in rich, bourgeois houses, with Grace. Rumour even had it that he had been seen in Sir Conrad's box at the Ascot races. None of this had done him much good with his Crew.

The Captain began by saying that it was quite essential for the Royal George to have a monetary success. If it did not, he pointed out, they would no longer be able to satisfy their serious public with plays that they alone were brave enough to produce. They would, in fact, be obliged to shut their doors and put out their lights and close, leaving a very serious gap in the intellectual life of London. The Crew knew that all this was so. They sat quite still listening. The Captain went on to praise Fiona very highly for her translation of *The Younker*. He said he had been re-reading it, that it was very good, that he thought it would do. He then branched off into a disquisition on the psychology of audiences through the ages.

'The two greatest dramatists of the modern world,' he said, 'are Shakespeare and Racine.'

There was no sign of life from the figures round him; faceless and dumb, bowed immovably over their bare, blue feet, they waited for him to go on. The Captain knew that had he said Sartre and Lorca there would have been some response, a tremor, perhaps, parting the silky blonde curtains, or a nodding of the veiled heads. No such tremor, no such nodding, occurred. He began to feel nervous, to wonder whether he was going to fail in what he was attempting. But he had never failed, as yet, to master his Crew, and he thought all would be well.

'Now Shakespeare and Racine,' he went on, nervously for him, 'understood the psychology of the playgoer, and they both knew that there are two things that audiences cannot resist. The first (and if we are to take a lesson from these great men, as I think we should, this will give scope to Ulra when designing her set) is the appeal of the past. The second, I am afraid, discloses a weakness in human nature, a weakness which exists as strongly today as it did in the 17th century. Not to put too fine a point on it, audiences like a lord. Shakespeare knew what he was about, that can't be denied. You'll hardly find a single commoner in Shakespeare's plays, and when they do occur he doesn't even trouble to invent names for them. 1st gravedigger, 2nd soldier, and so on. You'd think he might have written some very penetrating studies of the burghers of Stratford, he must have had plenty of copy. Not a bit. Kings and lords, queens and ladies made up his dramatis personae. Webster the same. And who's to say they're wrong? "I am Duchess of Malfi still" makes us cry. "I am Mrs Robinson still" wouldn't be at all the same thing.'

The Crew did not raise a titter at this joke, and the Captain had an uneasy feeling it had probably been made before. He hoped he was not losing his grip, and hurried on,

'As for Racine, his heroes and heroines are usually Imperial.

'Now I say that what was good enough for the Globe and the Théâtre Royal is good enough for the Royal George. Supposing, Fiona dear, that you were to rewrite *The Younker,* to set it in an English country house in the nineties, to change the violent old Communist into a violent old Earl? Write the part of the boy for our adorable little Sigismond – he should prove a tremendous attraction. If you do all this, as only you can, Fiòna, if Ulra makes a really amusing set for it – a Victorian castle, Ulra, in the Gothic style, lace collar, velvet suit for the Younker – I think I can prophesy certain success. I think we could count on six months with the house packed. After that we shall be able to go on with what we are trying to do in this theatre, don't be afraid that I've lost sight of that. I won't keep you now,' he looked at his watch, 'I have to go to London, but I will be home for dinner.' They always dined after the evening performance in the Captain's house. 'We can talk it over then —'

Not a movement, the curtained figures sat as in a trance. He did not quite like it, but was not seriously alarmed; he had weathered too many a storm in that ship with that Crew, those hearts of oak.

When the Captain arrived home rather late for dinner the house was in darkness, and empty as the *Marie Céleste*. There were signs of recent human activity, a meal had evidently just been eaten and not cleared away, but nobody was there.

The Captain supposed that his Crew must have gone on shore. They sometimes did so of an evening and always, on these occasions, left some delectable titbit sizzling in the oven for him. But the kitchen was in darkness, the oven cold and bare. He peered into the bedroom usually occupied by Ulra to see if a sulking figure were not perhaps lolling on the bed. If so it must be stirred up, made to minister to his needs. Not only was there no sulking figure, but nylon hairbrush and broken comb had vanished from the dressing-table, crumpled underclothes no longer brimmed from half-open drawers, duffle coats and ragged ball dresses no longer bulged behind the corner curtain, there were no old shoes lying about on the deal floor and no old hats on the deal shelf. Ulra had clearly gone, and taken all her belongings. Down in the Port Royal, up beneath the Toits de Paris, the same state of affairs existed in every bedroom. The Captain's heart sank within him. This was desertion. Mutiny he could have dealt with, his dreaded cat o' nine tails, sarcasm, had but to be seen by the Crew for them to come to heel, but desertion was far more serious. They had almost certainly, he knew, gone off in a body to join the staff of Neoterism.

The Captain passed a sleepless night, during which he decided that there was only one course left for him to take. He must go and see Grace and persuade her to marry him. Not a bad thing, perhaps, to do it on an impulse, though he would have preferred to lead up to it with the triumphant success on the boards of Sigismond. He must try and whirl her to a registry office before either she or he had any more chance of thinking it over. Thinking it over was no good now, the time had come for action. Breakfastless, feeling rather sea-sick, the Captain set out for Queen Anne's Gate.

Now it so happened that on this particular day Grace had woken up sadder and more hopeless than at any time since leaving Paris. Her divorce had just become absolute, and she had finished her carpet. She had made a sort of bet with herself that before these two things happened there would have been a sign from Charles-Edouard; none had come. The weather, which always affected her spirits, remained terrible, as it had been so far the whole summer. Day after day it was a question of putting on winter clothes and crowning them, for no other reason than that the month was June, with a straw hat, through which the cold wind whistled horribly. She was putting on one of these hats to go out to a dull luncheon when her maid came in and said that the Captain was downstairs. This news cheered her up.

'Give him a glass of vodka – I'm just coming.'

The Captain was already pouring vodka down his throat in great gulps like a Russian and feeling much more confident that all would yet be well. The door opened, and, instead of Grace, Sigismond appeared.

'Good morning, Old Salt,' he said, too cockily for a child of his age the Captain thought, irritated. He must get rid of him, he had got to see Grace alone while the action of the vodka on his doubly empty stomach (no dinner, no breakfast) was having its excellent effect.

'And when do I go into rehearsal, Cap?'

This was too much for the Captain's nerves. He took Sigi by the shoulder, propelled him to the door, gave him a sharp push and said,

'It's your Mummy I want to see, not you. Run along to Nanny, there's a good boy.'

Sigi gave him a very baleful glance. Aware that he had done himself no good, the Captain felt about in his pocket. He had a shilling and a fiver, and if one seemed too little the other seemed immeasurably too much. He fished out the shilling, which Sigi pocketed without a word, going furiously upstairs. Nobody had ever insulted him with so small a coin in his life before.

Grace appeared. She looked very pretty and was pleased to see the Captain, quite approachable, he thought. He took the plunge.

'I've come on an impulse, to ask you to marry me, Grace.'

'Good heavens, Captain!'

'I suppose you think I ought to lead up to it, pave the way, break it like bad news. I don't. We're both grown-up people, and I think if I want to marry you the easiest thing is to say so straight out.'

'Yes. I expect you're quite right.'

'And please don't think it over. I hate the sort of people who are for ever thinking things over, horrid, calculating thoughts. Say yes now – and I'll go off and get a licence.'

Grace was seriously tempted to do so. She was feeling furious with Charles-Edouard, with his attitude of 'come back whenever you like but don't expect me to bother about you, or make it any easier for you', and with his manner of conveying it to her, in-directly, through Sir Conrad. Why did he never telephone, write, or make any direct approach? It was intolerable. She felt it would punish him if she were to marry the Captain, brilliant, sparkling, friend of Paris intellectuals, much more than if she were to marry someone like Hughie. Hughie could only be a stopgap, the Captain might well be a great new love.

'I don't want to think it over,' she said, 'but I shall have to consult Sigismond.'

The Captain was very much taken aback. 'Consult Sigi?'

'Oh Captain, if Sigi didn't like it I could never do it, you know. I've given him my word never to marry without asking him first.'

'It's mad. Little boys of that age change their ideas every few minutes – he might say yes one day and no the next, it would mean nothing at all. According to whether – well for instance according to whether one had last tipped him with a shilling or five pounds. Sigi is very fond of me, you must have noticed that for yourself. I shan't turn out to be a Mr Murdstone, I can assure you – I am good-natured and I love children. I tell you this, so it must be true. What people say about themselves is always true. When they say "Don't fall in love with me, I shall make you very unhappy" you must believe them, just as you must believe me when I tell you that both you and Sigi will have happy lives once you are married to me. Quiet, uneventful, but happy.'

'Oh I do, Captain, I do believe it. I've known it really for a long time.'

As Grace said this she looked positively cuddlable, and the Captain was about to press her to his bosom when she saw the time, gave a tremendous jump, said she was half an hour late for luncheon already and fled – shouting from the staircase 'Come back at tea-time.'

'Tell me something, Sigi. You love the Captain, darling, don't you?'

'Shall I tell you what I think of the Captain?'

'Yes, that's what I'm asking you.'

'I think he's a bloody bastard, so there.'

'Sigismond – go to bed this instant. Nanny – Nanny —' Grace was running furiously upstairs, 'Please put Sigismond to bed without any supper and without Dick Barton. I won't have it, Sigi, you're not to speak of grown-up people like that, do you understand? Oh no, it's too much,' and she burst into tears. She had quite made up her mind that she was going to marry the Captain and now this consolation was to be denied her.

Sigi, rather puzzled and very cross, received pains and penalties, but he had hit his target first. That night the Captain left London, alone, for France. The Royal George had gone down, without her crew complete. Her new owner, having repainted, furbished up, and rechristened her, more in the spirit of the age, The Broadway, opened triumphantly that autumn with a dramatization of *Little Lord Fauntleroy*.

Chapter Eleven

MADAME ROCHER DES INNOUÏS, as old ladies sometimes do, now got an idea into her head, and decided that she would not rest until she had seen it carried out. The idea was that Grace and Charles-Edouard must be brought together again, must be married properly this time, that Grace must be converted, that they must have more children, and do their duty by the one they had already. The present situation had become impossible. Charles-Edouard quite clearly had no intention of marrying any of the nice, suitable girls vetted and presented by his aunt, and was now in trouble with half the husbands of Paris. Grace, according to information received by Madame Rocher through the French Embassy in London, was contemplating remarriage with some very unsuitable sailor, and the child was being outrageously spoilt on both sides of the Channel. Bad enough that a Valhubert should be written about and photographed in *Samedi Soir*, it now seemed that his mother contemplated putting him on the London stage, while Sir Conrad, whom Madame Rocher loved but whom she did not trust a yard, was no doubt initiating him into the terrible rites of Freemasonry. Charles-Edouard's heir was on the way to becoming a publicity-monger, an actor, and a Nihilist; what must poor Françoise be thinking?

Madame Rocher took action. She arrived in London to stay with the French Ambassador, sent for Grace, and weighed in at once with what she had to say.

'Grace, my child, it is your duty to return to Paris and marry Charles-Edouard. Picture this unfortunate man, lonely, unhappy, reduced to pursuing the wives of all his friends, forced to go to bed at the most inconvenient times, and always with the risk of his motive being misunderstood. He may find himself trapped into some perfectly incongruous marriage before we know where we are. Then think of your little boy, brought up like this between the two of you, no continuity in his education. Nothing can be worse for a child than these six months of hysterical spoiling from each of you in turn. You are very reasonable, Grace dear, surely you must understand where it is that your duty lies.

'I know the English are fond of duty, it is their great speciality. We all admire you so much for having no black market, but what is the good of no black market if you will not do your duty by your own family, Grace? Have you thought of that?'

Grace, sick to death of living alone, longing night and day for Charles-Edouard, was unable to conceal from Madame Rocher's experienced eye the happiness these words gave her, and that in her case duty and inclination were the same.

'But Charles-Edouard never asks me to go back,' she said. 'I'm always hearing from my father that he wants me, but I've never had a direct communication from him. It makes it rather difficult.'

Madame Rocher gave a sigh of relief. The day, she saw, was won.

'It is perhaps not so very strange,' she said. 'Charles-Edouard has never been left before by a woman. He fully understands the technique of leaving, one might say he has brought it to a fine art, but being left is a new experience. No doubt it puzzles him, he is not quite sure how to deal with it. Could you not take the first step?'

'Oh Tante Régine! Yes, perhaps. But then what about Juliette and Albertine?'

'Back to them again? You are behind the times, my dearest. Juliette is quite finished. But let's try and be sensible about it. Charles-Edouard was sleeping with you, I suppose?'

Grace became rather pink, but she nodded.

'Well then, that's all right. Why not look upon these others as his hobby? Like hunting or racing, a pursuit that takes him from you of an afternoon sometimes, amuses him, and does you no harm?

'There's another thing I wanted to tell you. Of course one never can say for certain, and people vary in this respect, but very often at Charles-Edouard's age a man does begin, all the same, to settle down with his own wife. If you go back to him it would not surprise me in the least to see a very different Charles-Edouard five or ten years from now.

'Tea with Albertine, yes I expect so, she is one whom people never quite get out of their systems, I'm afraid, and Charles-Edouard had her in his long before he ever met you. But the Juliettes of this world have their little day, it is soon over, and sometimes they are not replaced. I think Charles-Edouard is a particularly hopeful case because of the great love he has of his home. Consider the hours and the energy he expends on it, re-arranging his furniture and pictures, adding to his collections, pondering over almost insignificant details of the lighting, and so on. Think how much he hates to leave it, even for a short holiday at Bellandargues or in Venice. He goes away, complaining dreadfully, for a month while the servants have their holiday and is back before the dust sheets are off.

'All this can be very much on your side if you can manage to make him feel that you are part of his home, its goddess, in fact. I had a cousin, a terrible Don Juan, whose wife retrieved him, really, with her knitting. She sat through everything with this eternal ball of wool and click of needles – how we used to mock at her for it. But it was not stupid. In the end it became a symbol to him I think, a symbol of home life, and he so turned to her again that when they were old he seemed never to have cared for anybody else. Could you not try to see this whole problem rather differently, Grace? More like a Frenchwoman and less like a film star?'

Grace felt that she could, and knew that she longed to, since this different vision was clearly essential if she were to go home to Charles-Edouard.

'Yes, Tante Régine,' she said. 'I will try, I promise you. But Charles-Edouard must come and fetch me.'

'Oh – that! I shall have a word with him, and I can promise he'll be here next week. So all is settled then – good. And now, when do I see my dear Vénérable?'

'Ah well, the Vénérable dies for you. He rang up the Embassy to find out your plans – it seems they are taking you to the Ballet tonight, so he hopes that you will dine with us tomorrow. He's out shopping this very moment, trying to find something fit to offer you.'

'Wearing his apron, no doubt. But please tell him not to trouble. I love your English cuts, sirloins and saddles – you see how I remember, and I haven't been here since 1914. I love them just as they are. That excellent roast meat, those steak and kidney puddings, what could be more delicious? At eight o'clock then tomorrow?' She kissed Grace most affectionately on both cheeks.

Grace went home, a warm feeling at her heart. Everything was going to be all right now, she knew.

The dinner party for Madame Rocher consisted of an M.P., Clarkely by name, member of the Anglo-French Parliamentary Committee, Sir Henry and Lady Clarissa Teazle, owner of one of the big Sunday papers and his wife, noted francophiles, and, of course, Mrs O'Donovan. Madame Rocher arrived in full Paris fig. Her breasts were contained (but only just, it seemed that they might spring out at any moment, and then how to coax them back again?) in pale blue glass bubbles embroidered on yellow silk; her pale blue skirt, carved, as it were, out of hundreds of layers of tulle, was rather short, and when she sat down it could be seen that she wore yellow silk breeches also embroidered at the knee with bubbles. Mrs O'Donovan and Lady Clarissa could not take their eyes off bosom and knees, and exchanged many significant glances.

'What a joy,' Madame Rocher cried effusively, 'to see dear Meg. Why do you never come to Paris now? I know more than one who still dies of love for you there. Nobody,' she said to the company at large, 'certainly no foreigner, has ever had so much success in Paris as Madame Audonnevent.'

All the English guests had been chosen because they spoke excellent French, but they did not get much opportunity to air this accomplishment, since Madame Rocher was determined to practise her English, and, furthermore, never drew breath the whole evening.

Her theme was the delight, the ravishment, the ecstasies into which she had been thrown by her two days in London.

'This morning,' she said, 'I got up at eight, and imagine! I was ready for the opening at nine.'

'The opening?'

'Of the shops. Oh those shops! I have already bought all my hats for the Grande Semaine.'

'No! Where?' said Mrs O'Donovan, hoping for the name of a talented little French modiste, kept perhaps in some secret mews by the ladies of the French Embassy.

'My dear, can you ask? D. H. Heavens, of course – in the basement. I never saw such beauties – the straw! the workmanship! the chic! I have got Christmas presents for all my friends – how they will be thrilled – of your famous English scent, the Yardley – so delicious, so well presented, such chic bottles. Then all my cotillon favours for the bal des Innouïs at the Woolworth – oh the joy just to wander in the Woolworth. The very names of the shops are a poem – the Scotch House – I bought a hundred mètres of tartan to cover all my furniture, many country beréts, and a lovely fur bag, in the Scotch House, while as for the Army and the Fleet! The elegance! I shall come over once a month now for the elegance alone.

'At Oopers I ordered a new Rolls-Royce, of cane-work – you see the chic of that. From time to time, when I get a little tired, for all this shopping does tire me rather, I go to the Cadena Café and order a *café crême* and sit very happily watching your English beauties. They are a refreshment to the eye. I notice how sensible they are, they scorn the *demi-toilette*, and quite right too, there is nothing worse. They come out with no make-up, hardly having combed their hair even, to do their shopping. Then, of course, they go home and arrange themselves properly. Now I admire that. All or nothing, how I agree.

'So I had no time for luncheon as you can imagine, but who cares when you can have a bun and a cup of tea? The afternoon I spent in fittings!'

'Fittings?' Mrs O'Donovan and Lady Clarissa were stunned by this recital.

'Junior Miss, my dear. All my little dresses for the plage. Don't ask me what Dior will say when he hears of Junior Miss. I'd rather not think. No thank you, no wine – when I am in England I drink nothing but whisky.'

Mr Clarkely, more interested in French politics than English elegance, began asking a few questions about the Third Force, saying that he had made friends, through his Committee, with many of the Ministers, but Madame Rocher merely cried,

'Don't talk to me of these dreadful people – they think of nothing, day and night, but their stomachs and their mistresses.'

'Really?' said Mr Clarkely. 'Are you sure?' It had not been his impression at all.

'On what do you suppose they squander their salaries – those huge augmentations for which they are always and for ever voting?' (Madame Rocher would have complained very much if she had found herself compelled to dress on the amount annually earned by a French Minister.) 'Stomachs, dear sir, and mistresses. The vast sums that dreadful Dexter gives them for tanks and aeroplanes, what d'you suppose happens to them? My nephew, a commandant, tells me there are no tanks and no aeroplanes and hardly even a pop-gun. Why? Because, my dear sir, these sums are spent on the stomachs and the mistresses of your friends.'

Mr Clarkely was very much surprised. 'Surely not so and so,' he said, mentioning a certain prominent Minister noted for his dyspeptic austerity of life and devotion to work.

'All – all! Don't mention their names or I shall have an attack! All, I tell you, all! They take the best houses to live in, they have fleets of motors, they spend the day eating and drinking and all night the relays of mistresses are shown up the *escalier de service*. It has ever been so, but let me tell you that the scandals of Wilson and Panama, of the death of Félix Fauré even, are nothing, but nothing, to what goes on today. Give us back our King, my dear sir, and then speak to me of politics,' she said, rather as if her King were kept a prisoner in the Tower of London. 'More whisky, Vénérable, I pray.'

Mrs O'Donovan whispered to Mr Clarkely, 'It's no use asking that sort of Frenchwoman about politics – ask me. I know a great deal more than she does.'

But Mr Clarkely went to tea once a week at St Leonard's Terrace and had been told what Mrs O'Donovan knew already. He had hoped for something more direct from the horse's mouth.

'Is she really so royalist?' he turned to Grace. Madame Rocher was telling Sir Conrad her summer plans and begging him to go with her to Deauville, Venice, and Monte Carlo.

'Like all the Faubourg,' said Grace, 'she has a photograph of the King on her piano, but I don't think she'd raise a finger to get him back. My husband says the French hate all forms of authority quite equally.'

After dinner Madame Rocher took Sir Conrad aside, saying, 'And tell me, *mon cher Vénérable*, how goes the Grand Orient? You know,' she said, breathing a scented whisper (not Yardley's) into his ear, 'that I have designs on one of your adherents?'

'I am most glad to hear it,' he replied, delightfully drowning in the great billows of sex that emanated from her in spite of her seventy-odd years. 'Come in here a minute and we will discuss ways and means together.'

Chapter Twelve

MADAME ROCHER's journey turned out not to have been really necessary. The night of Sir Conrad's dinner party Sigismond was very sick and feverish; in the morning the doctor came, and said he must have his appendix out at once. He was taken by ambulance to a nursing home to be prepared for the operation, deeply interested in the whole affair.

'Shall I die? And go to the Père La Chaise? And see l'Empereur, like in Le Rêve? Well, I forgive Nanny for everything. Can I see the knife? I shall have a scar now, like Canari! oh good! When are you going to do it?'

'Not until tomorrow morning,' said the nurse, 'and don't get so excited.'

'Better give him something to keep him quiet,' said the doctor, after which Sigi became intensely drowsy. Grace sat with him until evening, when Nanny came, prepared to spend the night in the nursing home. As there seemed no point in them both being there and as Nanny insisted on staying, Grace went back to Queen Anne's Gate. Charles-Edouard was getting out of a cab just as she arrived.

It seemed quite natural to see him, she felt no embarrassment or constraint, and nor, quite obviously, did he.

'*Ravi de vous voir, ma chère Grace,*' he said, kissing her hand in his rapid way.

She opened the door with her key and they went into the house together.

'So how is he? And when is the operation? I was out when your father telephoned or I could have been here sooner.'

'It doesn't matter,' she said, 'he's been asleep more or less all day and the operation isn't till the morning. There's no danger, and no need to worry.' She sat down rather suddenly, feeling giddy.

'You look tired.'

'Yes. I was up most of the night, and I've been at the nursing home ever since without much to eat. I shall feel better after dinner.'

The butler came into the hall. He looked uncertainly at Charles-Edouard's bag, left it where it was and said, 'Sir Conrad won't be back from the House until late.'

'Perhaps we could have dinner at once then, please.'

Charles-Edouard was delightful at dinner; he told her all the Paris gossip.

'I'm so very pleased to see you,' he said from time to time, and towards the end of the meal, 'You don't know how much I've missed you.'

'Oh Charles-Edouard, I've been ill from missing you.'

'I thought I would open Bellandargues this summer. Sigi can get over his operation there. Won't you come?'

'For a week-end?'

'For good. Let's go upstairs.'

They went up. When they got to the drawing-room Grace opened the door, but Charles-Edouard took her hand and pointed further up.

'Charles-Edouard, we can't. We're not married.'

'We never have been married,' he said.

They went together into her bedroom.

'But I think we had better be,' he said, later on, 'and properly this time. For the sake of the child.'

Grace repeated happily and sleepily 'For the sake of the child.' Then she woke up a little more and said, 'But why, Charles-Edouard, did you never make a sign? A whole year and no sign?'

'No sign? When you refused to see me although I'd come all the way from Paris – when you told Sigi nothing would induce you to speak to me on the telephone – when you never answered the long letter I gave him for you. No sign? What more could I have done?'

So then it all came out. All poor Sigi's major acts of iniquity and minor acts of trouble-making were revealed before the horri-fied gaze of his parents.

'We seem to have given birth to a Borgia,' said Charles-Edouard at last.

'Rubbish!' Grace said indignantly, 'he's a dear, affectionate little boy. The whole thing was entirely our own fault for leaving him too much alone when we were happy and depending too much on him when we were lonely. We've been thoroughly selfish and awful with the poor darling from the very beginning, I see it all now. He only did it because he loves us and wants to be with us. When we were together we left him out and made him jealous, so of course he thought the best plan would be to keep us apart.'

'It's terrible all this jealousy. First you and then the child. What am I going to do about it?'

'You must try to be nicer, Charles-Edouard.'

'I must anyhow try to be more careful.'

'One thing, he did stop us marrying anybody else.'

'Were we seriously considering such a step?'

'I was, twice.'

'How extraordinary. Confess you would never have amused yourself so much as you do with me.'

'Amusement is not the only aim of marriage,' said Grace primly.

'Are you quite sure?'

They decided never to let Sigi realize that they knew all, but to keep a firm look-out for any underhand dealings in the future.

When Sir Conrad got back, very late, he found Charles-Edouard's suitcase still in the hall, the drawing-room empty and dark. He nodded to himself, and went happily to bed.

*

Next morning Sigismond, still very much interested, was lifted on to a trolley, 'Like the pudding tray at the Ritz,' he said, and was wheeled away. The last thing he knew was the surgeon's enormous eye gazing into his.

The very next minute, or half a lifetime later, he opened his eyes again. He was back in his bed. He saw the nurse and smiled at her. Then he saw his father and mother. They were holding hands. His mother leant over him. 'How d'you feel, darling?' Suddenly the full significance of all this became hideously apparent. He shut his eyes again with a shudder.

'He's not quite round,' said the nurse, 'he hasn't seen you yet.'

'Oh yes I have,' said Sigi, 'and I'm going to be sick.'

As soon as Sigismond was well enough to travel they all left for Paris on the Golden Arrow, complete with Nanny, the usual mountain of luggage, and Grace's carpet, a huge roll done up with straps.

'It will do for your bedroom at Bellandargues,' said Charles-Edouard.

'I meant it for your bedroom in Paris.'

But Charles-Edouard raised his hand, shook his head, and said, very kindly but firmly, 'No.'

Madame Rocher, who was already back in Paris and delighted by this turn of events, rang up Charles-Edouard the day before their journey. 'I've got Fr Lanvin,' she said, 'he'll marry you on Thursday morning at eleven, and then Grace must be converted by him. He's far the best and quickest, he did the Princesse de Louville in no time.'

But Albertine, whom Charles-Edouard rang up to make quite sure that all Paris should know the facts of the case, begged him to go to her priest. 'Fr Lanvin is quite all right, I'm sure, but I think you need somebody of a different calibre. Fr Strogonoff is so gentle and understanding, and then he specializes in foreign converts —'

'Yes, I'm sure, Albertine, but you see my aunt has made the appointment now, I think we'd better keep it. We can always change, if Grace doesn't like him.' Grace thought it was just the way people go on about their dentists.

'What?' said Charles-Edouard, still on the telephone. 'No! Are you sure?'

He was listening with all his ears. Grace could hear Albertine's voice, quack, quack, quack, down the receiver, but could not hear what she was saying. Charles-Edouard seemed entranced by whatever it was.

'Oh how interesting. Go on. Yes. What a sensation! Don't you know any more? Don't cut off – wait while I tell Grace. The Dexters,' he said to Grace, 'have flown to Russia. They've been Communist spies from the very beginning, and they've gone. It will be in the papers tomorrow. Salleté has just told Albertine the whole story. Well then, Albertine dearest, goodbye, and we'll count on you Thursday at eleven. Saint Louis des

Invalides. Nobody at all except Tante Régine and my father-in-law. Goodbye.'

'So —?' said Grace, all agog.

'Well, it seems the Americans have been rather suspicious of your friend Heck for quite a long time. At last they had enough evidence to arrest him – he must have got wind of it and he flew to Prague the day before yesterday. The latest information is that he has turned up in Moscow.'

'And Carolyn?'

'With Carolyn and little Foss.'

'Rather a comfort,' said Grace, 'to think that little Foss won't be ruling the world after all.'

'Rather a comfort,' said Charles-Edouard, 'to think that we shall never have to listen to Hector's views on anything again.'

'Poor Carolyn, will she like living in Russia? One thing, the Russians can't get on her nerves more than the French used to. So I was quite right, you see, she was a Communist at school. No wonder she got so cross when I reminded her.'

'And it seems that his real name is Dextrovitch.'

'He told me his mother was a Whale.'

'She was. His father, Dextrovitch, became an American just before he was born. They say they have evidence now that Hector has been a Bolshevist all his life, his father brought him up to be one. It's a most interesting story really. The father saw his two brothers shot by the Tsarist police, he escaped to America, married this rich Whale, and had Hector.'

'Can you beat it,' said Grace. 'Where's Papa – do let's go and tell him.'

Of course the journey to Paris was greatly enlivened for Grace, Charles-Edouard, and Nanny by the Dexter story, which now filled all the newspapers. Hector Dexter, it seemed, was worth at least ten atom bombs to the Russians. He had held jobs of the highest responsibility for years, had always been *persona grata* at the White House, where he knew his way about better than anybody except the President himself, had never been denied access to any information anywhere, and was one of the most brilliant of living men. Great stress was laid upon how deeply he was beloved by his countless friends (good old Heck) in London, Paris, and New York. Many of these refused to believe that he had gone to Russia of his own accord, but were quite certain that the whole family must have been kidnapped, putting forward as evidence that Carolyn had left her fur coat behind. 'I suppose they've never heard of Russian sables,' Charles-Edouard said when Grace read this out to him.

Asp Jorgmann and Charlie Jungfleisch were interviewed in Paris. 'Whatever Heck may have done,' they said, 'he remains a very very good friend of ours.'

But the French Ambassador to London, who was on the train and with whom Charles-Edouard went to sit for a while, told him that his American colleague regarded it as worth quite a lot of atom bombs to be relieved of good old Heck's company for ever. 'He's supposed to have gone straight off for a conference with Beria. Well, I feel awfully sorry for Beria.'

'Perhaps he won't mind as much as we do; we're always told the Russians have no sense of time,' said Charles-Edouard.

'It does seem strange, dear, such a good daddy. And fancy Mrs Dexter too. What will Nanny Dexter say?'

'You must ring her up the very minute we arrive and see if she's still there.'

Sigi sat by his mother in a fit of deep sulks, his mouth down at the corners, his clever little black eyes roving to and fro like those of an animal cornered at last. When the train was nearly at Dover the clever little black eyes suddenly had their attention fixed. The Bunbury burglar was walking up the Pullman on his way, no doubt, to the Trianon bar. Charles-Edouard was asleep in his corner, and Grace half-asleep in hers.

'Where are you going, Sigi?' she said, as he slipped out of his seat.

'Just to stretch my poor scar.'

'Well don't be long, we're nearly at Dover. You'll be able to lie down on the boat,' she said, 'poor darling.'

He sidled off, and found his burglar alone in the bar, drinking whisky.

'Good Lord,' said the burglar. 'It's you! Where are you off to?'

'Paris. I'm a French boy, like I told you. And I'm going home with my father and mother, but leaving my appendix in London.'

'Oh dear. They ought to have given it you in a bottle.'

'Are you coming to Paris too?'

'I hope so. If nothing awkward happens on the way.'

Sigi got very close to him and said confidentially, 'Have you got anything you'd rather I carried through the Customs for you? My papa travels to and fro the whole time, they all know him, he never has anything opened.'

The burglar looked at him and said, 'Whose side are you on now?'

Sigi began twisting up his curls. 'On your side, like I was last time, if you remember, until you sausaged me. But although it was very treacherous, what you did, I do feel I owe you a good turn to make up for shutting you in the cupboard.'

'Mm,' said the burglar doubtfully. They were passing through Dover Town station, sea and cliffs were in sight, seagulls mewed, and passengers began to fuss.

'White horses,' said Sigi. 'Poor Nanny.'

At last the burglar said, 'All right. If you like to give me a hand with this.' He passed him a small leather writing-case.

'Coo!' said Sigi. 'Heavy, isn't it?'

'Heavy because full of gold.'

'Can I see?'

'No. We're arriving. Be a good boy, bring it to me on the boat, cabin 11, can you remember? Then I'll give you a bit for a keepsake.'

'Oh here he is. You shouldn't wander off like that, darling, we were quite worried.' The train stopped with a bump.

'What's that satchel, dear?' Nanny asked as they went towards the Customs shed.

'I'm looking after it for Papa —'

'That makes eighteen pieces then – I'd only counted seventeen. Where is that porter going?'

Charles-Edouard told Grace and Nanny to go on board. 'I'll see to the luggage.' He gave Grace their tickets. 'And it's cabin No. 7.'

'Eighteen pieces of luggage, sir.'

'Thank you, Nanny. Run along, Sigi.'

'No, no,' said Sigi, 'this is the part I enjoy.'

Charles-Edouard laughed and said to Grace, 'We saw some

219

idiot taken away last time, for smuggling, I suppose he hopes for the best again.'

'I do. Very much indeed.'

A huge heap of luggage, mostly, of course, belonging to Sigi, was piled on to the counter in the Customs shed. Charles-Edouard stood by, with his back to the counter, talking to a friend who was in the Ambassador's party. They were both roaring with laughter still about the Dexters.

Sigi put his little writing-case on top of the other things and said, confidentially, to the Customs man, 'If I were you, officer, I would take a look inside that.'

'These all your things, sir?' The officer leant forward and spoke rather loudly to Charles-Edouard, who replied, half-looking round, 'Yes, yes, all mine', and went on talking with his friend. The officer, who knew Charles-Edouard by sight, began chalking the cases as he passed them.

Sigi, getting very fidgety, said, 'You mustn't mark that one without opening it first.'

The officer laughed. 'What are you up to? Smuggling?'

'Not me, my papa. Oh do look – do look inside.'

The officer good-naturedly snapped open the case, which seemed at first sight to contain coffee in half-pound bags. Still laughing, he took one out. Then his face changed. He tore open the bag and gave a loud whistle. Charles-Edouard was saying to his friend 'See you in a few minutes then.' The friend went on out of the shed and Charles-Edouard turned to the Customs officer who said, 'Excuse me, sir, is this your case?'

'I think so. If it's with the others,' he said, rather puzzled at the sudden gravity of the man's expression.

'Then I'm afraid I must ask you to follow me.'

'Follow you. Why?'

'This way, sir, please.'

'Yes, but why?'

'Your case is full of gold coins,' said the officer, showing him.

'*Nom de nom*,' said Charles-Edouard, very much taken aback. 'But wait a moment, that's not my case, I've never seen it before.'

'You've just said it was yours, sir.'

'Sigi – does this case belong to you?'

'Oh no, Papa, you gave it to me to hold, don't you remember?'
Sigi was wildly twisting up his hair.

Two Englishwomen said to each other, 'Shame, making the
child smuggle for him.'

Charles-Edouard gave Sigi a very searching look and said,
'Sigismond, what is all this? Now will you please go on board
this minute, go to cabin 1, find M. l'Ambassadeur and ask him
to come here.'

Sigi ran off and Charles-Edouard followed the Customs man
into a back office.

When Sigi got on to the ship he made no effort to find cabin 1
or the Ambassador. Since he had time to get rid of, and did not
want to run into his burglar, he made his way to the ladies' room,
where, as he knew he would, he found Nanny lying down with
her skirt off and occupying the entire attention of the stewardess,
who stood over her with a bottle of sea-sick tablets. 'Not as bad
as all that,' the stewardess was saying, 'bumpier this side. You
go right off to sleep, dear, that'll be the best.'

'And what about the little monkey?'

'I'll be all right,' said Sigi. 'I'm just waiting for the boat to
start and then I'll go and find Mummy. I've got some very interesting news for Mummy, but only when we've started.'

'Won't be long now,' said the stewardess, looking at her watch.

Meanwhile the Ambassador's servant had arrived in his cabin,
saying, 'M. le Marquis de Valhubert is in trouble with the
Customs and it doesn't look as if they will allow him to travel.'

The Ambassador did not hesitate. He had a word with the
ship's captain and immediately went on shore again, accompanied by an officer who took him straight to the room where
Charles-Edouard was talking with several Customs men.

'What is all this about?' said the Ambassador, in English.

Charles-Edouard said furiously, 'My child, who seems to be a
member of the criminal classes, has planted a case full of gold
coins on me. Don't ask me how he got them. I'm in a very
awkward position indeed.'

The Ambassador said to the senior official, 'It's absolutely out
of the question that M. de Valhubert should be smuggling gold.
You need not consider it even as a possibility. There must be a
mistake.'

'Yes, sir, we feel sure there is. But we must find out where all this gold comes from. Where is the little boy?'

'He went off to find you,' Charles-Edouard said to the Ambassador.

'I haven't seen him. My valet told me you'd been delayed, that's why I came.'

'It was most good of you, *mon cher*, I'm exceedingly grateful.'

'I could do no less.'

Another official now put his head round the door.

'Mr Porter, please, one moment.'

Mr Porter went out, and was back again almost at once.

'I think we've got to the bottom of it,' he said. 'A man has just been arrested on board. If I might have your name and address, sir, you've time to catch the boat, I'm very glad to say.'

Charles-Edouard gave him his card and hurried on board with the Ambassador.

Sigi's timing had gone a little bit wrong, and he had arrived in his mother's cabin rather before he meant to. Charles-Edouard, from outside, heard a well-known voice piping, 'He has always been wrapped up in Madame Novembre – it doesn't surprise me in the least. They're made for each other, and now they've gone off together – oh yes, Mummy, I saw them, I tell you, in her Cadillac.'

Charles-Edouard burst open the door, saying, in a voice which neither Sigi nor Grace had ever heard, and which turned Sigi to stone with terror, 'Sigismond'. This was followed by a tremendous box on the ears. The three of them stood looking at each other for a moment. Then Charles-Edouard, mastering his temper, said, 'What you need, my child, is a family of little brothers and sisters, and we must try to see that you get them. And now, please run along and find Nanny.'

READ MORE IN PENGUIN

In every corner of the world, on every subject under the sun, Penguin represents quality and variety – the very best in publishing today.

For complete information about books available from Penguin – including Puffins, Penguin Classics and Arkana – and how to order them, write to us at the appropriate address below. Please note that for copyright reasons the selection of books varies from country to country.

In the United Kingdom: Please write to *Dept. JC, Penguin Books Ltd, FREEPOST, West Drayton, Middlesex UB7 0BR*.

If you have any difficulty in obtaining a title, please send your order with the correct money, plus ten per cent for postage and packaging, to *PO Box No. 11, West Drayton, Middlesex UB7 0BR*

In the United States: Please write to *Consumer Sales, Penguin USA, P.O. Box 999, Dept. 17109, Bergenfield, New Jersey 07621-0120*. VISA and MasterCard holders call 1-800-253-6476 to order all Penguin titles

In Canada: Please write to *Penguin Books Canada Ltd, 10 Alcorn Avenue, Suite 300, Toronto, Ontario M4V 3B2*

In Australia: Please write to *Penguin Books Australia Ltd, P.O. Box 257, Ringwood, Victoria 3134*

In New Zealand: Please write to *Penguin Books (NZ) Ltd, Private Bag 102902, North Shore Mail Centre, Auckland 10*

In India: Please write to *Penguin Books India Pvt Ltd, 706 Eros Apartments, 56 Nehru Place, New Delhi 110 019*

In the Netherlands: Please write to *Penguin Books Netherlands bv, Postbus 3507, NL-1001 AH Amsterdam*

In Germany: Please write to *Penguin Books Deutschland GmbH, Metzlerstrasse 26, 60594 Frankfurt am Main*

In Spain: Please write to *Penguin Books S. A., Bravo Murillo 19, 1° B, 28015 Madrid*

In Italy: Please write to *Penguin Italia s.r.l., Via Felice Casati 20, I–20124 Milano*

In France: Please write to *Penguin France S. A., 17 rue Lejeune, F–31000 Toulouse*

In Japan: Please write to *Penguin Books Japan, Ishikiribashi Building, 2–5–4, Suido, Bunkyo-ku, Tokyo 112*

In Greece: Please write to *Penguin Hellas Ltd, Dimocritou 3, GR–106 71 Athens*

In South Africa: Please write to *Longman Penguin Southern Africa (Pty) Ltd, Private Bag X08, Bertsham 2013*